*A demon's whi...
to be feared. I...
person do anything...
if she let it.*

"My name is Galen. Galen McManus."

"And I'm Professor Dawn Maybank," she responded crisply. "But then, you already know that."

A chilly breeze swirled the fog around them, cooling her. But not nearly enough. When she asked, "What do you want for the diamond?" her voice cracked.

He stepped in closer. She could see his pulse beating strong and steady in a vein that disappeared beneath the collar of his mac. For some reason, she was not afraid. Not when he matched her movement so his buttons brushed her breasts; not even when he bent down and whispered in her ear with a voice as soft as black sable, "I want *you*."

In her rational mind, she knew it was a spell. But then she made the mistake of looking up, into his eyes.

"Five nights," he whispered. "Five nights in your bed and your body. That is my price for the Demon Stone."

Dear Nocturne Reader,

Can you believe it? I keep saying I'm not a paranormal writer! And up until now I haven't been. Not really.

Night Mischief, however, takes the plunge into the moody, twisty world of the genuinely dark and sexy that is NOCTURNE. Our hero is one very bad boy. In fact, he's a demon. Literally. Pretending to be an incubus, in order to seduce our heroine. And not for the reason he gives her. How could he get any darker or sexier? I love this guy!

Meanwhile, be sure to check out the other spine-tingling books in the DARK ENCHANTMENTS series. You won't want to miss a single one!

Drop me a line if you get a chance. I love to hear from readers! Let me know what you'd like to see from me next at www.NinaBruhns.com or email me at NinaBruhns@aol.com.

Take care, and happy reading!

Nina

Night Mischief

NINA BRUHNS

MILLS & BOON®

Pure reading pleasure™

First published in Great Britain 2009
by Harlequin Mills & Boon Limited,
Eton House, 18-24 Paradise Road, Richmond, Surrey TW9 1SR

© Nina Bruhns 2007

ISBN: 978 0 263 87282 8

46-0409

Harlequin Mills & Boon policy is to use papers that are
natural, renewable and recyclable products and made from
wood grown in sustainable forests. The logging and
manufacturing processes conform to the legal environmental
regulations of the country of origin.

Printed and bound in Spain
by Litografía Rosés S.A., Barcelona

ABOUT THE AUTHOR

Nina Bruhns credits her Gypsy great-grandfather for her great love of adventure. She has lived and travelled all over the world, including a six-year stint in Sweden. She has been on scientific expeditions from California to Spain to Egypt and Sudan, and has two graduate degrees in archaeology (with a speciality in Egyptology). She speaks four languages and writes a mean hieroglyphic!

But Nina's first love has always been writing. For her, writing is the ultimate adventure. Drawing on her many experiences gives her stories a colourful dimension, and allows her to create settings and characters out of the ordinary. She has won numerous awards for her previous titles, including a prestigious National Readers' Choice Award, two Daphne Du Maurier Awards of Excellence for Overall Best Romantic Suspense of the year, five Dorothy Parker Awards and two Golden Hearts Awards, among many others.

A native of Canada, Nina grew up in California and currently resides in Charleston, South Carolina, with her husband and three children.

She loves to hear from her readers, and can be reached at PO Box 2216, Summerville, SC 29484-2216, USA or by e-mail via her website at www.NinaBruhns.com.

This one is for my very great friends and long-time critique partners, celebrating our ten years together with this amazing series! To Michele Hauf, Cynthia Cooke and Pat White. You ladies are the best of the best.

Four hundred years ago a secret, hermetic order was created by the first Earl of St. Yve and a handful of initiates who pledged their lives to keep the world safe from evil paranormal beings. Ever since, the Cadre has been dedicated to maintaining the delicate balance between the mortal and Dark realms through research and observation of otherworldly entities. Seldom does the Cadre interfere.

But not all mortals seek peaceful understanding between the realms. In recent decades, an opposing force has been created by the British Security Service. This covert group, called P-Cell, has but one directive: destroy paranormal creatures of all kinds.

As the two organizations fight faithfully for their separate causes, unbeknownst to either of them the dark forces of evil gather, preparing to overtake the mortal realm....

Chapter 1

London, October, present day

Professor Dawn Maybank peered into the dense London fog and drew her trench coat tighter around her shoulders. Pressing the auto lock on her Jaguar, she shivered. She should not have parked on the street. She knew better. Anything could be out there, peering back at her. Vampires, demons, were-creatures: any of the paranormal beings that inhabited the dark shadows of the mortal realm. This was exactly the kind of cloaking fog that drew paras out to hunt. She knew that.

It would be her downfall someday, her impetuousness.

In the tomblike silence of the twilit morning, Dawn's high heels clicked loudly on the uneven cobblestones, echoing off the ancient walls that canted Old Trolly Road where the Department of Anachronistic Research, of which she was now the department head, was located. She should at least have worn flats. In case she had to run. Damn this job and damn the dress code, and damn her father for making her accept the position.

The thick mist crept slowly around her body like a moving shroud of unease. She could see sod all. Even her hearing was muffled, the cries of the gulls from the nearby Thames sounding more like whispers in the distance.

A drift of warm preternatural energy tingled over her skin.

Damn. There *was* something out there.

Instinctively she slid a hand into the pocket of her suit jacket, reaching for the emergency countermeasures she always kept close. Dead Sea salt for demons, a tiny but powerful UV flashlight for vampires, which also had a built-in high-frequency tone-emitter to ward off werewolves and other were-creatures. Gripping her briefcase tightly in her other hand, she quickened her pace. And murmured a spell of concealment, which she really should have said before she left the car. She never got to finish it.

Because suddenly he was there. A man. Looming over her.

She halted, scant inches from his towering body.

Never show your fear.

Their eyes met. For a moment they just stared at each other, her heart beating so quickly Dawn thought it would burst from her chest. He was huge, his broad shoulders made menacing by the black, ankle-length macintosh that swirled about his legs. Otherworldly power emanated from him, humming over her arms like a comb covered in warm wax paper.

For a split second she weighed the possibilities. Vampire? Unlikely. It was after sunrise, and very few vampires were able to venture out in the light, thank God. Demon? Maybe. Sidhe? The heated energy radiating around him did not feel like faerie glamour. Glamour was cooler, more tingly. A were? Maybe. Or a human with magic? No, the energy didn't feel human, either.

All at once the man's fingers were wrapped around her arm. She hadn't seen him move; they were just there. At the contact a prickly wash of power surged over her, hotter than before. The fine hairs on her arms raised.

Definitely not human.

"Let me go," she ordered, keeping her voice firm and steady. *What had happened to her instincts?* Three months away from her job as a demon tracker for the Cadre and already she was slacking off. Somehow she needed to get to the capture crystal in her briefcase, in case he was a demon. If he was some sort of were-creature, she was already toast. Still, a good bluff never hurt. "Let go *now!*"

"Lady Dawn?" the man asked. His deep voice was oddly hushed, like the fog surrounding them. Another clue.

Which immediately became lost in a more disturbing fact: *He knew her name.*

"Lady Dawn, I have something for you," he said softly, barely above a whisper. His voice trailed along her skin like the brush of fire-warmed velvet, sensual, erotic. "Something you've wanted for a long time."

A strange light flickered in his eyes as he spoke, as though he expected to tempt her with his low-spoken words.

She wasn't impressed. Or fooled. And he'd given himself away. *Demon.*

To be more precise, *daemon sapiens.* One of the two major genera of demon, this type was nearly indistinguishable from humans. On the outside.

But a demon's whisper was dangerous. Its power of suggestion could easily lure a mortal to her doom.

Dawn shielded her mind against it, and visualized a solid circle of protection around herself, both techniques the Cadre had taught her well. "What do you want?" she demanded.

One corner of the demon's mouth curved up, a wealth of meaning shining in those tempting black eyes. *Promises. Wicked promises.*

She jerked her arm, but his fingers were like a vise, her efforts useless. Demons were strong enough to bend steel with their bare hands, their preternatural energy even stronger. His hot, other-worldly power pulsed into her almost painfully, shattering her invisible circle of protection. Her heart pounded harder. She'd been caught in his net like a novice. She was going nowhere until he wished it.

Maybe the Cadre High Council was right. She didn't deserve adept status.

"I'm here to make a bargain with you," the demon said.

A devil's bargain. "Not interested."

"Trust me, you will be."

Unwilling curiosity tugged at her. He seemed so certain. Besides, she appeared to have little choice but to listen. Fine. If he'd intended to harm her, he would already have done so. Probably.

"All right," she said. "But keep your voice above a whisper. No more tricks."

He tilted his head in acquiescence.

"What kind of bargain?" she asked.

"I'll show you." He glanced at his fingers on her arm, then met her gaze with black brows raised.

She nodded and he released her. She wouldn't run because it would be no use. She could no longer feel his dark power flowing between them, but it was still there. He would easily catch her. And she would suffer his displeasure. Even Cadre novices knew that much. A demon's displeasure was not a pretty sight.

As though reading her thoughts, he smiled wickedly. For a second she was blinded. Lord, such a handsome devil. Her heartbeat took off, but this time not from fear. Then she came to her senses. What in God's name was this demon thinking of? Trying to *seduce* her? He knew her name; he had to know who she was. What she was. The man must be as recklessly impetuous as she! Maybe he'd been passed over for demon adept....

The small irony bolstered her courage. She took a deep breath as his hand disappeared beneath his mac, and came out with—

"Oh, my God." Her eyes widened.

Between two fingers he held a diamond. A very large black diamond. *The* diamond.

The Demon Stone!

Her gaze shot to his. The Demon Stone belonged to her family; it belonged at St. Yve Manor! The Saxon Crown from which it came had been found in a cache on the estate in the 1600s by the daughter of the very first Earl of St. Yve, Dawn's direct ancestor. It was stolen two centuries later by the infamous demon of destruction, Rofocale. Not the whole crown. Just the center diamond known as the Demon Stone.

The hair raised on the nape of her neck. *Could this man be Rofocale?*

Before her imagination could take off, she pulled in another calming breath, dismissing the idea. No. A minister of Hell, one of the dark realm's ruling Grigori, would hardly deign—or dare—to appear in the mortal realm. Not like this.

She focused on the stone between his fingers. Her fear abated as excitement began to build within her. "Where did you get the diamond?" she asked.

"You know where." He watched her carefully as she set down her briefcase on the cobblestones at her feet.

"Was it you who took it?" Never hurt to double-check.

"No." He shook his head. His thick black hair was long enough that it swayed back and forth with the movement. It reached his collar, glossy and rich, cut in a perfect style for his angular face. "It belonged to *Ba'al* Rofocale," he said. Lord Rofocale. *Ba'al* was a demonic term of rank, of respect.

So she was right. She'd heard the name many times in her work for the Cadre. *Evil.* As evil as it got. Some of the demons the Cadre had captured even claimed Rofocale was plotting to take over the mortal realm. Did this man work for him? She swallowed, and yanked her attention back to the demon's eyes.

"How did you get it?"

"I won it from *Ba'al* Rofocale in a game of chance," he said.

Dawn knew all about most demons' penchant for gambling. It was one of the few weapons a good demon tracker could use against them. But gambling with a demon was dangerous. Most of them, even the more evolved *daemon sapiens,* felt only two emotions—lust and anger. Both were legendary. You didn't want to piss a demon off. Even if you were another demon. This man had to be out of his mind to risk gambling with a ruling minister like Rofocale over something so...insignificant in the grand scheme of things.

And speaking of insignificant...

Why Dawn? What could he possibly want from her? Because there was no doubt he wanted something.

She shifted nervously as his gaze slid down the length of her body and back up again, almost as though he could see right through her trench coat. Lord, maybe he could. Did he have that power? One never knew, as each demon possessed different strengths and abilities.

Her cheeks warmed as his frank appraisal continued. She must remember to shield her thoughts. Most of them couldn't read your mind unless they were somehow able to put their demon essence into you, but this one seemed to know just what she was thinking.

Again she wondered. What did this nameless, handsome demon want from her?

"My name is Galen. Galen McManus."

Damn. Shields! "And I'm Professor Dawn Maybank," she responded crisply. "But then, you already know that."

"I do," he confessed. "Though I prefer Lady Dawn. *Professor* sounds so...impersonal."

He drew out the last word in a dark, sensual whisper that played inside her head, toying with her body like a warm physical touch. His hot power spilled over her. To her mortification her nipples tightened and a tight-throated thrum of sexual attraction seeped through her body.

She was horrified. *Galen McManus was a demon.* An entity she'd been fighting all her life. What was wrong with her?

A chill breeze swirled the fog around them, cooling her. But not nearly enough.

"What do you want for the diamond?" she asked, her voice cracking.

He stepped in closer. She could see his pulse beat strong and steady in a vein that disappeared beneath the collar of his mac. He smelled...exotic. Like rich spices from the Far East, like lush, verdant jungle foliage. He was so much taller than she that her nose was at his throat, almost tucked under his square jaw where the faint scent was strongest. Aftershave? Or him? She leaned in.

For some insane reason she was not afraid. Not when he matched her movement so his buttons brushed her breasts; not even when he bent down and whispered in her ear with a voice soft as black sable, "I want *you*."

She didn't move. She didn't move because she thought if she did she would probably start to shake. Not from fear, but from... *Oh, God.*

The demon wanted her. In all her years in the Cadre as a demon tracker, she had never been blindsided like this.

He could mean any number of things by that, she reasoned desperately. Her loyalty. Her help. Her soul.

Her body...

Oh, Lord in heaven. She squeezed her eyes shut. Which would be worse?

"Me?" she asked in a whisper.

His fingers brushed along her jaw, startling her eyes open with the prickle of preternatural energy, energy that was a living thing, leaving behind a rough, sparking-hot residue.

"I am an incubus," he said as though that explained everything.

Perhaps it did. The seductive whisper, the obvious heat of his energy. Every demon derived his power from one of the four elements: air, water, earth, fire. An incubus's element was fire, his power of possession sexual.

Suddenly she wondered if she was already dreaming this. Dreaming him.

His fingers tipped her chin up. He laid his cheek to hers. "Let me come to you," he ordered softly in her ear. His voice was like a lover's whisper in the night. Beckoning. Seductive. Promising those wicked, wonderful things.

In her rational mind she knew it was a spell. An illusion of intimacy, a cruel trick designed to rob her of her free will. A demon's whisper was a thing to be feared. It could make a person do…anything…if she let it.

She fought its power with all her strength, dredging up her simplest, most powerful spell of protection, the one she'd memorized at her mother's knee. But she made the mistake of looking up into his eyes. And was caught in the dark light of his gaze. Caught in their drowning magic.

"Five nights," he whispered. "Five nights in your bed and your body. That is my price for the Demon Stone."

The dense fog swirled. In the distance, some of it lifted, causing a pale haze of blue to shimmer above the billowy curls of gray cloud. But around the two of them, the shadowy gloom still lingered.

This was madness. She shouldn't even consider his devilish proposition.

But the Demon Stone glittered on his palm, calling to her. *Five nights. With an incubus.*

Thoughts sifted through her, mysterious and elusive as the dimming vapor that enveloped them. She couldn't. *She couldn't.*

Could she?

This man was a demon. Her enemy. He could be lying, tricking her. But here was the Demon Stone, not an illusion, and within Dawn's grasp. Finally an opportunity to reap vengeance for all the times she had been found wanting. By her perfectionist father. By her perfect sister. This would put an end to Father's indifference and Aurora's condescending smugness forever!

So very tempting.

Dawn licked her dry lips in a chaos of indecision, torn as never before in her life. "Let me see the diamond," she said, playing for time.

Galen obliged, holding it out on his palm for her to take. She picked it up. The stone was big, perhaps ten, fifteen carats. Crudely cut, as were all gems of such considerable antiquity. But no less brilliant for that. Even in the dim light of this dreary morning it sparkled and shone.

He held out a jeweler's loupe. She knew why. To check the inclusion. But she also knew without looking that it would be there. A five-pointed star, just off center in the middle of the diamond. An imperfection.

Demon stone was a jeweler's term for the one imperfect gem among a set of matching gems used in a piece of jewelry—in this case the Saxon Crown. The four other diamonds that still adorned it were perfect. While listening to her father tell the story of the crown and the missing demon stone, Dawn had often thought the term an apt description of herself. The imperfect one in a matched set—her twin sister Aurora being the flawless one.

The star inclusion was there. No surprise.

Yes, demons lied. All the time. It's what demons did. But seldom about outward things that could easily be checked. They lied, they cheated, they deceived. But they weren't stupid. Far from it.

"Why me?" she asked him, getting back to the heart of things.

He regarded her impassively. "Have you looked in a mirror lately?"

If he was trying to flatter her, he'd have to do better than that. She sent him a withering look. Still, demons might not be stupid, but they were often simple. And some of them did have a taste for human females.

"Sex? That's it? Nothing more?"

"Isn't it enough? I could ask—"

"No," she cut him off before he could up the stakes. Never dicker with a demon. You'd lose every time. "Sex is…plenty."

But could she do it? Could she open her mind and her dreams and her body to this stranger? Could she part her legs and let him—

She sucked in a breath at the all-too vivid image.

No. She couldn't!

But then she thought of all the years her father, the Earl of St. Yve, had searched for the Demon Stone, using all his considerable influence and endless resources to get it back for the family. All in vain. And here it was, sitting in the very palm of her hand. Hers, but for—

"Five nights," Galen murmured, plucking it from her grasp. It disappeared into a pocket under his mac. "Then it's all yours. I really don't think it's an unreasonable price." *He wouldn't.* "It's not like you have a boyfriend," he added.

Her mouth dropped open. Her love life might be pathetic, but did the entire universe know about it, dark realm as well as mortal?

He smiled. That blinding, sexy smile. "I know things about you that you don't even know about yourself. I've been watching."

She stared at him, scandalized. "Where?"

He shrugged expansively. "Everywhere." He leaned in. "Trust me, you have no secrets from me. None."

"Then you know I can call the wrath of the Cadre down upon

you with a single scream. The gargoyles will hear me and send for help." Two of them guarded the Department's doors, a stone's throw away.

"But you won't."

"How can you be so sure?"

"Because you want the Demon Stone."

She stared at him, hating that he was right. "How do I know you'll honor your agreement?"

"I give you my word," he said.

She almost laughed. "The word of a demon?"

Again he shrugged. "Very well. If you don't want it…" He turned.

"Wait!"

She closed her eyes, thinking furiously. If anyone could pull this off, she could. She knew how to handle demons. She'd had training, a lifetime's worth. And she wasn't afraid of sex, either. She'd be fine.

But… Could she trust him?

Maybe he was telling the truth, no tricks. Sometimes a bargain was simply a bargain. They had been his own terms, after all. He could have asked for far more….

But it still mystified her why this Galen McManus had chosen her, had sought out her, Dawn, rather than making his offer to her sister, Aurora. On second thought, if he'd really been watching her, he'd know. He'd have gotten nowhere with Aurora. Most probably he'd have lost the diamond and wound up imprisoned for all eternity in a crystal in the dungeon of St. Yve Manor.

Aurora didn't care much for demons.

Dawn was startled by the feel of Galen's fingertips feathering down the column of her throat, pausing to measure the pulse that beat there madly. She shivered in reaction. She still hadn't gotten used to the spill of hot, otherworldly energy from his touch. It was like liquid fire pouring between them.

His fingers continued downward, pushing aside the edges of her trench coat as they slowly, deliberately, brushed across the upper slope of her breast. Stopping just short of her nipple. It pebbled to a hard, aching point. She held her breath. His touch there would be electrifying. *Just an inch farther...*

"Well?" he murmured. "What's it to be? Yes or no?"

She needed more time. How could she decide something like this so quick—

"Yes," she said in a rush. Before she came to her senses and changed her mind. "You have a deal, Mr. McManus."

His eyes blazed over her body like flame over kindling. "Good," he murmured, and drew his fingers around the tip of her breast. His power surged, sending ribbons of fire through her insides. Searing away her will with its heat.

His face lowered, not quite touching hers. The heady masculine scent of him, peppery, musky, inundated her senses. She could almost feel the dark stubble of his shadowed jaw on her skin. His breath was hot on her ear. Hot like the dark realm.

"I'm going to have to kiss you," he whispered. The suggestion sifted through the inferno of her body like a cool spring snow, blanketing her reason in a comforting, soothing numbness. *It would be all right.*

Or would it? A niggle of doubt struggled to break through his powerful magic. Her mind stumbled, panicked, reaching for the words of her protection spell. Failed. Why couldn't she remember?

"I must do it now, Lady Dawn."

She sucked in a steadying breath and was again hit with the dizzying, alluring scent of him. She fought harder, and managed to jerk away. "Stop it!"

His black eyes regarded her with amusement. "It must be done."

"I know." She swallowed crossly.

"It's just a kiss."

Like hell. She knew how an incubus worked. To be able to visit your dreams he must leave a small quantity of his demon essence in you. Preferably in the mouth, through a kiss. But it was dangerous. So very dangerous. Accepting a demon's essence was the first step to a human's downfall. His essence in you created a connection, a bond, between you. The more essence, the stronger the bond. Too much and you became the demon's familiar. Then he'd be able to bend you to his will completely, if he so chose. You could become his slave.

"There's no other way?" She was grasping at straws and she knew it.

"I'm afraid not." His lips moved toward hers. "You must trust me."

She almost snorted at the thought.

"Just a little. Only enough to open your dreams to me."

"Do you swear you will take nothing more?"

"I swear."

She shuddered out the breath she'd been holding. "Try not to enjoy it."

He looked even more amused. "Impossible."

She couldn't believe she was doing this. Knowingly allowing a demon to put his essence in her, to kiss her, to seduce her. To give him the free use of her body. She, the daughter of the Earl of St. Yve, whose family had founded and led the Order of the Cadre in its fight against evil otherworldly entities, especially demons, for nearly four hundred years.

His lips lightly touched hers. His energy tingled over her, warm and arousing. His thumb traced her jaw and tugged at her chin, urging her to open for him. She did. Her heartbeat tripled at what she was about to do. Willingly allowing him to infuse her with his demon essence. Letting his demon tongue—

Oh, Lord, his tongue!

"Is it…?" she whispered.

"Yes," he said, and flicked his tongue over hers.

It was. She could sense it, subtly, the fork that divided his warm, moist tongue in two. A secret thrill raced up her spine. What forbidden, devilish things would he do to her with that wicked, wicked instrument?

His fingertips skimmed around her nipple, barely grazing it, a sizzling reminder of the liberties he intended to take. Later. In her dreams. She had an overwhelming urge to lean into those arrogant fingertips. More of his bespelling magic? She forced her body to remain apart from his.

Until his mouth covered hers and his tongue swept into her, and she forgot all about restraint and decorum and the fact that they stood not a hundred yards from the entrance to the university department she was head of. Forgot that this was the most dangerous, foolhardy thing she had ever done in a lifetime of dangerous, foolhardy behavior. And forgot that Galen McManus was a demon, her greatest hereditary enemy.

She quite simply melted.

He urged her to open wider, his free arm banding around her waist to prevent her from falling. He tasted so good. So exciting. So...*dangerous.* She knew well what could happen if she lost her senses and let him slide his tongue down her throat, all the way down, to touch her heart. She'd be lost, tapped as his familiar. Under his power completely. Forever.

She didn't care. She slid her hands into his hair and kissed him back. Tasting the dark, dusky flavor of his essence as it spurted into her. The tingling heat of its power started in her mouth and sparkled down her throat, circling into her abdomen and lower still, stroking between her legs like an invisible lover. *Sweet mercy.* She teetered near the edge...near the edge of... *So close.*

He pulled away. She gasped, and clutched his arms, clinging to him for balance. He stood for a moment, until she steadied herself, and stepped back. He gave her the smile of a man well pleased with himself.

"Until tonight, then," he said.

Then he turned and, with a swirl of his long, black mac, vanished into the fog.

Chapter 2

It took several long minutes for Dawn to get her limbs back, to be able to move with a fair certainty her knees wouldn't buckle under her. Quickly, she said her protection spell, for all the good it would do her now. She just stood there, increasingly mortified as the reality of what had just transpired seeped into her suddenly numb mind and body.

What had she done? Oh, Lord, *what had she done?* How could she have been so stupid?

She had let a demon bespell her! She'd never run into a demon able to bespell and command a human through his eyes. But this one must have done. She'd shielded herself from his whisper. What other explanation could there be for her witless, terminally foolish behavior other than that captive black gaze?

Damn! She might not be an adept, but she knew how potent a demon's powers of persuasion could be, even without the eyes. She'd dealt with demons all her life, tracking them and even capturing a couple. And yet she had let this one come near enough to whisper in her ear; had let him plant his demonic essence in her body. And agreed to do more than that. Much more.

She'd done insane, impetuous things before. But this…this went beyond the pale, even for her. What would her father say if he found out?

She covered her traitorous mouth with her hand and swallowed back a growing dread. And tasted demon on her tongue. Galen McManus. *Incubus.*

Taking a fortifying breath she staunchly quelled the panic threatening to undo her. *The diamond,* she reminded herself. She'd done it for the Demon Stone. *For her father.* To prove herself. To show him she was as worthy a daughter as her sister Aurora.

Not because Galen McManus was the most attractive man she'd ever met. Not because of the way he'd made her feel inside—all liquid, burning heat. Certainly not because she enjoyed the edge of danger and the recklessness of the situation. Though Aurora might say she did.

Okay, maybe she did enjoy it.

Oh, who was she kidding? This disaster had proven nothing less than that Aurora was right. There were four levels of achievement in the Cadre, each demanding years of rigorous training to reach: novice, apprentice, fellow and adept. Dawn had been a fellow since age ten, unable to rise further.

Aurora had been right all along. Dawn didn't deserve to be an adept.

But this situation was still salvageable.

She must find the demon immediately and tell him she'd changed her mind. He could strike some kind of a bargain with her father instead. There must be something else they could offer him in exchange. Something. Anything. Besides her body.

Yes, that was what she'd do. She'd go straight to her office and check her reference books for an incubus-summoning spell and get him back here. Then tell him. He'd let her out of their bargain. He must.

Swiping up her briefcase, she strode determinedly the half block to the Department of Anachronistic Research. Known to those who belonged simply as the Department, it was the university's most obscure, mysterious and archaic department. They specialized in all manner of human paranormal and parapsychological studies: ESP, telekinesis, out-of-body, mediums, that sort of thing. And well beyond. It was a legitimate university department, but a front, of course. The Department's most important function—although unknown to most staff and all students—and Dawn's real job, was to pinpoint and recruit new initiates for the Order of the Cadre.

The unique Department building which had seen three-and-a-half centuries of continuous use by the university poked its hexagonal verdigris cupola up through the last remnants of fog. A set of worn marble steps glittered in a beam of sunlight, leading up to a grand double-doored entryway. To either side of the front door, a pair of elaborately carved gargoyles guarded the entrance—complete with indwelling threshold demons who watched over the building by night. Only Cadre initiates could actually see and speak with the demons. To other humans they looked exactly like any of the hundreds of stone gargoyles around the city of London, or any other city in Europe and the world.

Maybe the guardians would know how to get hold of Galen McManus. Or maybe Huwa, the portal demon who protected her own office door. Though maybe not. Part of the lower demonic order, *daemon incultus,* locus demons were notoriously disinterested in anything not having to do with their own designated task—or Directive as it was called in the dark realm—which was why they were so good at their jobs. In nearly four hundred years, the Department had never been broken into by thieves or other evil-doers.

But she would ask them if they knew how to find Galen, just in case.

Unfortunately, as she approached the steps to the Department she ran into Roland Esterhaus. *Not* a Cadre member and therefore he would prevent the demons from speaking with her. Bugger.

Roland was a short, balding chauvinist pig who made a career out of making her life as department head as miserable as possible, probably to compensate for his own glaring inadequacies. Alas, he was an excellent researcher with strong ESP leanings, so she had to put up with him as a teacher. But there were times—such as now—when she wished he'd just break something and go away. Permanently.

"Good morning, Professor Maybank," he greeted her as they both reached the bottom of the steps. He was carrying a pile of computer readouts under his arm. His current project, "Double-Blind Study into the Occurrence of Pre-cognition among East End Britons," or some such nonsense.

"Morning, Roland." *Go away, Roland.*

It was more than unsettling to be talking to anyone, but particularly him, with the taste of demon lingering in her mouth and the tingle of masculine fingers still on her breast.

"Professor Dawn, here at dawn," he said in a singsong. "As usual."

"There are worse things than dedication, Roland." Like being a wanker.

"Trying to keep up with the rest of us, what, professor? How's the schedule for next semester coming along?"

Roland knew damn well she'd just started it yesterday. Gritting her teeth, she was considering whacking him over the head with her briefcase, when suddenly a misty shape swooped up the steps and whirled about their shoulders.

Roland gasped and batted at it. "What the bloody—"

Lord, not another one. She'd had her fill of demons this morning. She threw up a tractor spell so the primitive *daemon incultus* wouldn't get away, and fumbled with her briefcase, flipping it open. She'd grabbed a crystal and was starting to chant when the demon flew straight up and snapped the tractor spell like a rubber band. Bloody hell.

Screeching like a banshee, it swooped down on Roland. He screamed and started to bolt down the stairs. Big mistake. *Never run from a demon.* Always stand and fight. Usually it was only out to scare you; showing fear just fed its fun. Of course, Roland wouldn't know that. The Department staff all specialized in strictly human paranormal phenomena. It was part of the cover. Most didn't even know demons really existed. Or vampires, or any of the other paras that occasionally roamed the mortal realm.

"Roland, don't!" she shouted after him. Too late.

He tripped on the marble steps, and crashed down amid a snowstorm of papers. The demon vanished. Roland howled. She gazed down at him, and for a split second she thoroughly enjoyed the sound of his pain.

Immediately she felt massively guilty. She rushed to his aid. *What was wrong with her?* She'd never been mean-spirited before.

"Dear God, Roland. Are you all right?"

Roland was not all right. As it turned out, he had a femur broken in two places and a fractured kneecap. She wasn't enjoying it when she exited the hospital an hour and a half later, leaving him in the tender care of the doctors. It was terrible that he'd been injured. But she *was* relieved that he had already decided to take a three-week holiday to recover. Life would be so much easier without his Greek chorus singing over her shoulder, pointing out her myriad inadequacies.

Another good thing. The incident had taken her mind off Galen McManus. For a while, at least.

Right until she walked into her office at the Department and closed the door.

* * *

Galen McManus, vengeance demon and denizen of the dark realm, was feeling quite pleased with himself. After making mincemeat of that unbearable twit Roland, he'd headed up to Dawn's office and made himself comfortable. He was now lounging in her cozy leather chair with his feet propped up on her massive antique desk. Naturally, he'd leafed through the papers in and on her desk, and riffled through the locked filing cabinet, but hadn't found anything particularly interesting. All academic stuff, related to the running of the Department of Anachronistic Research and its silly projects. She wouldn't keep anything incriminating here, of course. Despite her job as chief recruiter for the mysterious hermetic Order of the Cadre, she must be scrupulous about keeping any and all Cadre information out of this building. He'd heard from various sources that the Department was subject to harassment by the British Security Service—in other words, MI5. Specifically the P-Cell section of MI5. Nasty buggers. A bunch of trigger-happy, macho human males with big guns and even bigger complexes. Bad combination. Especially if you happened to be a demon.

When his newest object of possession walked into her office, he laced his hands over his stomach, leaned back in her chair and smiled. Lady Dawn. Such a mouthwatering bit of work. Long auburn hair the color of an autumn sunset, even longer legs that went on forever. Large green meltingly expressive eyes and a luscious wide mouth. He could still taste her on his tongue. Sweet. Susceptible. Perfect.

"Hello."

She jumped, letting out a squeak. "How on earth did you get in here?" She glanced down at the keys in her hand.

"Huwa let me in."

Huwa, the peculiar little portal demon who lived in the angel sculpture hanging on her office door. Now, there was an interesting chap. Not. But at least he recognized a superior being when he saw one.

"I'll have to speak to him," she said, setting her things down on the desk.

She was trying desperately not to look at him, instead stopping in front of the coat rack where he'd hung his mac. But he'd seen her surreptitious glance at his white dress shirt, which he wore with sleeves rolled up, tucked into black Helmut Mann trousers. During his reconnaissance here, he'd noticed most of the teaching staff wore jeans and T-shirts, so this morning he'd dressed deliberately to set himself apart. The strategy had obviously worked. Her gaze lingered admiringly on his exposed forearms. Score one for the demon.

"Actually, I'm glad you've come," she said. She fussed nervously with her coat as she hung it up next to his mac.

"That's progress," he said. "What's on your mind?"

"I've changed it," she blurted out, as though she had to say it quickly or lose the nerve. "My mind. About our deal."

Ah. Now, there was a shock. He regarded her implacably. "Is that so?"

"I don't know what I was thinking. To be honest, I *wasn't* thinking." Her cheeks flushed a charming shade of rose. She attempted an embarrassed smile, but botched it. "I seem to have a problem with that. Not thinking things through properly."

"Indeed." He didn't move. Merely watched her as she paced back and forth, gesturing as she spoke. Not news to him. He wasn't worried.

"You can talk to the earl, my father, about the Demon Stone. Work something out with him. He's desperate to have it. Believe me, he'll give you whatever you want."

"I told you. I want you."

That brought her up short. Her cheeks flamed redder. "There must be something else."

"*You* are what I want, Dawn," he said, laying it all out in plain language so there would be no doubt as to his intentions and his expectations. "Your body. Your surrender. Nothing else will do."

He saw a shiver travel through her. "But that's not possible."

Wrong. "We've made our bargain, my sweet. It cannot be undone. Besides which, I no longer need your consent. You carry my essence within you, therefore I can come to you in dreams whenever I choose. You've no choice in the matter any longer."

She closed her eyes and took a deep breath. "That's not fair. I didn't know what I was doing."

"Oh, you knew very well what you were doing," he refuted.

"You bespelled me."

"No, you want me."

Her eyes squeezed tighter. "No."

"I'll be good to you, Dawn," he said, keeping his whisper as low and soothing as his promise. "You won't regret it. I swear." He felt her mental shields waver.

She opened her eyes and he regarded her with as sincere an expression as he could conjure. No reaction. Damn.

He tilted his head. "You don't believe me?"

"Would it matter?" she countered, an edge of anger in her voice. Or was it fear? Had he finally managed to scare her?

He didn't speak. She knew his answer.

With a short, sharp exhale, she busied herself with her brief-case, which she'd set on the desk. She spun it around and fumbled with the locks, but her fingers shook and she couldn't get it open, the only outward indication anything was wrong. She was good.

He laid a hand over hers. She snatched it back.

"Why are you here?" she demanded. "In my office. I thought we were to meet tonight."

"I missed you."

She glared at him. "Please. I don't need some sweet-talking

incubus filling my head with ridiculous fantasies. We both know what this is about."

He resisted a smile. He did know. She was the one with no idea. Sex? Just a pleasant diversion. A distraction so she wouldn't guess the real reason he was here.

"Okay." He held up his hands in mock surrender. "I came to ask a favor."

"What kind of favor?"

"Don't tell the Cadre about me," he said. "At least not until the five days are up and I'm gone."

Her mouth parted. "So you *do* know who I am. And still you dare—" She glanced toward her right desk drawer.

"Don't even think about it," he said. He didn't need essence or magical powers to read her thoughts. He'd found the small stash of crystals she kept there. Capture crystals. For demons. He shuddered.

Every denizen of the dark realm was well aware that the Cadre's method of containing evil demons was to chant a spell that captured their soul in a special crystal. Once imprisoned, the demon was then taken to a storage facility in the dungeon of Cadre headquarters at St. Yve Manor, and kept there forever. At least that was the rumor. No truly evil demon had ever returned to say for sure. Only mischief demons who'd been captured then released to be deported back to the dark realm. And their descriptions of the short stay in the crystals were bad enough.

He slid open Dawn's top drawer and pulled out one of the fist-sized pyramids. This one was ruby red.

"You're a brave man," she observed. "Handling that."

"I trust you," he said. The mild admiration in her face turned to shock. Until he added, "Besides, I know *you* have to be holding it for the imprisonment spell to work."

"Are you sure?" Her expression taunted.

"Now you insult me." He set the ruby pyramid down. "Doesn't the crystal frighten you?"

He pursed his mouth to hide a wince. "Admittedly, the whole idea gives me chills. What the devil would I do with myself for all eternity without books to read or beautiful women to seduce?"

She snorted softly. "You, read?"

He ran a reverent fingertip down the spines of the leather-bound books she had piled on her desk. He loved to read. Whatever realm he found himself in. Not the usual hobby for a Dark, admittedly. "Classics mostly. I'm especially partial to the Existentialists. And Dante, of course." He winked. "Such drama."

She rolled her eyes. "In between seducing all those beautiful women, I suppose."

His fingertip paused on a gold-embossed title, *Incubi et Succubae.* "Truthfully, it's been awhile," he said. "You will be the first in…an age."

"Stop."

"I wouldn't lie," he protested, then grinned unrepentantly. "At least about that." Anything else, all bets were off.

She crossed her arms over her breasts. "What *would* you lie about," she asked, "if not in aid of your seduction?"

"Seduction?" He slid his boots off her desk and came to his feet in a single move, his eyes never leaving hers. Demons had the ability to move in the blink of an eye, faster than any mortal could perceive. It was called apportment. A handy ability. Always impressive to humans. "As I recall, we struck a simple bargain," he said. "No need for seduction."

Enough of this cat-and-mouse game. She needed a lesson. It was time to reinforce his will. He walked around the desk, toward her.

She backed up. "You're right, of course. The Demon Stone was all you needed to assure my…cooperation. And you knew that."

"Did I?" He pursued her step for step. She was in such denial. She wanted him as much as he wanted her. Every shallow breath, every tremble of her hand, every blush on her cheek told him so. Bespelled? Certainly. But by her own lust. How had he gotten so lucky?

But she needed to be shown how thoroughly she had fallen. "So, if I had looked like a fat gargoyle with brimstone breath you would still have accepted my terms?" he asked.

"Don't be absurd." Her back bumped against the wall. "You're an incubus. Incubi are always ridiculously handsome."

More like it. "You think I'm ridiculously handsome?"

He didn't stop coming at her. Not until his body was touching hers from knee to breast.

"What are you doing?" she asked, her voice breathless.

His body reacted instantly. To the contact. To the look in her eyes—*desire*. He pressed even closer. Dipped his fingers under her skirt. "Thinking about moving up our timetable."

"You can't!" She grabbed his shoulders and squirmed as he slid his hands up her thighs. Her silken flesh felt warm, humid, acquiescent. *So good.* She gasped. "An incubus can't…do this in person! It has to be in a dream."

"Are you sure about that?"

"All the books say so. Anyway, someone might walk in."

He lifted a hand toward the door and twirled his fingers. There was a loud grate then a snick as the old-fashioned key turned home and locked. She seemed surprised. Good. He wanted to keep her guessing. Unsure of his powers. Unsure of everything about him. Because really, almost nothing was as he'd led her to believe.

"Any other objections?"

"Yes!" she blurted. He could smell her panic. Excellent.

He stepped away from her. "In that case, I'll stop. I'm not a savage. I can wait for tonight." Tonight she would be twice as vulnerable, her surrender twice as exciting. Anyway, his purpose here had been accomplished.

She blinked. Totally thrown.

He went to the coat rack and put on his mac. "In return, I trust you won't tell the earl or the Cadre about me. That would not be good for either of us."

"No," she agreed after a slight hesitation. "You're right. Better to keep this just between you and me."

He smiled. "Yes. Better by far."

Then he unlocked the door and strode through it as if he owned the place instead of being deep in the enemy's lair. Because he did own the place. By owning its mistress.

Oh, yes, he owned her, all right.

Whether she realized it or not, she was his.

Body and soul.

For as long as he wished.

Chapter 3

So far, the day's work had gone very well.

Galen hummed a dissonant tune as he released steamed milk from his shiny stainless-steel cappuccino maker into the demitasse of espresso he'd just brewed. He inhaled deeply of the mellow coffee aroma.

Unexpectedly well.

Walking from the window of his penthouse living room, he gazed out over the rooftops of London, sipping his cappuccino and watching the sun set in a dazzling display of oranges and reds. He'd been worried. Having a seasoned demon tracker as his newest victim was a tad unnerving, to say the least. Especially one with Lady Dawn's impressive credentials. He'd almost begged off the job when they'd told him who she was. Hell, along with her father and sister, the woman practically ran the notorious Cadre—one of the very few genuine threats that existed to his kind.

The Cadre was an old and venerated order—a hermetic order most would say—which claimed to be dedicated to the study of otherworldly beings, the containment of evil ones, and the maintenance of a positive balance between the mortal realm and the dark realm.

He had no quarrel with cosmic balance. That was, after all, what Galen himself was all about, too. And unlike their rival organization P-Cell, the Cadre never outright killed those they hunted. Instead they captured, interviewed and deported the benign, and held those entities they considered evil in crystal suspension until such a time as they discovered a "cure" for them.

Galen gave a disdainful snort. As if a demon could be "cured."

A demon was a demon, his nature inalterable. A wrath demon was a wrath demon, and would always be a wrath demon; a portal demon or a demon of gluttony was simply and only that. Each particular variation of his brethren, whether *daemon sapiens* like himself or *daemon incultus,* the more primitive, ancient type, had its own Directive, given by the Grigori themselves. The Grigori were those demons who ruled over the dark realm and saw its laws strictly enforced. Appointed by the Dark Lord himself, the Grigori council was made up of one member of each of the major demonic tribes.

The Cadre could do all the research they wanted. Nothing was going to change demonic nature.

Luckily, Galen's concerns about Dawn's twigging to him had been unwarranted. She was obviously clueless that she'd conjured up any kind of demon when she'd read from that old book of spells during her Demonology I class two weeks ago. But she had. Specifically, *him.* A bit surprising… But it seemed Lady Dawn hid a secret flaw deep beneath that serene professorial facade. One that had called to him, loud and clear.

Wouldn't she be surprised when she realized the truth? That Galen McManus was no ordinary incubus…

He was a demon of vengeance.

A pure stroke of genius, that incubus ruse. He'd been concerned that as a Cadre member she'd see right through the ploy. That she'd either immediately chant a spell to banish him, or school her thoughts not to include wicked prayers for vengeance. Because that would rather spoil his game. When planning his approach, he'd figured the best strategy would be to knock her so off balance she'd never question his real purpose. Thus the incubus idea. It had worked beautifully. Already he'd had one blazing success with his true Directive. His smile widened to a grin. Poor Roland.

And as a delightful bonus, Galen got to spend five sinful nights in Dawn's bed. Damn, he couldn't wait.

The sun disappeared below the rooftops, and a few moments later the radiant twilight ebbed into an enveloping shawl of inky blue and black. A thready fringe of fog was already rolling in from the east, smudging the bright city lights below into a murky blush of yellow.

A perfect night for mischief.

After finishing his coffee, he strode into the bedroom and considered his closet. Galen enjoyed his frequent stints in the mortal realm. He kept this high-end flat in London's fashionable Chelsea district, filled with trendy furnishings, techy gizmos and the latest designer togs, as his base of operations. Of course, he maintained smaller flats in Paris and New York, as well as a bungalow in old Hong Kong. He did like his sensual comforts. And clothes were one of his favorite indulgences.

He knew Dawn spent most of her nights in her London townhouse in Mayfair, but still stayed occasionally in her rooms at the Cadre's headquarters at St. Yve Manor. St. Yve was the luxurious country estate of her father, the Earl of St. Yve, located about an hour southwest of the city. The Manor was huge, more of a castle, really. He'd only seen the place from the relative safety of the enchanted wood that surrounded the castle. But the faeries who lived in the forest liked to sneak up and peer through its windows, and they said the inside was sumptuous. Tonight Dawn would undoubtedly seek the false security of sleeping within the walls of St. Yve. She should know better than to think he couldn't reach her there.

He chose his clothes carefully. Silk boxer briefs. A soft Ungaro shirt in cobalt blue and black Viktor & Rolf trousers. Van Noten loafers. No socks. They'd just be a bother to take off.

Laying out the clothing, he showered and dried his hair. Considered shaving. But decided against it. This morning he'd sensed how turned on Dawn had been by the subtle rasp of his two-day stubble on her smooth skin.

After he'd dressed, he stood still for a moment, closed his eyes and tested the connection between his mind and hers. Blocked. She was still awake. And shielding her mind from him. A damned annoying skill, taught by the Cadre no doubt. He'd never known another human who could do that.

Ah, well. It was early yet. And he had nothing but time. Time and purpose.

He lit a crackling blaze in the fireplace, picked up a book and settled down in his leather easy chair in front of the window to wait for her to fall asleep. Only then would her mind open up and let him in.

He waited. And waited. And waited some more.

When he finally sensed her defenses start to crumble, he glanced at the clock. It was 2:30 a.m.

He almost smiled. So predictable. He'd observed her over the past two weeks and knew full well she was an early riser. Which meant tonight she'd tried her best to delay the inevitable. Surely she, of all people, knew it was useless to fight your demon after you'd invited him in. He would win. And she would learn her needed lesson.

That was the way of things.

Did he feel sorry for the humans who fell into his clutches? Did he feel bad serving them up their cold, measured fates? To be honest, he wasn't so much into emotions. Feeling sorry wasn't in the nature of a demon. Nor was feeling love or affection, hate or even impatience. The only emotions he felt were lust and anger. Those were plenty. He did his job, and took his pleasure from the balance restored by it. And of course, from the sensual aspects of his life while in the mortal realm. Food. Drink. Color. Sound. Touch.

Sex.

Oh, yes. Sex was good. He took immense pleasure in sex— with a human female. And it happened all too rarely. Hell, his cock was already hard just thinking about it.

With a lusty feel of anticipation, he set his book down on the table next to his easy chair and settled into a relaxed position.

Closing his eyes, he pictured Dawn. And sent his mind spinning out toward her…

Chapter 4

The faeries were right. The inside of St. Yve Manor was sumptuous. High, coved ceilings. Rich wood paneling, elaborately carved moldings. Thick Persian carpets. Galen could even smell the luxury—a faint perfume of old roses blended with the scents of leather and furniture wax. A sensual paradise.

Suddenly, the air was charged with otherworldly presence. House demons swirled like vapor about the room, phantom fangs and claws extended toward him.

"Whhhooo aaarrre yooou?" they moaned.

"I am Galen," he told them, unperturbed. The faeries had warned him of them. "Here at your mistress's bidding."

They'd also told him about the house. Built upon an ancient temple site of hedonistic pagan fertility ritual, St. Yve Manor was a place bathed in sensuality. Its very foundations oozed with secret, erotic cravings and voyeuristic abandon, absorbed from ten thousand years of the worship of sex.

An incubus would be welcomed within, the faeries had told him. As long as he meant no harm.

He felt the house demons probe his mind and see his carnal intent. Their menace turned to delight. Claws and fangs disappeared.

"Yesss," they hissed excitedly. "You mussst haaave her."

"Go away," he said. "I want her to myself."

The lesser demons obeyed. But he sensed another presence in the room, in the very walls themselves, watching him. Like a living thing, the silent house crouched and waited, sending a low current of sexual energy flowing over him, encouraging him, quickening his body with its growing urgency.

"I said go!" he repeated. But his words had no effect. *So be it.*

He looked around. He appeared to be in a library. One wall was completely covered with cases holding all manner of books, from stately antique volumes to brightly colored paperbacks. There were *objets d'art*—vases and sculptures of glass, ceramic and metal—scattered about. A mammoth marble fireplace mantel held a giant bouquet of fragrant pink and yellow roses and a golden clock that ticked loudly.

Dawn was tucked into the curve of a glass-paned bow window, lying on a green velvet sofa in a sexy sprawl. The damask curtain behind her was drawn closed. Her head had lolled against the back cushion, the book she'd been reading lay splayed on the floor below her drooping hand.

Galen's body thrilled to the sight of her. The top button of her lilac-colored satin pajamas had come undone, and her hair was mussed as though she'd run agitated fingers through it many times. Or as if *he* had.

Just one of the many things he intended to do to her before the night was out. Starting with those pajamas.

He took a step toward her, the sound absorbed by the thick pile of the Oriental rug. Raising his hand, he brushed the air in a subtle gesture, causing the buttons to slip from their moorings. The pajama top gaped open, revealing her perfect, creamy breasts. *Beautiful.*

He didn't stop there, but used his powers to slither the top down her arms and off her body. She didn't stir, even when the material slid between her body and the green velvet of the sofa. So he did the same with the pajama bottoms. Leaving her gloriously nude.

For a moment he simply savored the sight. She was gorgeous. Long-legged and curvy. Lips made for sin. Breasts shaped for lust. *And all his.*

Even though he wasn't a true incubus, he, as most *daemons sapiens,* had the ability to call up his incubus, or parts of his incubus, at will. He couldn't resist conjuring an extra, invisible hand and sending it out to pass lightly over her breasts, relishing the feel of her soft flesh, letting it thumb the rosy peaks, which tightened to perfect, round points.

She came to with a gasp and sat up, blinking unfocused eyes.

But she was still asleep. Her dream of him had begun. In all ways, she would behave as though awake, unable to tell the difference between reality and illusion. For all intents, he *was* real. The best part of pretending to be an incubus was that he could do all sorts of mind tricks. And body tricks. As long as she remained asleep.

He tsked, spotting the oversized coffee cup that sat on the end table behind her. "You've been a very naughty girl, my sweet. You didn't really think you could stay awake all night to avoid me, did you?"

Her emerald-green eyes swam with trepidation. "Worth a try," she murmured. "I told you I'd changed my mind."

"And as I said, too late." He swiveled to indicate a gold-labeled bottle which he'd brought with him, sitting on a tall stand along with two crystal flutes. "Come, have a drink. I trust you like champagne?"

"Um. Yes." She seemed surprised by its appearance. Ah, she did have much to learn.

He filled the two glasses and held one out to her. She rose from the sofa, and that's when she realized she was naked.

She glanced down at her bareness, gasping in embarrassment. "What have you done to me?"

"Just remember," he reminded her, "that none of this is real. It's all just a dream." Which was a lie, of course. Just because it was a dream didn't mean it wasn't real.

"It *feels* very real," she said, turning away from him as her cheeks flushed dark-rose. Perhaps she was on to him. "Where are my pajamas?"

"You won't need them," he promised. He moved behind her and reached the glass around to her. "Here. Take it. It'll help you relax."

"This is *my* dream. I get to choose if I'm dressed or not," she said, but took the flute from his hand.

"Not with an incubus, you don't." He moved closer, so his body brushed down the length of her bare back. "I'm in charge now. It's part of the fantasy."

He felt her shiver. He liked when her body disobeyed her mind. "Fantasy? I thought you said this was just a straightforward bargain."

"You of all people should know better," he softly chided. He placed a gentle kiss to the side of her throat. "Open your mind to me, my sweet," he whispered in her ear. "Show me your deepest fantasies. I'll make every one of them come true."

Again, her body trembled. She shook her head. "Stop whispering."

"Afraid?" he murmured.

"Terrified," she confessed softly.

"Of me? Or of yourself?"

She turned around to face him, her expression tormented.

And something else simmered just below the surface. *Something that wanted him.* "Both," she whispered.

He smiled, his craving for her growing harder to ignore. He touched his champagne flute to hers. "To us."

He was pleased when she drank. Pinning her with his gaze, he reached out to her. Slowly, slowly, he drew his fingertips down her throat, and lower still. Her breaths became shallow and quick, and her flushed cheeks colored deeper.

When he reached her breast, her hand shot up to stop him. He easily caught her by the wrist, and held her with just enough firmness to prevent her from escaping. Or from covering herself. Tossing back the rest of his champagne, he set down his glass and took hers away, as well.

Gathering both wrists behind her back, he contemplated her naked body, and murmured, "Now, Lady Dawn, what would you like me to do to you?"

Her delicate rose nipples spiraled to tight little points, sitting up prettily for him. They jerked up toward him with each panting breath she took, as though begging for his tongue.

Not yet. Better to let the need build within her. He wanted *her* begging for his tongue first.

"Let me wake up," she said, her voice breathy and low.

He lowered his lips to her cheek. "I don't think so, my sweet."

He held her immobile and trailed his lips and his stubbled jaw down her cheek, under her chin, and up the other cheek, ending with his mouth hovering over hers. He felt an answering rush of energy from her as the warmth of their exhales mingled. Sexual energy.

"I arouse you," he murmured. *As much as she aroused him.*

"Yes," she admitted, trembling. "But I'm still afraid."

He wasn't about to allay her fears. Fear lent a dark edge of eroticism to her inevitable surrender that had him thickening and lengthening at the thought.

"It's time we sought your bed," he whispered. "Afraid or not, you must seal our bargain by surrendering your body to me."

She swallowed. "Surrender was never part of our bargain, Galen." she said, tipping up her wobbly chin. "Only sex."

His lips curved. He admired her courage. It couldn't be easy for a woman like her to find herself in this position. Yet he had every intention of commanding her complete surrender.

"We'll see," he said.

She waited for his next move with a hint of rebelliousness in her gaze. But she didn't fight him when he leaned in for a kiss. Didn't so much as resist. She was learning.

Though he preferred to think she wanted him as badly as he wanted her, and her defiance was all about self-delusion. He'd like that, too. Self-delusion he could use.

The kiss didn't last nearly long enough. He'd barely put his tongue to hers before she withdrew.

Perhaps it was time to banish this particular delusion—the one she held that she could in any way control him—by giving her a small demonstration of his powers.

He sent his demonic energy spinning over her, through her body. She gasped. The hairs rose on her arms. Her eyes squeezed shut. He poured his powerful lust into her, enslaving her blood, her muscles, her libidinous need.

He pulled her flush to his body and mercilessly covered her mouth with his. A mewl of protest escaped her throat, but immediately it turned to a low moan as he thrust his tongue deep into her mouth. Her body melted into his.

Satan's tears, she tasted sweet. Sweet and innocent.

How was it possible a woman of her background and experience could be so easily captured, so trusting of a man like him? She wasn't even attempting to fight him.

Not his problem. In fact, it played right into his hands. The more trusting she was, the better. It would make his real job that much easier. And it would give them both maximum physical pleasure as long as he was with her. And he planned to be with her in every way. Rule her in every way. Demand her surrender in every way. This little demonstration was just the beginning.

Around them, the room's walls seemed to close in, as though straining to hear and see what he was doing. The ancient ones craved their satisfaction.

Galen kissed Dawn thoroughly, using all his inborn skill to render her boneless and bring her to her knees before him—or it would have done if he hadn't banded her firmly against his chest. She moaned in pleasure, gratifyingly helpless against his all-out sensual assault. He didn't need his magic. She wanted him. Even his split tongue, so foreign to her kind, turned her on. He used it without pity, stroking its twin points along the top of her tongue, sent it exploring opposite sides of her moist, eager mouth. Tickled the back of her throat so she writhed and squirmed with need.

Then he conjured his tongue's incubus, its invisible double, and sent it slicking wetly down her body, its phantom substance curling around the tips of her breasts, trailing down her flat abdomen to dip into her belly button. And farther down, to slide boldly between her thighs, parting the swollen folds of her womanhood. At that, she cried out. So he let it linger there, licking and teasing her until she started to quiver and quake in his arms.

He shouldn't, he knew he shouldn't, but he couldn't stop himself from making one further carnal claim upon her. As the shuddering firestorm of climax roared through her body, he sent his demon essence flooding into her mouth for a second time.

His name tore from her lips. A deep, throaty sound of pure bliss such as no other woman had ever uttered for him before. Then she collapsed in his arms.

He scooped up her limp, wrung-out body with a dark, swirling sense of dominance, of possession, akin to what a vampire must feel after sucking the life force out of his victim.

It was an incredible feeling. Total dominion over another. And yet, he still had such an unsatisfied craving for the woman, he was about to crawl out of his skin.

He needed to feel her naked body under him. He needed to feel his cock push deep into her heat. He needed to feel his sex explode through her willing flesh. And he needed it to happen *now*.

Sweeping a turn, he stalked to the library door, her panting body still in his arms, and kicked it open.

"Take me to your bedroom," he commanded harshly. "Now, my sweet, I shall claim my due."

Chapter 5

The next morning, Dawn awoke slowly, by degrees. First came an awareness of sunlight streaming through the diamond panes of her bedroom window. Then of nearby birdsong and the distant musical laughter of the sidhe dancing in the enchanted wood. Finally, the surprising physical ache of her muscles, and the heavy—

Oh, my God!

She bolted upright in bed, grabbing for the sheet to cover her nakedness, recollections of the previous night streaking through her mind. Tangled and twisted, the bedclothes refused to cooperate as she scrambled back against the solid wood of the headboard. Yanking a corner of the sheet over her, she searched frantically around the room for...*him.*

Omigod, *omigod.*

What had she done?

Last night was *not* what she'd signed up for.

"Galen?" she ventured, her voice coming out raspy with trepidation, thinking he might be ensconced in the en suite bathroom.

The room virtually echoed back at her with tense silence. Not even a whisper of his power remained.

Rubbing a hand unsteadily over her eyes, she slid down on the mattress with a huge measure of relief. For a moment all she could think over and over was, *He's gone. Thank God.*

Because she honestly didn't think she could face Galen McManus ever again. Not after the things he'd done to her last night. And all the things she'd done to him...

She'd expected sex. A nice, civilized round of man-on-woman pleasure.

What she'd gotten was...*SEX.* Round after round of wild, lustful man-all-over-woman feral iniquity.

Lady Dawn Maybank didn't do feral iniquity.

Her face burned. Swallowing a desperate sound of embarrassment, she yanked a pillow over her face. Incubus? She didn't think so. If all that was merely a dream, then she was the bloody Queen of Sheba.

Damn. She could even *smell* him on the bedclothes. That exotic, musky, will-decimating scent of aroused male. *Aroused demon.* The scent that had plummeted her over the edge again and again last night. Even now, her body was reacting to its potency, quickening and slickening in readiness to receive him. The man's unique smell was so incredibly erotic it could practically make her come by itself. Let alone the rest of him... All through the night, she had been completely helpless to resist his seductive demonic powers.

Not that she'd wanted to resist. She'd been a total goner for Galen McManus the second he'd stepped out of the fog yesterday morning and made his indecent proposal. Though, at the time she'd had no idea just *how* indecent he'd intended to get.

Last night, she'd found out.

The man was incredible. A sexual demon in bed.

Her breath hitched. Well, what did she expect? Galen McManus really *was* a sexual demon. An incubus, whose specialty was driving women insane with his prowess. And it was working all too well. Even now, she had a fierce craving to close her eyes and go back to sleep, so he'd return to her bed. And they could do everything all over again.

He really was driving her insane.

Please, God. She couldn't do this. Four more nights! She wouldn't survive even one more! She must find some way out of their agreement. Or she'd end up—

The phone rang on her nightstand, startling her badly.

It was her private line. Probably her father or Aurora. Raking a hand through her hair, she gathered her scattered wits as best she could, and reached for the phone.

"It's Dawn," she said, making a stalwart effort to answer as her usual calm and collected self. Yeah, right.

"Actually, it's gone nine," said Galen's deep, whisky-smooth voice, laced with amusement. What was it about the man's voice that reminded her of the taste of sweet dark chocolate melting over tempting fudge brownies and the feel of soft kittens in the morning sun? "Still in bed, my sweet?"

Her throat seized up and for a second she couldn't utter a sound. Then his words penetrated.

"What?" She straightened in shock and fumbled for the alarm clock that sat next to the phone. "Just brilliant. I have a class at eleven!"

Her father would be sorely disappointed in her if she was late. In forty years the earl had never been late to a class he was teaching. And somehow he always knew every detail about what was going on at the Department, even now.

"Want me to take over for you?" Galen asked charitably.

"Good God, no," she choked out, imagining the havoc *that*

would wreak on her undeserving first-year students. Almost as much as he was wreaking on her. But at least she'd brought it on herself. "Where are you?" she asked, suddenly suspicious.

"Your office. Just dropped in to see how you were getting on after…everything." He almost purred out the last word. *There was that voice again.*

She squeezed her eyes shut as a mass of chaotic feelings seared through her. Disbelief, mistrust, frustration. Pleasure.

Damn it! He's a demon!

In twenty-four short hours he had succeeded in turning her world completely upside down. She *must* snatch it from his grasp and turn it back around, right side up.

"I'm fine," she said briskly, and vaulted out of bed. "Ouch!" She'd forgotten about the sore muscles.

"What?"

"Nothing."

She'd also forgotten his annoying ability to read her mind.

"Did I overdo it last night?"

"You think?"

"You seemed to enjoy yourself."

She tipped her head back and stared at the ceiling for a brief moment. "I did," she reluctantly admitted. "But you cheated. Don't think I didn't notice you planted more of your essence in me. I know how that works." Which was why he could read her thoughts and emotions so well, down to her physical desires.

"You seemed to enjoy that, too."

Lord, had she. The truth was, she'd never experienced an orgasm that incredible and intense. She hadn't known one could *be* that incredible and intense. Between the feel of Galen's tongues on her flesh and the taste of his essence sliding down her throat, her body had detonated like a landmine, shredding any resistance to his licentious advances in the wake of its explosive pleasure.

But having his essence flowing within her made her too vulnerable to him. The more essence he put in her the more vulnerable she became. Much more, and it would allow him to bend her completely to his will, if he should so wish. She'd been a fool to let him go this far.

"Galen, you're an incubus. You can make me enjoy whatever you do to me. But that doesn't mean I want it."

"We both know I didn't make you do a single thing last night you didn't want to do. And you enjoyed it all on your own. My essence merely enhanced your pleasure. Admit it, Dawn. You wanted me badly. Admit you still do."

A shiver coursed through her body at the raw truth of his declaration. But there was no way she would tell him that.

"There's no shame in it, my sweet," he purred, low and rough like a lion coaxing a lamb to lie down with him. "You were amazing. I've never had a more eager or generous lover. I'm counting the minutes until tonight."

She couldn't let his pretty words get to her.

"There won't be a tonight, Galen. You broke our agreement. I never consented to swallowing more essence. And I never consented to…all those things you did. I agreed to have sex. You went…beyond that. Our bargain is off."

He laughed softly. A dark, touchable laugh that was physical, like warm, uncut velvet sliding over her skin. "Your memory fails you, my sweet. You agreed to five nights in bed with me. No mention of what we'd do there. And as long as I don't hear you say no, I intend to do anything and everything I wish."

"I'm saying no now."

Again he laughed. The sound was thick, drowning, without an ounce of humor in it. "Doesn't count. Your refusal must be at the time I'm doing it."

"Says who?"

"Says me. I'm in charge. Remember?" His voice had gone very low, to his demonic whisper. The hushed pronouncement of dominance sent a spiral of desire purling through Dawn's insides. The words pulled at her, invading her mind and rolling over her will. For a moment she wanted nothing more than that he decide everything. He had but to say what he wished and she would obey.

His whisper was bespelling her. She fought the urge fiercely, struggling to shield herself from it.

"Stop," she said, compelling herself snap out of it. "Your tricks won't work on me."

"They worked fine last night."

"You're right," she admitted crossly. "I can't say no when I'm with you. Your power is too strong. But I don't like it. It's not fair."

She could practically hear the male within him preening at her admission. "Dawn, you knew what I was when we made our pact. You've studied my kind your whole life. If you came into this with false assumptions, whose fault is that?"

Hers. All hers. She'd been trained from birth to recognize and resist demonic powers and traps. In her days as an active Cadre tracker she'd single-handedly faced down demons of wrath, deflected demons of greed and ignored demons of terror. She'd even encountered lust demons, and felt scarcely a twinge of sexual need.

But with this man, she'd walked right into his ambush with her eyes wide open.

"You're mine," he whispered. The words leapt from the phone and churned through the room like a dark, hot wind.

You're mine. You're mine. You're mine.

Again she fought him. "I belong to no one, Galen."

He continued as though she hadn't spoken. "Our time together is short enough. Try to enjoy it while you can."

"You can only take what I am willing to give," she told him.

"I'll take whatever I desire," he refuted mildly. "Accept your fate, my sweet. Because there's nothing you can do to stop it now."

Chapter 6

After ending the call, Dawn shook off the disturbing conversation with Galen and hurried to the closet to grab some clothes in her usual style for teaching, a tailored business suit with a silk blouse and fashionable high heels. But as she dressed, a vague sense of unease trickled through her.

Something was off here.

Galen's parting shots had held an almost prophetic ring to them. Like…a warning. As though he meant that if she thought things were uncomfortable now, just wait.

What was going on? Could Galen want something from her besides the obvious?

It was possible. Demons were crafty, devious beings with no conscience. Galen could easily be lying about everything, spinning a web of deceit to conceal his true purpose.

The question was, *what* purpose?

Should she be worried? She thought about the Cadre, and

the Department. What damage could an incubus do to them through her?

Nothing, she assured herself. Because, as susceptible as she was to Galen's…charms, there was no way in hell she would ever let him harm those she loved. No bloody way.

Besides, his interest seemed focused strictly on her. He hadn't asked a single question about the Cadre, her father or Aurora; he'd even gone out of his way to avoid them knowing about him. His curiosity about the Department appeared incidental, more academic than personal.

Still. This unfortunate arrangement between herself and a demon could absolutely *not* be allowed to come back and bite her in the backside. If anyone, especially her father or Aurora, ever found out about it, Dawn would be deep in the muck.

She must take care. Be extra wary around Galen. Getting the Demon Stone back was important, but her first concern must always be to protect her family, and uphold her responsibilities to the Cadre.

Especially if Galen had some nefarious scheme up his sleeve.

Dawn made the drive into town in record time. Dashing up the round stone staircase to her third-floor classroom—after parking in the underground car park—she checked her wristwatch. Only ten minutes late to class. Not too awful.

Outside the classroom door, she paused to catch her breath. Having the Department in an historic registry building was wonderful, but it also had its drawbacks. The lack of a lift, for one.

However, she wouldn't change venues for the world. The Department of Anachronistic Research was housed in the oldest structure owned by London University. And Dawn had by far the coolest classroom in the entire place.

It was an old autopsy theater—in fact, the oldest such theater in all of England. It simply oozed atmosphere. On her express orders, minimal changes had been made to accommodate the modern props of teaching, and her unique classroom sat just under the three-hundred-forty-five-year-old hexagonal copper onion cupola adorning the building's roof. Below the exposed cupola, six rings of steeply graduated dark wood benches surrounded a small stage like a miniature sports arena. In the center of the stage stood a podium where, in the old days, a crude operating table had sat for autopsies conducted before the country's first medical students. Exposed copper runnels that used to drain the body's blood were still embedded in the heartwood floors.

It was the perfect place to teach young, impressionable minds about demons and sidhe, vampires and werewolves, and all manner of paranormal beings, which was her specialty at the Department. Luckily, the ghost seers, trance mediums and ESP specialists on the staff wouldn't touch this room with a ten-foot pole. Too much psychic interference, those teachers claimed. Which suited Dawn just fine. She had no such qualms.

She opened the door and strode through the short passage leading under the circular tiers of student-filled benches. When she emerged at the edge of the hexagonal center stage, she halted in consternation.

An all-too-familiar figure stood there, face and arms raised as though to the heavens. Her students watched him in silent awe, eyes wide and lips parted. Why hadn't she felt him, sensed his power, before she walked in? She could have used a warning.

"Galen! What on earth!" she snapped, breaking his spell. It was a spell of charisma, of personality. She realized he was shielding his preternatural energy very carefully. She couldn't detect even a hint that he wasn't a normal human. Amazing. And scary. If she couldn't tell, no one could.

His gaze dropped to her, and he flashed a roguish grin. "Behold, my sweet, and be astonished." He looked up again, spread his fingers like a magician, and called, "Now!"

Suddenly he was illuminated as though by a bright spotlight, his midnight hair turning to liquid onyx, his shirt to a white so dazzling it almost hurt to behold.

Gobsmacked, Dawn followed his line of sight to the upper walls of the room where mullioned windows of wavy glass circled the cupola to bring in three-hundred-sixty degrees of sunlight. Four students stood at the windows opposite the sun, manipulating the angle of the casements so the glass panes reflected the sunbeams directly on him.

She *was* astonished. So much so that she forgot he'd just called her his sweet in front of all her students.

She gaped at him. "H-how did you know about that?" She'd done extensive research on the building and had never read anything even hinting at this unique feature. Although it made perfect sense when you thought about it. And explained the curvy glass in the windows.

"How? I'm older than I look," he said with a wink, and the students laughed. "Why, I remember one autopsy in particular. A victim of Jack the Ripper, I believe—"

She snapped her jaw closed and with a grimace strode to the podium, poking him aside with a finger. "That will be all, Mr. McManus. I'm sure you've more than entertained my students with your tall tales, but I can take over now, thank you very much." She put a hand to her eyes and motioned to the students at the windows above. "And please change the angle on those casements! I feel like an angel ascending to heaven in the bright light."

"And you look like one, too, my angel," Galen said, bowing over her hand and giving it a courtly kiss, to the delighted whistles and cheers of her students. "You don't mind if I stay and listen?"

She snatched her hand back. "As a matter of fact—"

"Good!" With his long-legged stride he'd reached the fourth tier of seats before she could draw breath to protest. "Since I'll be in London less than a week, I'd hate to spend a single moment apart from you. Right, darling?"

"Who is he, Professor Maybank?" one of the female students asked her with a worshipful glance at Galen. "Your fiancé?"

Dawn ground her teeth together. "Absolutely not. Mr. McManus is a… He's an antiquities dealer. We're doing some business together."

"Just so," he said, and leaned back in a smug, you-aren't-fooling-anyone pose. "Business partners. Nothing else."

Setting her briefcase down, she endeavored to ignore him and start the day's lecture. The subject of which, as soon as she pulled out her notes, she remembered to her horror was "Lust Demons."

She nearly succumbed to the supreme temptation of pushing the bright-red panic button mounted under the podium top which would summon a Cadre member to dispose of the pesky man. Demons did occasionally drop into her lectures—mostly mischief demons looking for a new, gullible victim among her students—thus the panic button. But if she pressed it now, she'd have to explain her obvious acquaintanceship with her demon tormentor…since counting on him to keep his mouth shut was a fool's hope.

No, the panic button was not an option.

Battling back a sinking feeling that anything she did today was bound to go wrong, she slapped her notes onto the lectern, shot Galen a warning glare, and began her talk. Surprisingly, he minded his manners and sat there with an interested, if mildly amused, expression on his face. And didn't say a word.

Well. Until she got to the part about him: the incubus, and his female counterpart, the succubus. Then apparently he couldn't resist making her squirm.

"I read somewhere," he announced into a pause in her lecture, raising his hand, "that an incubus is actually just a fantasy. That the woman is simply having erotic dreams to make up for a boring sex life in the real world."

She pressed her lips together and narrowed her eyes at him. "Yes, well, that is one interpretation," she said reasonably, determined not to let him fluster her. "And in many cases I'm sure that's exactly what is happening with both incubi and succubae. However, it doesn't explain the times when there is actual physical evidence of a man having been with the woman."

One of the students suggested, "Maybe she's having a forbidden affair and blames it on an incubus, or is making up a story to explain an awkward pregnancy."

"Also likely possibilities." Dawn folded her arms under her breasts as she warmed to her subject. "Certainly, not all so-called 'possessions' involve real demons, including sexual possessions."

"What are you talking about? There's no such thing as real demons," the student said, making a face.

"Are you sure about that?" she countered. "True, there has always been a fine line between what lives in the human psyche and what is a true demonic being."

"How do you mean?" asked another student.

"Regardless of whether the demon is real or in the person's head, the mechanism is the same. When a demon selects his victim," she explained, "there is nearly always a corresponding weakness, or flaw, in the makeup of the human he chooses, which correlates to his…demonic calling, if you will."

"You mean the person's flaw is what conjures the demon, and allows it entry into the person?"

She nodded. "Exactly. A rage demon victimizes a human who is either predisposed to rages, or is so afraid of going into a rage that the demon is able to possess the person and slowly influence her to express all that pent-up rage. Nearly always inappropriately."

"So…" Galen asked with transparent innocence, "What would that say about a woman who is possessed by an incubus?"

She stared at him, taken aback for a moment before answering. Surely, it wasn't some deep, hidden sexual fantasy that had brought him to her? A particularly embarrassing fantasy… Her earlier concerns about his reason for being here came rushing back. *Did* it involve more than their simple bargain?

"I, um…" She tore her gaze away from him and glanced around at her students, all watching her curiously. She decided just to blurt it out. "Incubi, as all lust demons, can be a bit more complicated than other types of demons. The victimology can be similar, where the chosen human in this case is particularly susceptible, or averse, to sexual domination."

A male student perked up, interrupting her train of thought. *"Domination?"*

She took a breath. "Both incubi and succubae have a predilection for mercilessly dominating their victims."

Goose bumps broke out on her arms. Why hadn't she remembered that yesterday during their negotiations? No wonder Galen was so insistent on having his way about everything.

"Don't sound complicated to me," a young woman said with a sniff. "Sounds like a typical bloke."

Dawn forced a chuckle as the other students laughed, then went on, "Well, it gets complicated because sexual desire is one of the few 'human' feelings a demon usually has. Therefore, this type of possession can simply be a case of a demon feeling lust for a specific person, totally at random."

The laughter died. "An innocent, in other words?" the young woman, said, clearly appalled. "Who has done nothing to provoke the demon?"

"Other than appear sexually attractive to him, yes. Exactly." Dawn hazarded a glance at Galen, who had a satisfied smile on his face. As though she'd just said exactly what he'd wanted her to say. She frowned. "Then again, because of its very randomness, a clever demon of a different kind could be using this type of possession and his natural ability to summon his incubus, to cover some other, more sinister intent."

Galen's smile froze in place and for a second his expression turned murderous. Then it was gone, his serene mien restored. "What could be more sinister than complete sexual domination?" he suggested in a final, rhetorical kind of way.

Which made her think the question was likely far from rhetorical. Or the answer final.

What *could* be more sinister than that, she wondered?

"Come to my place."

Galen had followed Dawn to her office. He wanted to get her naked, but couldn't even get her to look him in the eye.

"No," she said, fussing with the things on her desk. "I have too much work to do."

"Work later," he urged, coming up behind her. He stroked his hands down her arms to still her movements. "I want you," he murmured. "Now."

"Do you?"

"Oh, yes." He pressed his cock against her bottom so she would know exactly how much, and whispered in her ear exactly what he wanted to do to her.

To his surprise, she asked quietly, "Is that all?"

He gave a deep hum of approval. That had been easy. "It is just the beginning of what I want to do, my sweet, I assure you."

She turned in his arms. "No. I mean, is sex all you have in store for me? Or should I be worried about something…else?"

He schooled his features while tamping down a flick of anger. Okay, not so easy. She had been shielding herself from him. A habit he needed to break her of. Still, after her comments in class earlier he'd been expecting this line of questioning. And was prepared. "Something else, such as?"

"You tell me."

He tipped her chin up and gave her a look that would melt steel. "You must be able to tell how I feel about you, Dawn."

"Galen. Weren't you listening to my lecture? I'm perfectly aware demons don't have feelings, other than of the basest sort. Lust and anger are the extent of your repertoire. So don't try to have me on. If you've caught me in a honeytrap, at least have the decency to warn me what's coming."

For a split second he actually considered her request, then quickly banished the heretical thought. *The Devil.* What the hell was that about?

As fate would have it, he was spared a response. A mousy woman with thick, black-framed glasses hurried into Dawn's office.

"Professor Maybank," she said agitatedly. "I need to speak with you urgently."

Dawn jetted out a breath and he could see her jaw muscle work. "What is it, Marta?"

The woman glanced pointedly at him. "Privately."

He took his cue. "I'll step out for a moment, shall I?"

He did so and closed the door behind him. The white stone angel hanging on it opened its eyes and shuddered. Long claws extended, then curled back into its fingertips. "Horrid woman. Wish I could bar her permanently from the room. The mistress is always in foul humor after she leaves."

"Indeed?" Galen said, leaning his back against the cold, roughhewn wall opposite. "Why is that, Huwa?"

"Running feud with another professor, Dr. Cornell. Claims he's harassing her. Cornell claims she's trying to get him fired."

"Is she?"

The guardian demon shuddered again and closed his eyes, apparently already bored with the conversation. "Bitch," was all he said.

A few minutes later the door burst open and Marta marched primly past Galen without so much as a glance. He strolled back into Dawn's office and found her clutching her head as if it were about to explode.

He came around and perched on the desk next to her, running his knuckles down her cheek. "Anything I can do?"

She groaned. "That woman seriously needs to get laid. Want to volunteer?"

"I don't think she fancies me." He kissed the top of Dawn's head. "What about her nemesis, Dr. Cornell?"

"A match made in heaven," she muttered. "Too bad neither of them can see it."

Well, he couldn't make promises for heaven, but he could clearly read Dawn's thoughts, and they were less than angelic concerning the troublesome pair. He felt a job coming on. Excellent.

Winding his hand in her hair, he compelled her face up and put his lips to hers. "Forget about them," he murmured. "Think about this instead."

Then he kissed her. Long, hard, wet, and wickedly, arousingly sinful. And when he finally lifted, ages later, he could sense the only thought she had in her head, the only craving she had in her body, was for him.

Which was exactly how he'd planned it.

What he hadn't planned on, however, was that the same was true for him.

And when he came to that realization, it was just about the scariest moment of his life.

Chapter 7

Despite that incredible kiss, Galen still hadn't been able to talk Dawn into going to his flat. In fact, she'd thrown him out of her office. She'd seemed upset. Though, for the life of him he couldn't figure out why.

He was the one who should be upset. This whole possession was getting out of hand.

To be sure, the first part of his plan had gone well. He'd talked himself into her bed easily enough. And he'd made good progress on his assigned vengeance task—Roland was history, and right after leaving the Department he'd arranged that the uptight Marta would run into Dr. Cornell—literally—tonight at a local pub, with enough drinks in both to land them in the back seat of the good doctor's car. What happened after that should prove entertaining. And should disrupt their little feud badly enough that one of them would leave in disgrace, fulfilling all Dawn's wishes.

But despite his successes, Galen was unnerved. Why?

Because for the past three hours he'd been wandering aimlessly around the British Museum—a place that had always been able to hold his rapt attention for days on end—and the only paintings he could remember seeing were all of the same subject matter: female, pretty, titian-haired and nude.

He was becoming obsessed with the pretty, titian-haired, preferably nude Dawn Maybank.

Obsessed! In all his stints to the mortal realm Galen had *never* become obsessed with a human he was working a possession on. Or anyone else, for that matter. Devil take it, Dawn was supposed to become obsessed with *him*—or at least with what he was doing to her. Certainly not the other way around.

The situation was unsettling. And unacceptable.

But what to do about it?

Irritated and randy, and irritated that he was randy, Galen turned on a heel, stalked out of the museum's entrance and down the front steps. He'd seen enough naked pictures for one day. What he wanted was the real thing. In the flesh this time, not in some stupid dream. Since he wasn't an actual incubus he didn't have that bothersome restriction on his behavior. Wouldn't Dawn be surprised to learn that little tidbit…too late.

For the first time since leaving her office he smiled. Yeah. That was all he needed to cure what ailed him. A long, gratifying night of lustful demon sex with Dawn. He'd use all his powers on her. In the morning they'd see who was obsessed with whom.

Good. He'd stop at the shops and pick up something for dinner, then he'd buzz by the Department and pick her up. And he wouldn't take no for an answer. She'd come to his flat if he had to throw her over his shoulder and carry her.

An hour later Galen parked his red vintage Austin Healey Sprite illegally in front of the Department, threw up a spell of invisibility around it, then went in and trotted up the echoing staircase toward Dawn's office. As he approached, he heard raised voices. Dawn, and an unidentified male. Arguing.

Galen's first instinct was to burst into the room and rain a deluge of fire and brimstone over the man's head, burning him to a crisp for daring to raise his voice to Dawn.

An overreaction, admittedly. Galen's unruly demonic nature straining to come out.

He halted at the partially open door, putting a finger to his lips when Huwa trained a gimlet eye at him.

"I'm telling you, miss," the man inside was saying loudly, "we have the latest detection equipment, and our instruments are never wrong."

Miss? Galen nearly changed his mind about the fire and brimstone at the man's deliberate rudeness. He should be calling her Lady Dawn, or Professor Maybank at the very least.

"Well, your instruments are wrong," Dawn said coolly. "I'm telling *you,* there is no otherworldly activity going on in this department. If there were, I can assure you as department head I'd know about it *and* put an end to it. The Department of Anachronistic Research deals exclusively in *human* paranormal phenomena."

The man's voice rose. "Check the readouts yourself." There was a rustle as papers were smacked onto the desk. "They clearly indicate—"

"*Mr.* Marcolf," Dawn interrupted, her voice changing character. "I am frankly surprised by these allegations your man is making. I know P-Cell is no friend to the Department, but we have always accorded you our fullest cooperation. Why would I be hiding something now?"

P-Cell?

The hair rose on the back of Galen's neck. *P-Cell is here? Satan's devils.* And where had he heard the name Marcolf before?

A different male voice, dark and deep, said, "We've no quarrel with you or your department, Professor Maybank. We'd merely like your permission to conduct a closer search of the premises. Or I should say *cooperation,* since as you know we don't really need your permission...." Marcolf's voice trailed off on that not-so-subtle note of insufferable governmental authority.

Galen was torn between going in there and striking both men dead with a bolt of lightning, or turning tail and running as fast as he could, straight back to the dark realm and away from the two P-Cell officers.

P-Cell was a highly covert black-ops unit of the British Security Service popularly known as MI5. The sole purpose of the P-Cell section was to locate non-human entities—such as demons, vampires, faeries and were-creatures—which entered the mortal realm, and eradicate them by any means necessary. Generally that meant blasting them off the face of the earth with any one of a number of high-tech weapons they'd developed specifically for the task. Their close-up detection equipment was pretty darn sophisticated, too. Could they have already spotted his presence? *The devil.*

He gave an involuntary shudder, and nodded when Huwa pointed a long claw at the closed door opposite. Making quick work of the lock, Galen slipped into the darkened room as Dawn answered Marcolf.

"Be my guest. You'll find nothing. But if I hear of a single incident involving one of my teaching staff or students, I promise you will live to regret it."

"A threat, Lady Dawn?" Marcolf asked silkily. There was something about the man...his tone, his manner...that made Galen's eyes narrow.

"No. A promise, Mr. Marcolf," Dawn answered archly.

Good girl. Don't let the bastard push you around.

Her office door banged open just as Galen shut his to a tiny crack. He peered through it as a cropped-haired young man emerged carrying a sleek, silver, twin-barreled machine gun sporting a digital readout panel and what looked like a night scope. He'd never seen anything like it. He didn't even want to imagine what damage it could inflict on his body. Demons were generally thought of as immortal, but it was in fact possible to kill them. Dead Sea salt was the traditional method. Exposure to more than a few grains of this special mineral could burn a demon so badly it incapacitated him. Cut a hole in his chest and pour Dead Sea salt into it, he'd die. Or you could simply rip out his heart while he was down. Or cut off his head. These days, guns and explosives were just as effective. Hell, more effective. And blowing a demon's body to bits was P-Cell's specialty.

Galen did a quick concealment spell around himself and continued to watch. The spell wouldn't stop their techno gadgets, but it would prevent the humans from deciding to point them in his direction. For now, anyway.

"I'll be round with my officers in the morning, Lady Dawn," Marcolf said, then emerged from her office. Tall and dark as Galen, the man had an arrogant air of command that lent his features an intimidating, almost menacing aspect. He didn't need weapons. Everything about the man spelled efficiency and danger.

If Galen had been human, Marcolf might have frightened him.

But he wasn't. So it wasn't fear that tingled along Galen's spine when the other man turned his hard, black gaze toward the door behind which Galen was standing and stared directly at him. For a long moment Galen stared right back through the crack. And wondered just who the hell this human, Marcolf, was.

But then he was gone, sweeping down the stairs after his mate with the blaster.

"Wanker," Dawn muttered from across the hall, pulling Galen out of his thoughts to see her locking up her office.

"And you think *I'm* scary," Galen drawled, coming out and leaning a shoulder against the doorframe.

She spun. "You! What are you doing here? My God, Galen, you could have been—"

He waved a dismissive hand. "Splattered across the walls and ceiling?" He sent her a wry smile. "Would you have cared?"

"Of course I—Galen, do you have any idea who those men were?"

"P-Cell weasels."

"That was the Deputy Director General of P-Cell himself, Dirk Marcolf," she intoned. "And he was looking for *you*."

So that was why the name was so familiar. The DDG of P-Cell was known far and wide to be a ruthless, take-no-prisoners adversary to all things demonic. Where he walked, death was sure to follow in his wake. On the other hand, he mostly tended to target evil demons and those involved in sinister plots against humanity. Galen wasn't evil. He dealt in cosmic justice.

"Dirk Marcolf couldn't have been looking for me. There's no way P-Cell could know I'm here."

"Trust me, they have their ways. It must be you. No outside demon has been sighted here in weeks. I just don't understand how…" She frowned suspiciously at him. "Galen, have you been up to no good?"

He pushed off the doorframe, dismissing Marcolf. Time to get back to why he was here. "On the contrary, it's all been *very* good," he murmured.

Her cheeks pinkened and she took a step back at his shift in mood. "Besides that."

Walking her slowly backward, he leaned down to meet her lips. "You know I'm not interested in anything but you, my sweet."

"Don't. They could come back." Her bottom hit the wall next to the door.

"Let them." He kissed her.

She allowed the kiss, but when he lifted, said, "They'll kill you."

He caught her up and kissed her again. "They won't."

This time she pulled away, insistent. "They will! They're murdering thugs, Galen. Please. You've got to leave. Go back to the dark realm before they find you."

Tugging her back to him, he murmured into her mouth, "Trying to get out of our bargain again?"

The exchange was beginning to anger him. He was sorely tempted to give her another taste of his essence. The more she swallowed the easier it would be to make her obey.

But no. When it came right down to it, he enjoyed their sparring. He liked her willfulness, how she tried to defy him but couldn't quite pull it off. He preferred her feisty, yet at times helpless against his magnetism. He didn't want her to be soft and acquiescent. He wanted her…just the way she was.

The real sport with humans was in the persuasion. When sex was involved, even more so.

"Yes," she said. "I *am* trying to get out of it. And you should be, too. For your own good."

"I'll be the judge of that," he said. "Right now, *you're* what's good for me." He shifted his arm around her waist and steered her toward the stairs. "Come on, I'm hungry. How about some dinner?"

She balked. "What if we run into Marcolf and his goon? They could be watching the building."

He kept walking. "Just give me a big kiss. They'd never believe the famous demon hunter Lady Dawn of St. Yve would willingly kiss a demon. Therefore, I can't be one."

"Tracker. Not hunter. And don't be too sure about that," she muttered. "P-Cell thinks the Cadre is a bunch of spineless bleeding hearts. Marcolf's not my greatest personal fan, either. He's convinced I'm lying to him, that there's a connection between the Department and the Cadre that I'm keeping secret."

Galen chuckled, scanning the foyer below the stairway. "You can't blame them, can you? There *is* a connection and you *are* lying to them, official government agency and all."

She sniffed. "Official, nothing. They don't officially exist. Neither does the Cadre. Sounds to me like we're even."

"True." He held up a hand while he slotted open the heavy wooden outside door. "The bad guys gone?" he asked one of the guardian gargoyles.

The gargoyle ruffled his wing feathers and hissed, "No thanksss to you. Leave, demon, and don't commme back. You endanger usss all."

Tetchy little sod. "I'll leave when my business here is finished," he stated, took Dawn's hand and led her out of the building and down the steps to the Austin Healey Sprite, snapping his fingers to disable the concealment spell.

"This is yours?" she asked, brightening when it popped into view.

He tossed her briefcase into the back and helped her in. "I realize the weather's a bit brisk for a convertible. I hope you don't mind a little wind?" All the better to warm her up when they got to his flat.

She produced a scarf from her coat pocket, tied it around her hair and flipped up her collar. "All set," she said with a smile. "Where are we going?"

He winked and buckled up. "Surprise."

"I love surprises," she said, settling deep into her bucket seat with a grin.

"Good. Because I'm full of them."

"So I've noticed."

"Yeah?" He pointed the car in the direction of his flat.

"You're not exactly one's stereotype of a demon, Galen."

"Really? How so?"

"Fishing for compliments again, darling?"

He slanted her a glance, irrationally pleased at the endearment. No one had ever called him darling before. No one had ever called him anything but his name. "Absolutely."

She laughed, an easy, carefree sound that lit up his insides. "You are incorrigible."

"I do my best." He grinned back at her. "So, about those compliments?"

She tipped her head. "I'm sure you're well aware of your attributes."

"I am." But damn, he wanted to hear them spilling from her delectable mouth. "Are you?"

"Oh, yes." Her eyes danced as she said, "You're handsome as sin. Your kisses turn me to jelly. And you've got pretty nice taste in cars, too."

He smiled. "Interesting list. Too bad there's no back seat or we could stop for a snog. Next time I'll have to bring a bigger car."

"I thought you were hungry."

"Ravenous." And getting more so by the second. But not for food.

Fifteen minutes later, he whipped into the car park under his building and squealed into his designated spot.

Confused, Dawn looked around. "Where are we? I thought we were having dinner."

"We are." Eventually. "I thought I'd cook for you." Her mouth dropped open. "Surprised?"

Her eyes widened, and in a flash every trace of lightness fled. She shook her head, at once wary. "No. I'm not going to your flat, Galen. It's not happening."

He raised a brow. "Why not?"

"Hello? You're a demon. I'd be mad to let you lure me into your lair." Now she really did look afraid, as though saying it out loud had doubly reminded her.

"My *lair?* How quaint. What do you think will happen that hasn't already?" He touched her chin, ignoring her flinch. "Besides, I'm an incubus. You said yourself you have to be asleep for my powers to work."

She swallowed. "I could be wrong."

"Ever heard of an incubus being with a woman who's awake?"

She swallowed again. "No. But how do I know you won't drug me?"

"A remarkable thought. But you should know I prefer my lovers sober, even if they are asleep."

She appeared unconvinced. He couldn't believe she was putting up so much resistance.

"It's just dinner," he argued. "I promise, I have no plans to enslave you or make you my familiar, if that's what's worrying you."

"How do I know you're not lying to me?"

He ground his teeth. "I guess you'll just have to take my word for it."

She nibbled her bottom lip, as though trying to decide whether or not he was trustworthy.

"I can *make* you come up," he said, losing patience. Inwardly lashing back at a glaringly alien prick of guilty conscience that he *wasn't* trustworthy. Far from it. He was deceiving her and using her, and in the end, fulfilling his Directive would hurt her more than she could ever imagine.

Because that was what his kind did.

But there was absolutely no reason to feel guilty. Trustworthy? Who gave a damn?

"Very well," he said, preparing to summon his powers of persuasion.

"Force won't be necessary," she said quietly. "Because I do trust you."

Chapter 8

Demons weren't the only ones who could lie. Because Dawn had just told a whopper.

Trust him? Not likely.

But at the moment she saw little option but to obey. For whatever reason, he wanted her in his flat. She silently visualized her protection circle and hoped for the best. She couldn't understand why it never seemed to work against him....

The look Galen gave her as he punched the lift call button unnerved her. Dark, edgy. *Ominous.* Despite his reassurances, she was certain something was about to happen to her. She knew better than to willingly go to a demon's abode. She *knew* better. His magic would be far more powerful where he lived, and he'd have countermeasures in place to render her mind shield and protection spells totally useless. She bet even her mobile phone wouldn't work. If she got in trouble, nothing and no one would be able to help her. She should be fighting him tooth and nail. It was a supreme mystery why she wasn't.

Stepping into the lift she felt suddenly lightheaded, and stumbled. He caught her, holding her in his strong arms. His hot energy tightened around her insides, coiling into her center like a glowing steel spring.

She forced herself to shut out the sizzling feeling and concentrate on her surroundings. It was an old building with gleaming wood and marble everywhere. Probably Georgian, or even older, though there had been renovations through the years, such as the lift that carried them. That was old, too, a black curly wrought-iron cage that crept slowly up floor after floor amid soft mechanical creaks and groans.

Galen didn't say a word. Just held her close to his chest, the sure, steady beat of his heart thudding against her breasts, the coarse collar of his long black mac rubbing her jaw. His subtle, distinctive scent teased her senses. The spice of his skin and the feel of his hard body pressing against hers flooded through her, reminding her all too vividly of last night.

The allure of him was too powerful. Against her will, she twined her arms about his neck, putting her nose to the warm skin of his throat to inhale of it more deeply. It was unsettling how much she wanted him, in spite of her uncertainties about him and his true reasons for wanting her.

Had he already worked his potent magic on her? Bewitched her so thoroughly she saw only the man she desperately desired, and not the demon within?

As a Cadre tracker, she'd seen for herself what inner chaos one of his lot could wreak on the unsuspecting or naive. Dawn was neither. She was strong, and more than knowledgeable of his ways. It was true, no normal woman was immune to the charms of an incubus. He could wile his way into her mind, change her perceptions, convince her that she was in love with him. After that, she'd do anything for him. With him. While he used her to his own purpose, and then discarded her. Dawn had seen it time and time again in her work for the Cadre. But she knew how to resist such charms and wiles. She'd done it before and would do it again. But this…this wasn't like that.

Why did this relationship with Galen feel so different? So…real? It left her reeling, uncertain of anything.

They took the lift all the way up to the top floor. He swept her off her feet and strode out with her, barely slowing as the stately door to his flat flew open by itself. He entered and it shut behind them with a whoosh and a snick. Inside, the air felt warm and electric as it pressed in on them, charged with power. Hot, other-worldly energy spilled over her, seeping through her pores, filling her lungs so she absorbed it into her very blood. Her heartbeat took off. What had she gotten herself into?

He let her down gently, holding her around the waist until she found her feet. Wordlessly he peeled off her coat and hung it from a peg on an elaborately carved oak Victorian hall stand. As soon as he let her go, the energy stopped, as if he had somehow switched it off. Leaning in relief against the cool, red-painted door, she watched him shuck off his black mac and hang it beside her white wool coat.

"Good thing you're not into symbolism," he remarked, breaking the crackling silence as he turned to her. Her body welcomed his with a sigh as he pressed its towering hardness against her. A sharp tension tightened between them.

"Who says I'm not?" she answered, the words barely a whisper. His shirt smelled faintly of cloves and vanilla.

"I do." He gripped her jaw in his fingers and lifted her face, covering her mouth with his. His forked tongue flicked at her, and of their own volition her lips opened to him. Leisurely, as though he had all the time in the world, he parted his tongue and sank it deep into the sensitive recesses of her mouth. Exploring. Tempting.

His kiss was hypnotic. Drugging. Filling her with an overpowering need to merge her body with his. She should stop him. Now. But she couldn't. The more he kissed her, the more she wanted. She wanted...more.

When he slid off her suit jacket she stepped out of her shoes. She was tall for a woman, but looking up at him she felt dwarfed by his height. For a second she thought about her lecture this morning, the part about an incubus wanting to dominate his partner. There was really no need with Galen. His sheer size did that all by itself.

As he kissed her, his fingers trailed down her throat to the buttons of her blouse, and undid the top one. She pulled away quickly. So quickly she saw his tongue cleave and glide back into his mouth. It was blue. She gave a little gasp. She'd read that a demon's tongue could change color when he was sexually aroused. As could his penis. Though she'd never actually seen it happen before. Last night it had been too dark to tell. Aside from which, she'd kept her eyes squeezed shut most of the night. Her senses had been overloaded, even without the added dimension of sight.

His energy returned, a dark, erotic vibration against her skin. Its heat poured through her, making her shiver.

"Am I scaring you again?" he asked, his long-lashed eyelids at half mast, his look slumberous, enticing.

"You never stopped."

His lips curved as he fingered her second button. "In that case, I suggest a drink. Shall we open a bottle of wine?"

Wine. Not a brilliant move. Just look where the champagne last night had taken her.

"Or would you prefer champagne?"

She gave her head a shake. "Mineral water's fine for me."

His look was withering. "Not at my table. Come."

He led her across a grand foyer with a magnificent gold-leaf ceiling medallion and gorgeous inlaid floors, and down a wide expanse of hallway which ended in a sliding panel door. Again it opened without a touch, and she found herself in a large gourmet kitchen, complete with stainless-steel appliances, glass-fronted cabinets and black granite counters with a giant matching center island. The kitchen smelled of baking bread, and she wondered if that was real or part of the house magic.

He waved a hand at a walk-in wine cooler the size of a small country. "Pick something and open it," he ordered, going to the fridge and starting to pull things out. When she hesitated, he warned, "If you don't, I will."

He would, too. She battled back a sudden deluge of panic. She'd been putting off the inevitable, ignoring the danger because of his power over her body, but it was past time to decide. Would she run? Would she gather her strength and try to fight him? Or would she just go along with whatever he wanted, leaving her fate in the hands of a man she desperately wanted, but didn't trust?

"Why am I here, Galen?" she asked uneasily. Wishing she knew what to do. Wishing he didn't tempt her so thoroughly. So blindingly. "What do you want of me?"

"I've told you," he said, his intense gaze pinioning her. "First I want to feed you dinner. Then I want you naked in my bed. I want your body under mine and I want your complete surrender, Dawn. Nothing less."

The desire within her flared again at his bald declaration. Perhaps he was telling the truth. He'd claimed much the same last night. And had been true to his word. She had surrendered and he had taken her, but nothing more than carnally. Despite the added essence.

"What if I do that? Fall asleep here, in your bed. If I surrender to you again. What then?"

The cruelly set angles of his face softened. "I hope you'll see you've nothing to fear from joining your body with mine. That what is happening here is exactly as it appears to be—exquisite pleasure for two people who crave each other. Nothing more."

The term *people* might be a stretch. Nevertheless, a trickle of relief purled through her. Along with another, less definable emotion. A different kind of fear. One she hadn't thought about before.

What if she surrendered to him, and found that she had given up more than her body? What about her *heart?* Was it possible to get so close to a man, to allow him complete reign over her person, and not develop feelings for him? Not start pinning hopes and dreams on their relationship? The kind of hopes and dreams a man—a demon—like Galen McManus would never be able to fulfill.

Anything beyond sex between them was impossible. Absurd, even if it were possible. Could she do it?

"My dear, you act as though you have a choice," Galen said with the assurance of a man who could read her mind and had the means to enforce his rulings. "You made your bargain, and I've every right to demand you keep it."

She closed her eyes and took a deep, cleansing breath.

He pursed his lips. "But…I'll tell you what," he said, setting a bowl of brown liquid on the counter. It seemed to be stirring itself. "If I really frighten you so much, I'll do the unprecedented and let you take back your word. You can walk out of here right now, if you like."

Her eyes popped open and she stared at him, stunned by his change of attitude. "Really?" The buzzing energy of his power had switched off again.

He nodded. "Really. But know this. If you do, you'll be walking out on the Demon Stone. You'll never see it again. Nor will anyone in your family. I'll make sure it is lost in the dark realm for two thousand years this time."

She continued to stare as his threat hit home. *What was wrong with her?* Her damn cowardice was about to cost her the Demon Stone! She thought about her father, and how badly he wanted it. How he'd searched the world over for it, for decades. How pleased he would be if she brought it back to the family.

In a turmoil of indecision, she watched Galen pick up the bowl of liquid and pour it over two thick steaks in a glass pan.

"Oh," he said, almost as an afterthought. "And you'll be walking out on me, too. For good. If you go, you'll never see me again. Ever."

Her heart stalled. She had to have heard wrong. "But… You can't mean—"

"Oh, but I do." His haughty black eyes met hers in challenge. "I have no use for a lover who trembles from my touch—at least not because of fear," he added with a tinge of irony.

Oh, God. She was about to lose the Demon Stone, and Galen, too! *Forever.*

Suddenly she couldn't imagine never seeing him again. His roguish smile. His shiver-inducing touch. She knew her need, her desire, were just illusion, created by his demonic powers. But her cravings felt no less real for that. What should she do?

"Surrender or flee," he said with a finality that left no doubt in her mind that he meant it. "Your choice, Dawn. You have thirty seconds to decide."

Desperation bubbled up within her, sick and agonizingly painful. *Thirty seconds?* He had to be joking!

The clock ticked. Her mind whirled.

"Twenty seconds," he said. Dead serious.

"Galen, please. This is insane." She reached out to him, but he stepped away.

"No. What's insane is me giving you a choice!" He looked angry and disgusted with himself. "Even a demon wouldn't go back on a sealed bargain. By Satan, it's *me* who's insane!" Hot, powerful fury suddenly vibrated in his voice. "I should take you by force." His power cracked around them like thunder.

Her pulse spun out of control. "You can't! I'm not asleep."

"Shall we test that theory?" he ground out. "Or I can truly bespell you. Trust me, you wouldn't stand a chance."

His energy swirling like a tornado, he stormed to the wine cooler and went in, coming out a few seconds later with a bottle the color of blood. Banging open a drawer, he scattered utensils violently, then slammed it shut again. He glared at the cork and it popped out of the bottle, flying into the wall with the force of a missile. The air was thick and charged.

"Five seconds."

"Please, can't we talk about this?"

"No."

Fire burned in his eyes as he sloshed the blood-red liquid into two crystal goblets. A shower of sparks flew from the base when he crashed one down on the black granite island in front of her. It was a miracle the glass didn't shatter in a million pieces. Like her nerves.

Next to the goblet, he slapped down a twenty-pound note.

"The choice is simple, my sweet," he growled. "What's it going to be? A taxi? Or complete surrender to my will?"

Chapter 9

The whole room pulsed with the hot, drowning spell of Galen's anger. Of his desire.

The choice he had given Dawn was untenable. Impossible.

She knew what she should choose. She was of the Cadre. This man represented everything she had fought against her whole life....

And everything she had yearned for.

The way he made her feel when she was with him, she'd never experienced anything like it, ever before. Warm, accepted.

Wanted. Unconditionally.

Was it only his magic? Merely an illusion? Probably. Did it matter?

Now, that was the bigger question.

And *that* answer was, indeed, simple.

She'd no doubt regret it. Probably for the rest of her life. But she just couldn't make herself...let him go.

With two trembling hands, she picked up the goblet of wine. Slowly she brought it to her lips and drank. It was sweet and tart all at the same time, full-bodied and aromatic. Surprisingly light for the rich color. Strawberries and chocolate and green apples all in a delightful jumble. A shimmering drift of enchantment wafted up from the glass like heat from pavement.

Faerie wine. She recognized the vintage.

She would be drunk in seconds. But fully sober. Wine brewed by the Daoine Sidhe painted the world for you exactly as you would have it appear. Liquid truth serum. Except idyllic. Real but not real.

Exactly what this situation called for.

Not.

Her only consolation was that Galen drank his own glass down in a single gulp. Were demons immune to the magic of the sidhe? God, she hoped not.

As for herself, she was feeling better already.

The man she wanted more than any other in the whole world, the only man she'd ever wanted quite this badly, was standing right in front of her. Smiling seductively.

Apparently he was feeling better, too.

She lifted her glass. The thing about faerie wine was that you could drink as much of it as you liked. The effect was the same whether you had two sips or two bottles. It just lasted longer.

His smile lifted. "You know what you're drinking?"

"Oh, yes," she assured him. "The sidhe who live in the forest at St. Yve make it."

"That's who I got it from." He refilled her glass, then his own.

"You've been to St. Yve Wood? The enchanted forest?" she asked, surprised.

"I've been watching you for a good while, Lady Dawn. Remember? The faefolk living in your wood were very helpful to my pursuit."

"At *St. Yve?*" She blinked. He'd said he watched her, but this was— "You *stalked* me?"

The revelation should have upset her. But for some inexplicable reason it thrilled her to the core.

He lowered the lashes of his dark, seductive eyes. "Like a satyr stalks a virgin."

She tingled at the analogy. Tingled at his look. Tingled even more as the enchanted wine slid down her throat. "But I'm no virgin."

"Don't I know it. And thank the fates for that."

Images from last night came tumbling through her mind and body, bringing heat to her cheeks. She took another cooling sip of wine. It didn't help. So she unbuttoned her blouse. All the way. Why not? It was obvious where this was headed.

And she wanted him.

He watched her with feral interest.

"Why?" she asked. He'd never answered that question.

His eyes didn't leave her breasts. "Why what?"

"Why did you stalk me? Um, come to me?"

His head tipped. "You called to me. I came."

"I didn't."

He looked up. "You did. You summoned me."

She shook her head confidently and took another sip of the sidhe wine. "Impossible. I may be impetuous at times, but I think I'd remember summoning an incubus."

"It was a few weeks ago. In class. You read a spell aloud to the students, as an example."

Ah. *That* she remembered clearly. She'd been upset yet again by something that had happened at a departmental staff meeting, and had perhaps been overly emphatic in her pronunciation of the ancient Latin curse. Wishing she could curse a couple members of her staff instead. Wait. No. It wasn't a curse, but a spell. And—

"I left the crucial words out!" she protested. That she was sure of. From age two, her father had drilled into her to be extra careful around spells.

"Apparently not."

After a second, she whispered, "My God, you're serious." Ironic laughter percolated from deep inside. "I brought you here from the dark realm *myself*?"

His lips curved wryly. "It's the usual way."

She searched his face, trying to remember the exact nature of the ancient spell. She was positive it had not mentioned an incubus. But maybe something about granting dark desires…

Recalling the gist of her lecture from this morning gave a bit of comfort. "If that's true, I have nothing to fear from you. I'm only afraid because you bring that which I fear most."

"Or that which you most desire," he said, taking a step toward her. There was that word again. *Desire*. Oddly, every time it entered her mind, her whole body quivered. He reached out to touch her. "What is it you desire, Dawn? Most of all?"

"I want…"

It must have been the wine, but at once a myriad of vibrantly poignant inner desires tumbled through her. *The desire for love, a desire to succeed brilliantly at her job, to finally gain the respect of her father, to wreak revenge on those who belittled her, for once to outshine her perfect sister, to return the Demon Stone to her family. To find a man like Galen with whom to live out her days….*

Suddenly her mind cleared, like a lens coming into focus, and she knew everything she wanted was possible. If only she were brave enough.

She stretched up and brushed her lips over his. "I want you to show me the rest of your home."

"I thought you'd never ask." His teeth nipped her bottom lip.

"Ow! What was that for?"

"For putting up so much resistance."

"No more," she murmured. "I brought you here to the mortal realm. I may as well take full advantage."

"I do like the sound of that." His hand slipped under her open shirt and found her breast. "Perhaps the bedroom first?"

"You're reading my mind again." But this time, it was just fine with her.

He didn't bother showing her the rest of the flat. By the time Galen had backed Dawn out of the kitchen and down the hall to the grand staircase leading to the upper story, kissing her the whole way, her blouse and tights had been left on the floor like a trail of breadcrumbs.

"Wait," she said breathlessly, and shimmied out of her pencil skirt. She wanted to be naked. Because she could feel that was what he wanted. The air around them pulsed with the power of his craving for her, like a living, breathing thing. The floor pulsed with it. Even the walls pulsed with it. And it was contagious.

Without breaking the kiss he lifted her up as though she weighed no more than a whisper. She hooked her arms around his neck and her legs around his waist as he apported to the top of the stairs in less than the blink of an eye. She'd seen apportment countless times, but had never experienced it herself before. One second they'd been at the bottom of the stairs, the next, they were at the top, like an old home movie that had been badly spliced.

At the landing he paused while she untangled her limbs, then helped strip off her bra and panties.

"Now yours," she urged, tugging his shirt from his trousers.

"Not yet."

She managed to unbutton the shirt and suddenly they were in his bedroom. This time she barely noticed the dizzy sensation. He crawled onto the huge bed with her in tow, lowering his towering frame onto her. She could feel every hard ridge and muscle of his magnificent body as he pressed her deep into the feather-soft mattress. She could feel his cock, long and thick and throbbing hot between her thighs. Covered by too much clothing.

"Off," she said, grappling for his waistband. "I want them off."

"Later. First I want you off."

He was strong. Domineering. Big. And exquisitely skilled. His mouth came down on her breast and suddenly she couldn't draw breath to argue. At the same time a second, phantom mouth sucked the other crown into its wet, invisible vacuum.

She cried out. "Not fair!"

He'd done that last night. Somehow conjured the illusion of double pleasure. Two mouths. Two tongues. Almost as though two men were making love to her. But the sensation of it was ten times more vivid in Galen's bed than in hers. More magic? The wine? Or merely anticipation of what she now knew would follow?

"Let me pleasure you, my sweet," he said, his power filling her like the buzz from the wine, his voice low and warm, as intimate as the promise of his words. "Tonight is all for you."

Every woman's fantasy.

"Yes, oh, yes."

His tongues played erotically with her nipples, impossible pleasure tightening within her like a wire being pulled to the snapping point. She flung her arms above her head with gasp after gasp, grappling for purchase on something, anything, as her body bowed beneath him. Fingers slid between her legs, and a hand seized her wrists, holding them fast above her head.

She bucked and writhed, giving herself over to the incredible pleasure he brought her. A dazzling blackout climax shimmered just at the edge of an almost painful ecstasy. She felt it swell closer, closer, robbing her of breath, robbing her of thought. Robbing her of self. She didn't care. She cried out again, reaching, reaching, and in the split second before it hit, she opened her eyes to look at her lover, her demon lover, and saw him smile down at her, his midnight eyes glittering like the Demon Stone.

"Mine," he whispered.

And she was ripped into the maelstrom.

Chapter 10

Normally, Galen liked his lovers as active as he. But it pleased him enormously that long after the orgasm he'd given Dawn subsided, she could barely move. Only her eyes shifted as she watched him undress and return to the bed, then open her legs, settle himself between them and mount her.

He pushed his cock deep into her, groaning low at the fine slick heat that greeted him.

She finally stirred, her body undulating under his like a wave on a sea of molten lava. Her thighs tried to grip his hips, trembling with the effort, but fell apart again.

She was conquered. He'd conquered her completely.

"Do you surrender?" he asked as he drew his cock slowly out of her, to the very tip.

"Yes," she murmured on a quivering sigh.

He rewarded her by pushing it back in, just as slowly. Then languidly pulled it out again.

"Say it," he commanded gently.

"I surrender," she murmured. No hesitation. No argument. The male beast within him crowed in triumph.

He rewarded her again. He gripped the mattress, tightening his muscles against the urge to go faster. Because he wasn't ready yet. He wanted more.

"To whom, my sweet? To whom do you surrender?"

"To you." Her eyes softened. "You possess me, Galen."

Her whispered confession made his entire being swell with pride and gratification. Including the already large part she held within her. She gasped, so he halted, afraid to hurt her.

"Don't stop," she pleaded, her voice ragged with need. "Don't stop."

His heart beat hard and wild. *This* was what he wanted. To hold her completely in his thrall. In his power.

"Please, I need you," she whispered.

Blind happiness splintered through him, taking him by surprise. And total shock, because he'd never before felt… anything like it.

Was this…an emotion? Other than lust?

He wanted to turn the awesome feeling into movement and share it with her. To thrust and plunge. To take her to the heights all over again, and lose himself in the sheer exhilaration of the taking.

Then do it a second time. And a third. And when she fell asleep, exhausted in his arms, he'd visit her dreams and do even more.

He climbed his knees up beneath her inner thighs, pushing them wide apart, and started to pump hard. She caught the rhythm, moving with him. He kissed her and she moaned, tasting eagerly of his mouth, encouraging his tongue as its tines twined with hers. He pounded into her, swallowing her gasps and cries like fuel to his fire.

She sucked at his tongue and he let it follow the pull to the back of her throat. She tried to swallow, pulling it back even farther. Instinctively it thinned, and slid deeper. And deeper still.

His pulse kicked up. He must stop. *This was forbidden.*

Her legs tightened around his waist, drawing him closer. She mewled, swallowed again. Her inner muscles gripped his cock mercilessly, and in that split second he lost control. His tongue went down, down, down, far inside her. Almost to her heart. He jerked it back just in time.

She was panting hard, writhing with need, her body coming off the bed as she met his forceful thrusts. Straining for completion. Blissfully unaware, blinded by the magic of the wine and the strength of his powers and the dizzy aphrodisiac of his tongue being so close to its mark.

If it touched her heart he would make her his familiar. His slave, if he so chose.

But he'd promised....

Do it! the devil within him urged. *Demons lie. It's what they do best. She knows that. It is her fault for not being more careful.*

So close. *So close.* The dark power built within him, spilling into her, working its corrupting magic on her will.

He could have her like this, under him, in his control, forever.

He scythed his cock deep, deep. The tips of his tongue tingled with the intensity of his dark energy. Keen to do his bidding.

The Grigori would be pleased if he claimed her. Galen's status would be raised considerably in the demonic order, having taken a love familiar.

Against her will, the fallen angel within him reproved.

I promised not to. I promised.

He gripped her wrists and rammed home again, to the very hilt, trying to banish the disturbingly unfamiliar voice. Conscience?

She moaned, vibrating his tongue all the way down. It quivered in excited indecision. Her inner muscles shimmered. She swallowed hard. He rammed again.

Please, she begged with her eyes, her voice muted by his tongue's incursion.

"I will," he growled. *"I will."*

He uncoiled the tips, ready to strike directly at her heart. He gave one, two more forceful thrusts with his hips. She began to shudder and quake. *Now!* her eyes said.

"Yes!" he rasped, with one last, violent plunge.

But couldn't do it.

He couldn't do it.

With a tortured howl of anguish, he swiftly pulled his tongue up, up, up from her throat as climax roared over them both.

As soon as his tongue was out of her, she screamed. From orgasm, disappointment or anger, he couldn't guess. For himself, all he knew was exquisite, sublime pleasure shooting through his entire body. His power thrilled over them like a torrent of hot wind, exploding in a firestorm of sensual pleasure. It went on and on and on as he emptied himself into her—the vital essence of his loins and the demon essence from his mouth. And then he collapsed in a glittering cloud of hot, sated energy.

She was unnaturally still when he finally dragged himself from the dense fog of sexual repletion he'd become lost in for longer than ever in his three thousand years of existence.

"Are you all right?" he gently asked, lifting on his elbows to peer down at her.

She wouldn't open her eyes.

"Dawn, my sweet?"

Her body was limp and trembling. He suspected it wasn't just from her climax.

"My angel, say something."

"What just happened?" she whispered threadily.

"Nothing happened," he said. "We had sex."

Her eyes fluttered open. "No," was all she said.

"Yes," he refuted. Though in his heart he knew she was right.

But the Devil alone knew what had really transpired between them. Something entirely outside his experience. When the hell had he grown a conscience?

"No. That wasn't just sex. I know it wasn't." Yet her voice was laced with uncertainty. "I think…I think we made love."

The word took him aback. *Love?*

No. *Hell, no.* That was the damned faerie wine talking.

"Demons don't make love," he reminded her gruffly. "We don't know what love is."

But even as he said it, panic spurted through his veins. Because now that the words had been spoken aloud, damn if it didn't *feel* like they'd made love, in some bright, hopeful spot hidden deep in his soul. A spot so well hidden he'd never known it was there, until this very moment.

"If that's true," she whispered, "you can't be a demon."

"But I am," he countered. Wanting to deny the spot's existence. Needing to deny it. *He was what he was.* She had to accept that. *And so did he.*

Satan's minions. He'd heard of a rare demon or two who'd "gone native" while in the mortal realm. Everyone had. Reviled throughout the dark realm as weaklings, the poor sods had been summarily excommunicated and declared persona non grata there by the Grigori.

No, the thought of turning human horrified Galen. All those sticky, complicated emotions, like regret and empathy and love. Not an attractive thought.

"I don't love you, Dawn. I can never love you."

Her face fell. "Galen—"

"Love? Are you mad? I nearly raped your soul!" he bit out. Harshly, so she could have absolutely no delusions. Because he certainly didn't.

"But you couldn't do it. Even though I practically begged you to." Her eyes were liquid with gratitude. Or some other distasteful human emotion he wanted absolutely nothing to do with. "You saved me. You spared me."

"Hardly. I put more of my essence into you. A lot more."

"A pale substitute for making me your familiar. Why, Galen?"

He jetted out an impatient breath. Anger whipped at him. "Because I felt like it. Drop the subject. Please."

"Admit it. You have feelings for me."

"This is absurd. You're drunk on faerie wine. What you're experiencing is not real."

"Why, Galen? Why did you stop?"

His anger spiked hot and brilliant that she should pin him down like this. And that he should feel compelled to answer. "Because I promised!" he barked. "All right?"

She regarded him solemnly with large, luminous eyes. On the white pillow beneath her head, her auburn hair was spread about her face in a tangle, like a fiery nimbus.

She was so beautiful.

Suddenly, he was seized with a fierce need to cradle her in his arms and hold her close, to protect her from all the evil that existed in the world, both in his and hers. And from all the evil he himself was destined to bring forth upon her.

No!

He rolled off her, unnerved by the strength and magnitude of these unbidden, completely alien feelings.

Scrubbing his hands over his face, he ignored her as she rearranged her limbs and pulled the sheet over her nakedness. They both stared at the ceiling for a long time.

"Galen?" she finally said.

"Yeah."

"I'm not asleep, am I." It wasn't a question. More of a guarded observation.

Nevertheless, he answered, "No. You're not asleep."

"How can that be?"

"You know how."

There was another long pause before she said, "You're not really an incubus. Are you." Another observation; this one more wary. With a slight tinge of fear.

This was more like it. It didn't matter if he admitted he'd lied about himself. By now he had more than enough control over her to do everything he must, and then some.

"No. I'm not an incubus."

"What are you, then?" she asked. This time a real question. Posed in a voice that spilled dread from it like blood from an open wound.

He rolled his head on the pillow and looked at her. Looked into her beautiful, frightened, lake-green eyes and decided to exercise some of his vast control over her. Just because he could. She needed a wake-up call, to be jolted out of her state of denial.

So did he. Maybe asserting his dominance would make him forget all those other unsettling and unwanted feelings he'd had about her.

"I am the unholy destiny you've wrought upon yourself," he said, and watched with satisfaction as the rosy blush was bleached from her cheeks. "I, my sweet, am the man who will teach you what it is to be truly possessed."

Chapter 11

Galen expected Dawn to react with hysterics. Or pleading. Maybe even to run screaming from the room. But the last thing he expected from her was angered disbelief.

"Don't even try," she retorted.

He frowned. What the hell was that supposed to mean?

She flipped back the sheet and started to slide out of bed.

"Oh, no you don't." He grabbed her arm and hauled her back. At the same time he summoned his belt from the floor so it flew to him with a loud crack of energy. "Shall I demonstrate?"

Her eyes narrowed as he gathered her wrists in his hand, the threat implicit. "Is this supposed to scare me?"

Hell, the little witch didn't even look frightened. "That's right, I nearly forgot. You like a bit of rough, don't you?"

Her breath sucked in sharply. *"Me?"* She grabbed the belt and pelted it back onto the floor. "Why, you bloody domineering bastard!"

"Tsk, tsk, tsk," he muttered. "Insults won't work on me, my angel. I have no feelings, remember?"

"Oh, you have feelings, all right." She spoke with such conviction that he glared at her. "Go ahead and try to deny it," she said, poking him in the chest. "You do have feelings. For me. Otherwise I'd be your familiar right now, and you wouldn't be warning me against whatever the hell you're talking about." She glared right back at him, daring him to deny that, too.

He was so appalled he couldn't even come up with a retort. The very thought—

"Tell me," she demanded, poking him again. Hard. "What have you been sent here to do to me?"

"I wasn't sent," he snapped, the pointed question finally knocking some sense back into him. He grabbed her finger and held it. "*You* conjured me. I'm here to fulfill *your* fondest wish."

"What wish?"

Kicking the sheet completely off both of them, he moved his grip back to her wrists and ran his other hand slowly over her breast to hip. So there could be no doubt he was still in command of her. *All* of her. "You know I can't tell you that."

"I know nothing of the sort."

A bluff. Demons never revealed their true purpose. She had to know that. It was part of the game. But what was hers? Why was she not afraid of him, or even intimidated? She should be. Any other mortal would be shaking with fear and trepidation at the thought of being possessed. Her reaction was the opposite. His hand on her body seemed to be calming her. Did she really believe he had feelings for her? *Delusional as well as temperamental.*

"Search your heart for what you wished for," he advised harshly. "You'll figure it out, I'm sure."

He sure as hell hoped he would, too.

"Whatever desires brought you here to me, they can't be that bad." She sounded almost relieved. "I don't have evil thoughts or wishes."

A matter of definition, perhaps. "Then you've nothing to worry about," he said with a false smile.

She didn't notice the irony. "Maybe I should reread that spell."

"More carefully this time, I trust. Wouldn't want any competition showing up." That part was true. If she summoned another demon, he'd be forced to fight for her. He wouldn't give her up. Not to anyone, demon or mortal.

His anger boiled again, irrational and ugly. He rolled her to face him and yanked her close. Her body was still warm and humid from their earlier sex. His own scent perfumed her skin, musky and dark, a subtle declaration of his possession. Nay, his ownership. His arousal sprang back to life.

She sifted her fingers through the black hair on his chest. "Competition doesn't worry me. I can take care of myself."

His blood pounded with sudden need. "Can you?"

"If I can't, you'll protect me."

Pride teased through him momentarily that she should think so. Then acute displeasure. He was *not* that predictable. "Are you sure about that? Maybe I like sharing."

She snorted. Her fingers traced over his pecs. "Men like you don't share."

"Says you."

"And I don't, either."

He raised a brow. Suddenly she pushed at his chest, landing him on his back. "Possession works both ways, darling."

His pulse lurched. So did a few body parts. "Indeed?"

"Believe it." Bending over him, she caught his nipple between her teeth and gave it a bite.

He came off the bed. "Satan's tears, woman!"

She enclosed it with her mouth and tongued the sting from the kernelled disc of flesh. A rash of goose bumps flushed over his body. He groaned, immobilized with confusion and an unexpected quiver of pleasure.

For the first time in his life he allowed a woman to climb on top of him.

If she didn't feel so damn good straddling his body, he might have been alarmed. Or maybe amused. He wasn't sure which. But at the moment, he didn't much care. He just wanted her to get on with it.

Her tongue sought his other nipple and teased it to a hard pearl. He threaded his fingers through her hair and held her in place, savoring the novelty of the sensation. He'd had no idea being on the receiving end could be so pleasurable. His power purred around them like a prowling cat. Or was it hers? The magic of her touch had him bespelled.

She kissed his chest and lapped at his appreciatively sensitized nipples. Her silky hair fell about her face, long auburn tendrils trailing over his skin. It felt so good. All of it. The tickle of her hair, the wet velvet of her tongue, the subtle spill of human magic. What was she doing to him?

"You like that," she murmured.

"I'd like it even more a bit lower down," he suggested.

She glanced up. Her lips glistened with moisture, full and lush. Her smile was sensually knowing. He wanted those lips on him. Around him.

She read his mind and gave him what he wanted.

But she took her time. She tortured him with those sinful lips and even more with her wanton tongue, drawing out the pleasure, making him pant, making him wait, making him grow harder and thicker and longer until he was about to burst. Until he was prepared to beg if he had to, if only she'd finish him off.

"Do it now," he gritted out. "Do it or I'll make you." His energy flared hotly, as though to prove his point.

Her own batted back, rendering him powerless against her.

His body sang with frustrated need. Just when he couldn't take it a second longer, an instant before he would dig his fingers into her scalp and give her no choice in the matter, she lifted her green temptress eyes to his and smiled her enticing temptress smile.

"Mine," she whispered.

And his whole world exploded.

Dawn didn't know what had come over her. What she'd just done was so out of character for her. But incredible. It was a heady feeling, having a demon lying utterly helpless beneath you.

Almost like her old days as a tracker. Like the time she'd be-spelled a new vampire punk who'd been biting little girls up in York, and managed to shackle him in silver handcuffs until the disposal team arrived. But this was better. Much better.

"You think I'm helpless?" Galen's voice was thick and smooth as sweet molasses from the lingering aftereffects of climax, his chest still rising with rapid breaths. He cracked open an eye and peered down the line of his torso to where her head rested on his abdomen. "Silver doesn't work on me, you know. Though… handcuffs could be interesting. On you, of course."

"Stop reading my mind," she admonished. It was getting worse. Before, he could only pick up vague images and emotions. Now he was quoting actual sentences from inside her head.

"For your information, I'm *not* helpless. Not by a long shot." His sensual, otherworldly energy swirled around her.

She sent him a frown. "It was just a figure of speech, Galen. And I mean it about reading my mind."

"If you don't want me in your thoughts, just shield them. I know you can do it. You've done it often enough."

"I shouldn't have to."

"No, you're right." He stared down at her for a long time. So long, he started to make her nervous. "What?"

"What do you think?" he said at last. His flesh was hot and

sweat-slick where she lay sprawled on top of him like pale icing on spice cake. He even smelled of cloves and exotic spices. But his energy had curled in on itself and disappeared.

She lifted her head. "Didn't you like what I did?"

He reached up and touched his thumb to her bottom lip, smearing a bead of moisture along its swell. His moisture. "You were perfection, my angel."

He touched his thumb to her tongue. She tasted him anew. Like musky, rich, fecund earth. A shiver of yearning sifted through her.

His fingers carefully raked fallen strands of hair from her face. "You claimed me," he said quietly. "Did you mean it?"

She laid her head back down on his abdomen. His breathing had slowed, and the strong, fast beat of his heart pounded rhythmically. She kissed his heated skin, considering.

Did she mean it? It hadn't been a conscious decision, to say what she had. The words had just slipped out in the heat of passion.

She sighed. "Even if I did mean it, it wouldn't matter. You and I, we can never happen. Not in a claiming way. It's impossible and we both know it."

He caressed the back of her neck. "Yes. But did you mean it?"

"I'm a demon tracker, Galen. The daughter of the leader of the Cadre. If my father or the High Council even suspected you seduced me, you'd find yourself locked in a crystal prison for the rest of eternity. Or worse."

He looked thoughtful. "Do they make crystals for two?"

She jerked up, scandalized, and smacked his hand away. "Not on your life," she huffed, then added, "Besides, eventually the sex would get boring. After about ten thousand years."

He smiled at her then, and it was as though the room filled with brilliant light. He was so incredibly handsome her heart ached. Or was it something else that suddenly made it hurt so badly?

"Besides, I didn't seduce you," he said with a shake of his

head. "You seduced me. The first time I watched you from behind a tree in the enchanted forest at St. Yve, I knew I had to have you, in every way possible. It's why I got the faerie wine. Hoping to waylay you, snare you in its magical spell."

"A case of demon lust," she said, smiling back. "And me, the innocent random victim."

"Hardly random," he said. "And certainly not innocent." She frowned and considered rolling off him. But before she could, he lifted her with strong arms, pulling her up his chest so her cheek met his jaw, and he wrapped those powerful arms around her. "But definitely lust."

Those last words he murmured in her ear just before spinning her under him. She landed beneath his body, his muscular thighs parting hers. Then he was inside her, filling her.

She gasped. And accepted his invasion, welcomed it. Drowned in it. She didn't want to have to think. About what was happening to her life. To her perceptions.

To her heart.

He kissed her as though he really meant it. As though he really did have feelings for her. But she knew that was just a faerie fantasy. Because he was right. It would take nothing short of a miracle for Galen to be able to love her.

So she lost herself in the here and now, in the inferno of their passion, in the transitory pleasure their bodies could give each other.

Because that was all she had of him.

And all she would ever have.

Chapter 12

They made love—Dawn refused to think of it as anything else—
and afterward Galen grilled the steaks on his fancy gas hob and
they sat down to a delicious meal. He'd also prepared a crisp
salad, steaming asparagus with a handmade béarnaise sauce,
and he hinted at a scrumptious treat for their after-dinner coffee.
One thing about demons, they enjoyed anything and everything
sensual, including eating. Good thing he wasn't staying, or she'd
soon be big as a house.

She downed two more goblets of faerie wine with dinner, pre-
ferring the blissful oblivion of illusion to the harsh light of reality.
What could it hurt? Galen already had her where he wanted her.
And for whatever reason, he seemed to relish her demonstrative
fantasy-induced crush on him. She should have felt embarrassed,
a bit like Titania under the spell of the donkey-eared Bottom, but
what the heck. Galen really *was* the handsomest man on earth,
and his ears…er, horns were nowhere in sight.

"Do you even *have* horns?" she asked, making him blink. And her as well. She hadn't really meant to wonder about that aloud.

"Pardon me?"

"You know." She curled her forefingers, put them up to her temples and wiggled them. And giggled. "Horns."

His mouth curved wryly. "No. Just the one big one."

Her gaze lowered as her hands covered another giggle. "And a very pretty one it is."

He grabbed the bottle of faerie wine and corked it. "That's it. I'm cutting you off, my dear."

She propped her chin in her hand with a grin and tilted her head. "Why not?"

"Any more of this stuff and things could get really embarrassing."

"No, I mean the horns."

"Ah." He rolled his eyes. "Really, now. Horns are *so* last millennium. My lot have changed with the times just as mortals have."

"How so?"

He leaned back in his Heppelwhite dining chair and folded his white linen napkin onto the table. "Demons like me are simply the projection of the shadow side of the human mind. As people's fears have become more sophisticated, so have we, to reflect those fears. Little red men with horns and pitchforks no longer frighten. Nowadays, people's deepest fears can appear nearly identical to their deepest desires. As you know." He said it with a little smile.

It sent a shiver down her spine. Did she ever.

But at the moment she was in no condition to think straight, let alone carry on a philosophical discussion on the nature of demons or the quality of human fear.

"You might be right about the wine," she said. She stood up to clear the table and was hit by a wave of dizziness. She plopped down again. "Could we have coffee by the fire?"

"Of course. Leave those." He indicated the dishes. "Coffee is already prepared and waiting for us."

"You have a brownie, too?" she guessed. They had one at St. Yve, and she was a wonder. All you had to do was leave her gifts and all the tidying and washing up was magically done while you weren't looking. A shy creature, in all her years at St. Yve, the helpful brownie had never once been glimpsed.

"More like she has me," he said. "I'd be lost without her."

Brownies were very rare. And very loyal—if you could attract their services in the first place. Dawn was impressed.

"What do you give her?" Her father left their fresh flowers from the conservatory, and CDs. But she'd heard some brownies preferred a more personal reward. She sucked in a breath and shot Galen a look. "Surely not…"

He returned her accusing gaze with composure. "Would you be jealous?"

"Yes," she admitted. Grudgingly. "I'd be forced to find her and scratch her eyes out."

He put his arms around Dawn and kissed her temple. "Then it's a good thing I just leave her books."

She frowned. "Books?"

"Apparently it's boring…wherever brownies live. She goes through paperback novels like butter. Four or five a week. She especially likes spy thrillers and sweet romances."

Unexpected. But comforting. Dawn let Galen lead her into the vast, high-ceilinged living room where a fire burned cozily in the massive marble-surrounded fireplace. Before it, steaming coffee in fine porcelain cups waited on a silver tray on the floor next to a scatter of large damask pillows.

"Her doing? Or yours?" Dawn was feeling cross again.

"Mine." He lowered himself to the luxurious oriental carpet as gracefully as a cat, gathering a couple of pillows to lean his elbow upon. "Come, my sweet. Join me."

Her tension fled at the inviting picture he made.

Neither of them had dressed for dinner after making love. Upon rising, Galen had produced two matching burgundy silk robes which they'd worn to the table, floor-length with full, cuffed sleeves. As he sprawled before the fire, he undid his belt so the robe fell open, revealing his splendid body.

She knew it must be the wine's influence, but the perfection of it literally left her breathless. Angles and hollows, lean sinew and thick muscle, sculpted lips and stallion-like manhood. He belonged in a museum, carved in marble or formed in bronze. Except, what a shame for him not to be animated by flesh and blood, to be gazed upon for the pleasure of the world as she gazed upon him now. Talk about performance art.

She undid her own belt and let her robe slide down her shoulders and fall to the floor. His eyes glittered languorously. Slowly, he extended his hand toward her. The pull of him was impossible to resist, and it had nothing to do with the prickle of energy that fanned out from his fingertips and washed over her like a breeze of sparks.

How lucky she was!

She went to him, captured by the magic that was Galen, dizzy with the thrill of being his.

This was all she wanted. In the whole world, he was all she wanted. And if that made her a fool and a dreamer, so be it.

Galen was content.

More than content. He awoke the next morning with a lightness of heart he'd never before experienced, no doubt thanks to all the sex he'd been getting the last forty-eight hours. But no, it wasn't only that. The warmth of the early-morning sun as it dappled his skin, the cozy softness of the feather bed and quilt, the smell of Dawn's skin and the silken feel of her hair draped across his chest as she lay dozing in his arms, it all filled his senses to overflowing and made him smile.

She stirred, and snuggled closer to his side. His heart tugged with some mysterious pull, and for the first time he found himself wondering what it would be like to be human. To wake like this for the rest of his life. To really experience the kind of feelings Dawn had mistakenly attributed to him last night.

It terrified him.

Galen liked being a demon. He enjoyed fulfilling his Directive, helping to maintain the delicate balance in the world between darkness and light. Humans often painted demons with a universally black brush, thinking all of them pure evil with no redeeming value. But nothing could be further from the truth.

Without the shadows that demons brought to the mortal realm, how would humans recognize the light? By highlighting the dark side of humanity, demons allowed people to compare and experience the opposite: the compassion found within mortals, the goodness, the forgiveness. The love. It was an important service his kind performed, and deep down, humans valued the function, even if they didn't always see it clearly.

And after all, it was the black thoughts of humans themselves which called the demons up from the dark realm. Galen was only here with Dawn because she'd had vengeful thoughts about other mortals, wishing harm upon them in her mind. The conjuring spell she'd spoken aloud had only been a convenient vehicle.

She murmured softly in her sleep, then her eyes opened slowly, blinking as though she was trying to figure out where she was. She glanced up. He smiled.

"Good morning, my sweet. Sleep well?" What little they'd gotten.

She looked a bit disoriented. "What time is it?" She raised up, searching for a clock.

"Early."

She flung back the covers. "I have to get to the Department. I don't want Dirk Marcolf and his P-Cell hooligans to conduct their damned search without me."

"Plenty of time for that," Galen said, displeased with her haste to leave his bed. He caught her around the wrist. "Stay with me."

"It's daytime, Galen. Our bargain was only for the nights."

He scowled. Quite a change from his adoring lover of last night. "So that's how it's to be, is it?"

She slid out of bed. "I'm sorry." Her gaze stuttered to him, then flitted off. "Last night was lovely." She shook her head. "I should know better than to drink that faerie stuff. I probably embarrassed you terribly. I am sorry."

Embarrassed?

"You didn't." In fact, he'd never felt more comfortable with a woman in his life, mortal or not. She'd brought out…things in him that he'd had no idea existed. Almost like…feelings. They were confusing, maybe even unnerving, but not embarrassing. "But obviously you are, or you wouldn't be running away."

"I have to get to the Department. That's not running away."

"Then let me come with you."

She spun to him, eyes wide. "No! P-Cell is out for blood. I'd just as soon it wasn't yours."

Better. "Very well, but I insist on driving you."

She gave one nod, then headed for the en suite.

He heard the shower turn on a few minutes later, and decided to join her. He didn't think he'd need to use much persuasion. As it turned out, he was right.

And they still managed to make it to the Department of Anachronistic Research before P-Cell's arrival.

At least that was what he thought. Right up until the shooting started. And his car was the target.

Chapter 13

By all the devils!

Disbelief froze Galen's hand on the Sprite's gear shift. A high-pitched whine and the echoes of machine-gun blasts ricocheted from the walls of the Department where he was about to drop off Dawn. He counted four men with M4s. Not great odds.

Bullets whizzed past his ears through the open convertible. The puff of an exploding white pellet blew off a fender.

Satan's tears. They were packing salt!

Dawn had just bent to retrieve her purse from the floor at her feet. "Stay down!" Galen shouted at her, throwing up a quick deflection spell around their bodies. Magic wouldn't protect him against the salt bullets P-Cell used in their demon-killer M4s, but it would help slow down the normal metal bullets dinging off the car.

"Is someone *shooting* at us?" Shock stained Dawn's astonished face.

Galen gathered a fireball in his fist and hurled it at one of the attackers. The man screamed. Better odds. But still not great. Galen slammed his foot on the accelerator to beat a retreat. "It's me they want. I doubt they saw you." Alone, he might have stayed and fought them, but he didn't want Dawn hurt.

"In that case—" She popped upright in her seat, glancing around. "My God!" she exclaimed, spotting one of the assailants. "It's that tosser who was with Marcolf yesterday! Why, the bloody cheek!"

"Damn it, Dawn!" Galen shoved her back down as far down as she would go. He barely missed hitting a sign post in the struggle. "Would you stay the hell down!"

"I should show myself so they stop shooting!"

"No!" He jerked the car back onto the road and threw another fireball. Another scream. "Dirk Marcolf would probably consider killing you a bonus."

A ferocious volley of gunfire splattered across the Sprite's pristine front, leaving gaping holes in the metal and crackling the passenger side of the wind screen like a spiderweb.

"Now they've gone too bloody far," Galen hissed, ripping the safety glass from the frame so he could see.

Baring his teeth in fury, he pointed the car straight at an officer who'd run into the middle of the road blasting his M4. More high-pitched whining, then a headlight exploded in a puff of salt. With an oath, Galen reached out with his power, jerking the machine gun from the man's hands and pitching it over the roof of the Department. Momentarily frozen in surprise, the officer glanced up just as the Sprite bore down on him. The wanker jumped away and landed with a rolling crash on sidewalk.

Galen whipped the car around the next corner on two wheels, getting the hell out of there. The pop-pop-pop of shots faded into the distance. He probably should have just grabbed Dawn and apported far away, but he loved the car too much to abandon it.

Driving at top speed he took streets at random to be sure no one was on their tail. Finally, he merged into the thankfully heavy morning commuter traffic that was headed to the London business districts.

What the devil had that been all about? P-Cell was targeting him deliberately. Why? He needed information, fast. Unfortunately, he could think of only one place to get it. Making a quick decision, he turned the car back toward his flat.

Dawn slid back up onto the bucket seat and tightened her seatbelt. Her eyes widened at the missing chunk of wind screen and the bullet-ridden bonnet. "Good lord, Galen! They really *were* trying to kill us!"

"Me," he corrected. Still mystified over the why of it.

Dawn's face went pale and troubled. "Galen, why are they doing this to you?"

He shook his head. "I wish to hell I knew."

A broad daylight execution on a public thoroughfare was a rarity even for P-Cell. The involvement of the deputy director himself meant it had to have been an officially sanctioned action. But there was definitely something not right here....

P-Cell was infamous for their shoot-first-and-ask-questions-never policy, but they usually had a fairly obvious reason for specifically targeting an actual individual. A sexual predator vampire, a sadistic blood demon, a child-killing werewolf, anything that murdered or mutilated humans. Demi-beings of any kind that plotted to upset the balance between the mortal and dark realms. That was more Marcolf's style. Those things quickly put you at the top of P-Cell's most-wanted list. Galen was small potatoes, a common vengeance demon, hardly meriting the kind of deliberate fireworks displayed this morning.

"Are you sure you haven't done anything to piss off Dirk Marcolf?" Dawn asked. "Personally, I mean?"

"Not that I can think of." He glanced at her and hiked a brow. "Unless, of course, he has the hots for you." That could do it.

Marcolf was a man, wasn't he? Dawn was an incredibly attractive woman.

She actually looked horrified. "You must be joking. Besides, that wouldn't explain it. They couldn't possibly know you and I are…together."

Galen pursed his lips. "True. If they did, they probably would have waited for me at your townhouse instead of at the Department."

"Or your flat. Which means they can't know where you live."

"The one bit of good news."

"Maybe it's just a mix-up," she suggested, "and they're not after you at all, but some other demon they expected for whatever reason to show up at the Department."

"Maybe," he said. But he doubted it. P-Cell generally didn't make that kind of mistake, which reemphasized that the first thing on his agenda must be to find out exactly what was going on—and why.

And that brought him around to his current destination and dilemma. "I'm taking you back to my place," he told her firmly. "And I want you to stay there until I come for you."

She regarded him suspiciously for several long seconds. "Not likely." She shook her head. "You're up to something dangerous. I can feel it."

Blast. He'd forgotten that the mind-reading thing eventually started working both ways. "Nonsense," he bluffed, banking his anger at Marcolf and making his mind a blank.

She scowled. "Don't try to hide from me, Galen. Whatever you're planning, I can help you. I know how P-Cell works."

"Absolutely not." On this he was adamant. "It's far too dangerous for you."

"I'm a big girl, Galen," she said, her mouth set in a mulish downward curve. "I'm coming with you. And that's final."

"You can't," he said flatly. Not a chance in hell. "Where I'm going, they eat big girls like you for breakfast."

* * *

It took all of Dawn's concentration and every last bit of her training to fool Galen into believing she'd given in gracefully and planned to stay put in his flat like a good little girlfriend while he went gallivanting off to battle P-Cell on his own.

As if.

She didn't know what he thought he was doing. The attack they'd just been through should have given him an idea of the kind of enemy he was facing. Mindless. Violent. P-Cell would stop at nothing to kill him if he was on their list of most-wanted demons.

But Galen was wrong. Dirk Marcolf wouldn't let his men kill *her.* Not deliberately, anyway. Her visible presence with Galen would only help him survive. She must follow him, in case they showed up again.

After he let her off in front of his building and handed her the key to his flat, she quickly hailed a cab and managed not to lose sight of the Austin Healey in the dwindling rush of commuter traffic, nor along the winding streets of the increasingly rundown neighborhoods he drove through before arriving at a rare section of abandoned dockside warehouses along the river. The buildings sagged, the planks of the quay had long since rotted through. The stench of refuse clung to everything, nearly gagging her.

"You sure about this, miss?" the white-haired taxi driver asked, eyeing the dilapidated warehouses and crumbling docks with distaste. Bits of fluttering waste paper skipped along the uneven ground. "Not safe fer a nice lady like yerself, you want my opinion."

"Just let me off when the sports car we've been following pulls over."

"If you say so, miss."

Galen parked, glanced around then slipped into a seemingly deserted alley. She could almost taste the adrenaline surge as she paid the cabbie and watched the taxi speed away, leaving her as the only creature in sight—living or dead. It was beginning to feel like her old demon-tracking days.

The alley into which Galen had disappeared loomed in front of her. A cold breeze stirred and lifted tendrils of her hair with skeletal fingers, sending a chill down her spine. She felt something…a tingle of otherworldly presence. But it wasn't Galen. It felt more…evil. Maybe it was P-Cell she felt?

Though the sun had not yet chased away the frigid chill of morning, a few stingy rays of sunlight managed to poke through the mist hovering over the slate-gray river. She glanced around, searching for anything that might be hidden out there, observing her movements. Unbidden, Aurora's voice of warning sounded in the back of her mind. *Don't go into dangerous situations alone. Always call for backup.*

Except she couldn't. If Dawn called the Cadre for backup she'd have to tell them why. Which meant explaining Galen, and her relationship with him. And the fact that P-Cell was hunting him. Aurora would just decline her request anyway. She would never allow Dawn to risk her safety for a demon. She just didn't understand. A demon lover? No way would Aurora allow that. She'd send Galen away, deport him back to the dark realm. If he was lucky. If he wasn't, he'd end up in a crystal. Either way, Dawn would never see him again. But first Aurora would no doubt waltz in and somehow wrest the Demon Stone from him and return it to their father, grabbing all the glory for herself. Once again.

No, calling for backup was not an option.

But was Aurora right in principle? Was Dawn being a tad too impetuous here? Armed only with a handful of magic spells, a pocketful of salt and her own, some might say questionable, wits, she was probably mad to go into an unknown situation. God alone knew what awaited her in that alley. Or maybe the Devil…

Should she just turn around and leave?

No way. She could handle this. It was just an alley. The feeling she'd gotten was probably just because the place was so disgusting. There were no scary monsters peering back at her from the shadows. Probably.

And madness or no, she could not leave Galen's fate to the likes of P-Cell. He might need her. He could be walking into a trap. Taking a deep breath, Dawn turned determinedly and went into the alley.

It was empty. Galen had vanished.

Closing her eyes, she tried to feel for his energy, but felt nothing.

A terrible thought occurred to her. Had Galen known all along she was following him, and led her astray?

No. He couldn't have known. She'd shielded her thoughts well. And she refused to believe her lover would just leave her out here in this awful place, alone and vulnerable.

There was only one door to be seen. It lay far down in the dark bowels of the alley, barely visible in a patchwork of shadows that crawled across the dingy brick wall. She paused to consider the door and what might lie behind it. She fingered the handful of Dead Sea salt and the UV flashlight in her suit pocket, wishing she had something a bit more substantial. Like her silver handcuffs and a crystal or two. She didn't have a single one with her; she'd left them in her briefcase at Galen's flat.

The air was unnaturally silent as she crept down the alley and approached the door. The fog seemed thicker back here, darker, as though the sun's rays had been choked off at the throat. She could almost taste the menacing energy of the place and roll its bitterness on her tongue.

This was it. Galen must be somewhere behind this door. His preternatural presence wafted over her. Or…*a* presence. A dark, evil presence. *No, not Galen.*

A shiver crawled down her spine like invisible demon claws. Was he in trouble?

What was this place? Only one way to find out.

She lifted her hand and knocked.

Chapter 14

The door opened slowly. Evenly. As though it weren't a real person holding the knob on the other side controlling its movement. It wasn't. A hulking, gristle-bound brute of a low-level *daemon incultus* stood there. A murk. Gross, but harmless.

Still, Dawn slid her hand in her pocket, reaching for the salt. Just in case.

"Who are you?" she asked authoritatively. Establishing dominance was always the first thing you did with a primitive demon. The murk's ugly, nauseating energy wiggled through her like a worm. But it didn't answer, simply stared at her. She took a deep breath. Mistake. The foul creature smelled as bad as it looked.

"I'm looking for Galen McManus," she said in a commanding tone, craning to peer around its massive body to the room beyond, hoping to catch a glimpse of Galen. She could see sod all in the darkness. "Is he here?"

The murk just kept staring at her. This was getting annoying.

Suddenly a deep male voice, smooth as silk, whispered, "Did you knock at our door, mortal?" The voice was low and close, as if the speaker were standing just beside her.

She startled. "Yes!" she answered, whirling. "Who—" But no one was there.

The murk was suddenly gone, too. He'd apported—somewhere. In his place stood a willowy man with glowing skin, waves of shoulder-length golden hair, and the most vivid emerald-green eyes Dawn had ever seen. They sparkled like fireworks.

He had on soft brown boots over tight, fawn-colored breeches of the kind men wore two hundred years ago. They fitted him like a second skin, showing off athletic thighs—and everything else—to advantage. A flowing white, open-necked shirt emphasized his broad chest and shoulders. No wings. But she recognized a sidhe when she saw one.

Good lord. Things were getting downright strange.

Had she stumbled onto some kind of dark realm/mortal realm borderland? Or a tear in the dimensional fabric? Why hadn't she felt it? Usually she could feel the overwhelming preternatural power of such a place down to her very bones. Like out in the enchanted wood at St. Yve. Was the place somehow shielded against humans? Why? *Daemons incultus* and faeries she could handle. But what other, more dangerous, beings had leaked through here? A handful of salt only went so far. She wanted her handcuffs and crystals.

The sidhe's lips curved in a smile as he returned her inspection. But far more thoroughly.

"Well, well, well. What do we have here?" A touch of delight colored his silvery tone, as though her appearance at the door amused him, and he couldn't wait to see what happened next. His faerie glamour twinkled like bright stars.

She frowned. Sidhe were mischievous and malicious beasts, despite their outwardly carefree and cheerful demeanors. Tinkerbell? Hardly. Dawn would not trust one further than she could spit.

He moved toward her. The air around him shimmered and flowed, like a pulsing, sparkling ripple of energy.

Magic. Living, breathing magic that crawled up her spine from the inside. *Black Court magic.*

She backed away in apprehension. "What is this place?" she asked.

"A little bit of Hell on earth," he said with a sly smile and an evil glitter in his eyes. "I bid you welcome to Pandora's Box."

Dawn's heart nearly stopped. The most notorious Dark club in the western hemisphere! She took another step backward as her heartbeat recovered and went into hyperspace. Good lord!

Pandora's Box.

She'd heard whispers about the place all her life. A secret underground seraglio where seductive otherworld beings tempted impressionable mortals over to the dark side. In hidden corners of the luxurious club beautiful demons, erotic vampires, ethereal sidhe and other members of the dark realm's demi-monde encouraged human victims to practice every sin imaginable.

It was said one could buy anything in Pandora's Box. For a price.

"My name is Loroth," the faerie said, sweeping a gentlemanly bow.

His bold emerald eyes captured hers and she said without thinking, "I'm Dawn."

Realizing with a start what he was doing, she tore her gaze from his. In case he had the power to bespell with his eyes. Many sidhe did.

"And you are as pretty as the woods at dawn," Loroth murmured. "Won't you come in, dear mortal?"

"No, thank you," she said, her nervousness increasing exponentially.

Once admitted, no human had ever spoken of what they'd seen, after they emerged. *If* they emerged.

Over the centuries, the Cadre had sent several adepts into the club for reconnaissance or to chase and capture a particular para who'd gone to ground there. Some adepts had disappeared forever; some had returned tapped as familiars, unable to remember anything that happened inside—others had simply refused to talk about it. A few had changed so fundamentally they'd been useless to the Cadre after that, eventually sinking completely under the sinful spell of whatever manner of demi-being had claimed their soul within the confines of the club.

"Oh, but you must enter," Loroth said. "Because you knocked. It's the rule, you know."

She shook her head. "No. I'm just looking for Galen McManus," she said. "He arrived a few minutes ago."

"I shall help you find him. *Inside.*"

Loroth bid her enter with an elegant sweep of his hand. But his emerald eyes were like hard gems. Uncompromising.

For a split second she considered running. But wings or no, the sidhe would catch her easily. And what about Galen? Why, oh, why hadn't she listened to Aurora's voice in her head?

Loroth's steady gaze told her he would give her no choice. She had to go in. To Pandora's Box.

God help her.

And yet… And yet, in the darkest recesses of her mind, the allure of the forbidden called to her. Like a dark siren, an irresistible madness impossible to resist, it bade her throw down her fears and step over the threshold of forbidden desires.

It was the same madness that always, always got her in trouble.

Loroth smiled. *He knew.*

Taking a deep breath, she walked past him. Into the dark and mysterious unknown.

Galen regarded the vampire lounging on the sofa across from him. The vampire looked like a modern-day gypsy. Or maybe a rock star. Black hair, black two-day stubble, black clothing. Marceau Demolay was well over three hundred years old but didn't look a day above thirty. Except in his black eyes. Those shadowed orbs showed every year of his three and a half centuries, and then some.

The man was intelligent. Ruthless. Perhaps even evil. But then, Galen had no problem with ruthless and evil. Not on principle, anyway. It was all relative.

"The information will cost you," Marceau said.

"I'm aware of that," Galen answered impassively. For the past half hour he'd searched the luxurious warren of back rooms at Pandora's Box for someone with answers. He'd never expected them to come cheap. "Can you help me?"

The corner of the vampire's lip curled condescendingly, showing just a tip of fang. "I believe I can find out what you need to know."

"How quickly?"

Marceau's shoulder rose and fell under his black leather jacket. "How quickly do you need it?"

"They're trying to kill me."

Galen smiled as he said it. He wasn't particularly worried about dying. He'd gotten out of worse jams. But the idea of Dawn getting caught in the crossfire made him absolutely furious.

"All right. I should have something for you by tonight."

"What do you want in exchange?" he asked.

Marceau rose from the gray silk sofa and went to a lighted sideboard where a slick platinum tray held cut-crystal glasses. After a moment of consideration, he chose a slim bottle from among the wide variety of offerings and poured dark-blue liquid into two of the glasses. The crystal facets flashed like sapphires in the low artificial light.

He handed one to Galen and gazed at him steadily as he took a measured sip. "Your blood," he finally answered.

Original. Still, Galen's brow arched. There was no love lost between demons and vampires, even at the best of times. Sucking blood was an almost...intimate procedure. And also—

"I thought demon blood was poison to you lot," he ventured. If the man keeled over, Galen wouldn't get his information.

Marceau smiled disdainfully. "It is poisonous to us, ordinarily. But then again, I am no ordinary vampire."

Galen granted him that much. He was definitely a piece of work. However, a little blood was a small price to pay for peace of mind. As long as it didn't get out of hand. He was already Dark and immortal. He didn't want to end up with fangs, too.

"All right," he said. "It's a deal. When?"

The other man wet his lips. "Right now."

There was a knock and the paneled door opened. A scantily clad faerie with brilliant orange eyes looked in at Galen and said, "A woman is asking for you out front. A human."

Galen blinked. "For me?"

"She says her name is Dawn."

Dawn? Here at Pandora's Box? How the hell had she found him? More importantly, why hadn't he felt her calling him?

"Are these walls shielded?" he asked, shooting to his feet.

"Of course," the faerie answered, surprised. "There's a complete protection ward surrounding the whole club, and each of the rooms. For the security and privacy of our patrons."

Damn. "Take me to the woman," he commanded.

And prayed he'd get to her in time.

Dawn had followed Loroth as he led her through a maze of black-as-night passages for what seemed like hours, though in reality it may have been just a few minutes. Impossible to say. One thing was certain, they were far underground by now. Perhaps even below the river.

The glamour around Loroth's body glowed luminescent

green, a delicate radiance that lit their path in a wavering sphere around the two of them. But other than that, she felt only a distant trace of any, otherworldly energy. They came to a double door at the end of a long, wide hallway. It appeared to be made of pure gold.

Loroth halted, turned and tilted his head. She had to admit, he really was an incredibly handsome man, tall and broad and golden as the door. Perfectly proportioned. An illusion? Probably not. The sidhe were a beautiful race. But shallow. His thoughts were as transparent as white faerie wine.

He lifted a hand and was about to touch her. "I belong to Galen," she said, careful to avoid his gaze.

His hand hovered. "You are the demon's familiar?"

"Yes," she lied. Paras were territorial. Generally, they respected what belonged to others. Because if they didn't, a fight was sure to result. Usually fatal to one of them.

The sidhe regarded her curiously. Could he tell she was lying? "You are his familiar willingly?" he asked.

She felt her face heat. A trick question. "We made a satisfactory bargain," she evaded.

His long fingers touched her cheek, caressed it lightly. "What did the demon offer you for your favors?"

She turned her face from his touch. "Enough."

"I can offer you more," he murmured, letting his fingertips glide down the side of her throat. "And I can protect you."

"I can protect myself," she said.

He inclined his head with a knowing smile. "Very well, human. You had your chance."

He waved a hand and the doors of gold slowly opened.

She blinked. Loud, jarring music poured through the widening gap. But the room beyond was completely, utterly dark. Darker than anything Dawn had ever experienced. She could see nothing, but she sensed a stirring...

Suddenly it hit her—a roiling, boiling wall of power that crashed into her from a wellspring of dark beings hidden in there in the blackness. She couldn't hear them over the music, couldn't see them, but they were there. Their power reached out like a huge, physical thing from the depths of the room, pressing in around her like thick water, rushing over her skin like liquid nettles, leaving a rash of goose flesh and terror in its wake.

Dark power. Evil power.

Power that could capture a person's innocence in the space between two seconds. Power that could strip a mortal of her willpower and compel her to do the unimaginable. Power that could make it all seem like a splendid idea.

Eyes suddenly materialized in the darkness. Red eyes, yellow eyes, moon eyes, cat's eyes, eyes of every color, shape and distinction imaginable, all of them focused on her.

Oh, God, this was so wrong. A colossal mistake. Galen couldn't possibly be here in this hideous place.

Something pushed hard against her back. She stumbled forward. The golden doors clanged shut behind her with the dull echo of finality. Her heartbeat screamed. Because her mouth didn't dare.

Never show your fear.

From somewhere in the middle of the room, a pair of half-lidded, red eyes slowly floated upward and separated from the rest, as though their owner had risen lithely from his seat and was now walking toward her. The height of them, and the way they studied her as they approached—measuring, calculating, greedy—left no doubt as to the creature's male gender. She shrank back.

"You can't hide, you know," a gravelly, disembodied voice, separate from the music, intoned in her ear. "I can see in the dark. We all can. The darkness is our element."

"It's not mine," she answered, forcing herself to stand straight and not cower. But her own voice sounded thready in her throat, terrified, even to herself.

A sense of hideous foreboding raked over her. She must get out of here!

"I want to leave," she said. "Now."

But the monster just laughed.

Chapter 15

Like a sunrise in Hell, the house lights slowly rose to bathe the room in a dim red flush. It reminded Dawn of being in an old-fashioned photographic darkroom, just bigger. But the light made things worse. A lot worse.

Now she could see the fiends. All of them. *Oh, God.*

The room was vast. From the low ceiling were suspended a dozen or more crystal cages, each holding a prisoner. The prisoners were human. They appeared to be drugged, or bespelled, their pupils black gulfs, their physical movements languorous. All were naked.

Sweet Jesus.

In the middle of the room stood a glass stage upon which were scattered strange-looking apparati. Around the stage floated a sea of squat crystal tables surrounded by drifts of gray silk chairs and sofas. Dark, shadowy figures of all shapes and sizes lounged upon them. She'd never seen so many demons and other paras at one time. Scores. Maybe hundreds.

Far too many for one handful of salt.

Hot spikes of panic began to burn in her veins. "Galen!" she called out. "Galen, are you here?" *Where was he?*

The demon with the red eyes tipped his head. He wasn't laughing now. He was studying her. The way an entomologist might study a new pet bug. It made her shiver, and not in a good way.

"Who is this Galen you seek?" he asked.

"He's… He is my d-demon m-master," she stammered, stumbling badly over the words, realizing with a sinking heart that coming away from this as Galen's full familiar was probably one of the better outcomes she could hope for.

If he was even here. Why wasn't he answering? Why couldn't he sense her panic? What good was carrying his essence if he didn't hear her when he called?

"I'm his," she said in what she hoped was a convincing manner. "I belong to him."

"We'll see about that," her tormentor chided. "Bring her to the stage, Loroth."

"Yes, *Ba'al* Chaddiel."

Loroth's green glow shimmered, and at once Dawn's arms were locked behind her, wrists gripped in the sidhe's strong hands. Then they were standing on the round translucent stage in the middle of the room. Apported, as though someone had pressed the skip button on the Tivo and she'd missed a whole minute of the movie. Except she was in it. She didn't like the sensation one bit.

There was a blur of motion and the demon with the eyes— Chaddiel—towered in front of her.

He wasn't handsome. Not remotely. But he had…presence. He looked like a man of fifty or more, with graying temples in his brown hair, but the muscles in his arms and chest were impressively defined under a well-fitting black T-shirt. She wondered what kind of a demon he was. Probably best not to know.

Chaddiel reached for her jacket. In a single quick motion, he stripped it off her and threw it onto the stage.

"No!" She fought her way out of his reach, horrified. "What do you think you're doing?"

He laughed again, a vicious baring of sharp teeth in the dark. His gaze swept over the naked humans in the cages, and a few she hadn't noticed before reclining on sofas, their nude bodies draped over the laps and limbs of their demon possessors. Some wore shiny red collars around their necks.

Chaddiel stepped forward and sinewy fingers grasped the front of her blouse. She screamed. His sickening laughter filled the room, echoing inside her head, drowning out her screams of protest. His red eyes burned brighter and brighter, feeding on her fear and desperation.

The audience leaned in, tense excitement charging the air, their energy growing hot and oppressive.

"I demand an auction!" one demon called out.

"Yes, sell her to the highest bidder!"

"She should go to the winner at the gaming tables tonight!" another yelled.

"No!" Chaddiel's guttural voice cut through the rise of shouts like a scythe. "This one is mine!"

Evil flowed from every pore of his body, snaking around the room, reaching its poison fangs out to silence the low, muttered objections of the crowd.

They feared him. They all feared him.

God help her, Dawn most of all.

"Does anyone dare challenge my right to this mortal?" Chaddiel growled.

Dawn's heart quailed. No one spoke. *She was doomed.*

Until, from the very back of the room, an answer boomed forth like the rolling crack of thunder.

"She belongs to me."

Fury didn't begin to describe what Galen felt as he stalked between tables and chairs toward his adversary, knocking aside anything that stood in his path. Fiery showers of sparks erupted from all he touched. Tables cracked, goblets shattered, plates of food flew in his wake. He made no attempt to rein in the power of his rage.

He would kill the man. Rip his heart out with his bare hands.

He reached the stage and leaped upon it, setting off bursts of sparks with his boot heels.

Chaddiel approached him, arms straight and rising up like a sorcerer's. Galen gathered his powers and flung his hands before him in a pre-emptive parry, streaming laser-sharp fire from his fingertips. Chaddiel spun. Blood sprayed from blackened slashes across his cheek and arm.

His cries of outrage echoed through the room. "You dare to defy me! You, who are nothing but a lowly insect!"

"She. Belongs. To. *Me!*" Galen thundered. The winds of his fury burst across the stage, whipping hair, clothing and objects into a hot tempest. He heard Dawn scream. She was on her hands and knees trying to crawl away.

Suddenly he was hit by a force like a locomotive. Airborne, he felt invisible fists of iron close around his throat, yanking him roughly back down to the stage. He choked, unable to draw breath, and was slammed onto the glass floor so hard he blacked out for a few precarious seconds. When he came to, he was lying on his back, his whole body in blinding pain.

"Galen!" Dawn screamed. Chaddiel had an arm banded around her waist, lifting her to carry her off. Her feet kicked and her nails scratched.

"Leave her!" Galen vaulted to his feet, ignoring the excruciating pain. He flung a fireball at Chaddiel's retreating back. It bounced off harmlessly. The bastard had put up a shield.

Galen's powers were no match for Chaddiel's. The man was some kind of demon lord, maybe even a prince. His only chance was to confuse him. Fight like a human. Go for the heart.

Galen summoned a crystal goblet from the nearest table, then swooped down to crack it against the floor, splintering the edge to razor-sharp shards. Brandishing it in one hand, he fisted the other and sent a smashing spell against Chaddiel's shield. The air around the other demon shattered like broken glass. Galen leapt, slicing the ragged goblet across Chaddiel's throat and down his chest.

Blood spurted everywhere. The wounds would heal quickly, but hopefully not quickly enough. With a howl of rage, Chaddiel dropped Dawn and came at Galen.

"Run!" he shouted at her. "Run now!"

A blinding pain seared across Galen's cheek and shoulder, and his head snapped back. He tried to lift the broken goblet as a defense, but suddenly couldn't move his arms. Chaddiel's laughter pitched high and maniacal. He rose up, shifting into the shape of a huge hooded snake, all blackness and evil. He grew larger and larger, until he towered over Galen, big as the Devil himself. Then the snake's giant jaws opened wide, poison-dripping fangs extended to deliver the killing blow.

Suddenly the audience gasped; those sitting nearest the stage scrambled back in panic. The snake screamed. It screamed and screamed and writhed and coiled in on itself until the reptilian illusion crumbled and it was just Chaddiel writhing on the stage in agony.

Galen rolled to a crouch. What the hell was going on? Then he saw it, sprinkled on the stage.

Salt.

He froze and glanced up. Dawn was kneeling behind Chaddiel, her suit jacket clutched in one hand, coarse grains of salt in the other. Their eyes met.

"He was going to kill you," she breathed in a strangled croak.

Inside Galen, something hard and cold broke wide open. His chest filled with the strangest sensation he'd ever experienced. It felt warm and gooey and…inevitable. Even more inevitable than his death at the hands of Chaddiel had been just moments before.

"Throw the rest, my sweet," he ordered softly. "And try not to hit me."

She nodded, and tossed the rest of her salt onto the thrashing body of their enemy.

Without waiting to see the results, Galen went to his lover and scooped her into his arms, closed his eyes and apported them away. A heartbeat later he stood next to the Austin Healey, clutching her close to his pounding heart.

They were both alive. And free. At least for now.

For a precious minute he just held her, savoring the feel of her warm body in his arms, and counting his blessings. Then he glanced over his shoulder checking for Chaddiel or others in pursuit. He and Dawn were probably safe. Defeating a demon lord generally brought the Grigori down on you—eventually— but raised the respect level of other demons. Mostly they left you alone after that. At least if you were a demon. Humans might be a different story, though.

"That was close," he murmured, wondering why she felt so rigid. "But we should—"

"Clever girl," a smooth voice said from close by. It sounded almost approving. A man stepped from behind a wall. "Very clever, indeed." It was the vampire.

Galen held Dawn's stiff body a bit tighter. Marceau raised a hand. She stopped moving in the middle of a gasp. Stopped dead.

"Tell your little mortal that I am a friend, Galen."

He glanced down at Dawn. She was absolutely, perfectly still. Her eyes were wide.

Anger swamped over him, fresh and potent. "What are you doing to her?"

"No harm. Tell your woman I am here to help you." Marceau held his hands palms up, almost in supplication.

Galen checked his anger. Just. "It's true, Dawn. I sought him out myself. About the P-Cell attack this morning."

Her body jerked and came to life. She sucked down a breath. "He's a vampire!"

"Yes. He is."

She shuddered with visible distaste, shifting her body to be put down. "What can a vampire know about P-Cell?"

"I have many contacts in the mortal realm," Marceau said, addressing Dawn with an odd smile. "And in the dark realm, too. I'll find out who is after your…demon. If he accepts my terms."

Galen set her down on her feet, but kept his arm firmly around her rigid shoulder. "We've already agreed on terms," he said. "I'll hold up my end."

His frown grew as Marceau's smile spread.

"I'm afraid our bargain was never…sealed," the vampire said silkily. "So there has been a slight change."

"What change?"

"The blood," Marceau said. "In addition to yours, I want to taste—" his black eyes landed on Dawn "—hers."

Chapter 16

"*What?*"

Galen didn't like the wary mistrust on Dawn's face when she turned to him for confirmation. But he liked the smugness on Marceau's even less. "That wasn't our agreement," he gritted out.

"That was before," Marceau said, unmoved.

"Before what?"

"Galen, what is he talking about?" She sounded angry.

He slid his hand behind her neck, caressing her with his thumb. "I agreed to donate blood in exchange for information. *My* blood. Not yours."

Horror replaced the anger. She stepped away from him. "You must be joking! Galen, he's a *vampire*."

"Thus the deal."

Marceau grinned. No fangs showed. Except for an overly pallid complexion, he looked almost human. Almost. "I take it you don't care for us?"

Dawn's spine stiffened even more than it already was. "Your whole species is an abomination," she spat out, then turned to Galen, her expression serious. "You mustn't trust him."

A surge of hostility emanated from the vampire, rushing through Galen like a freezing river of hatred. But as quickly as it hit, it ebbed. Marceau slowly ran a finger along the bullet-riddled fender of the Austin Healey, pausing to touch each bullet hole lightly, flicking salt residue off with a fingertip. "What reason would I have to deceive you?"

"I have no idea, Marceau, but—"

Dawn spun around. *"Marceau?"* She stared at the vampire. "You are Jason's brother, Marceau?"

The vampire stared back warily. Suddenly his eyes flared. His body went perfectly still. Galen had never before seen a vampire shocked lifeless. Bloodless. "He called you Dawn... You are Lady Dawn, Professor Maybank. Tracker for the Cadre."

Alarm shot through Galen. Please don't say they'd had a previous encounter...with a wooden stake involved. No, the Cadre didn't kill. "You two know each other?"

"Don't have that pleasure yet." Marceau inclined his head. "But apparently we know *of* each other."

Dawn gripped Galen's arm. "You mustn't do business with this...this monster. He's evil and immoral."

"Some would say *I'm* evil and immoral," Galen argued. "If he can help us—"

For a second she looked stricken, then glanced away and said, "He won't help you. He'll use you and betray you."

"Like I did my brother, you mean?" Marceau was smug again. Almost triumphant.

Dawn blanched nearly as pale as the vampire. Perhaps her warning merited closer consideration. She was acting strangely. And Galen had a bad feeling it wasn't all directed at the vamp.

Fine. He'd demand an explanation later, but right now they should get the hell out of there.

"Where can I get in touch with you?" he asked Marceau, cutting off any further discussion. Or confrontation.

Wordlessly, the other man produced a business card from the inside pocket of his leather jacket. Red numbers on a shiny black background. Just a phone number. No name. Cute.

"Call if you hear anything," Galen said, handing him one of his own. He turned to open the Austin Healey's door for Dawn. When he turned back, the vampire was gone.

Galen banked his growing unease until he and Dawn were safely back in his flat, giving her the chance to gather herself and her thoughts during the moody drive. He'd taken the long way home to be sure nobody followed them.

They were now in his kitchen and he was preparing a lunch of salad and seafood chowder. It had been a long morning and he was starving. The chowder bubbled on the stove, smelling delicious. Dawn unconsciously worried bits of sourdough bread from the loaf she was supposed to be slicing. She hadn't said more than a few mumbled monosyllables the whole time.

"Are you okay?" he asked.

"Fine," she said.

Right. "Why are you shielding your thoughts from me?"

Her gaze skittered to him, then away again. "No reason."

"Then let me in."

She shook her head.

A small, dull ache began to unfurl in his chest. She was shutting herself off from him. Not just her thoughts. Her whole self. "Dawn, what's going on?"

She looked up. Her expression was carefully even. "Why didn't you answer my calls? In the club?"

"The walls were warded. They interfered in our connection. I came as soon as I found out you were there. If I'd known—"

She gazed at him as though she wasn't listening to his explanation. As though she were seeing him for the very first time. He shut his mouth.

"My God, Galen, you're one of them."

It wasn't an accusation, exactly. More of a statement. But damn, if it didn't feel like an accusation. He wasn't sure what she was getting at, or how to respond. "I am a demon. You've known that from the beginning. Is there a problem?"

Again she shook her head. "No problem."

The ache grew sharper and twisted in his gut. *Sure there wasn't.*

He got out a wooden bowl and salad fixings. She'd been upset by the vampire. Maybe that held a clue. "You warned me about Marceau. What do you know of him?"

She pried off another bit of bread. "Marceau's brother, Jason, is…was…an adept with the Cadre, up until last year."

Galen frowned as he selected a sharp knife to slice tomatoes. "Marceau is over three hundred years old. How—"

"So is Jason."

It was Galen's turn to be shocked. Well, not really shocked, but—

Okay, he was shocked. "The Cadre has vampires working for it?" How had he not heard this?

"A few. And familiars, faerfolk, weres, shapeshifters. Not many, but some. It's not knowledge we spread around."

Satan's bollocks. "Demons, too? Besides portal guardians and house demons, I mean?"

She nodded. She didn't look particularly happy about that, either.

"Paras hunting paras?" He tried not to be so stunned. After all, Dawn had hunted demons professionally for years. But then, she was a human. He could accept that. Hunting your own kind seemed…distasteful.

"Sometimes it takes one to know one," she said. Pointedly?

He concentrated hard on the tomatoes. What was she trying to say? "Why? Why would they do it?"

"I suppose because they agree with the Cadre's philosophy."

"Which is?"

He knew perfectly well what it was, but he wanted to hear it from her mouth. He suddenly wondered where sleeping with a demon fitted into *her* philosophy. Where he—they—fitted into it.

"To study and learn as much as we can about the inhabitants of the dark realm," she answered. A teacher reciting a syllabus.

"Like we're some kind of science project," he retorted.

"I suppose in a way." She didn't even blink when she said it.

Anger spiked, fast and irrational. "And am I part of your science project?"

She ignored him and continued, "We humans must protect the mortal realm from harmful paras or risk perishing ourselves."

Ah. The crux of the matter.

"And who gets to decide what is harmful?" he asked. Striving hard for equanimity.

She gazed at him with somber eyes. He must be slipping. She knew it was a trap. "You're starting to sound like Jason."

So, obviously he *didn't* fit in. Too harmful…for what? Her peace of mind? And here he'd been feeling all squishy and…*human* toward her.

He ground his teeth. Equanimity lost. "Perhaps he's right."

"I don't confuse duty and honor with personal feelings, Galen."

Anger nearly paralyzed him. He stabbed the knife he was using into the cutting board. It sank in a full half inch, vibrating like hummingbird wings.

"I see," he growled. *Unlike him, apparently. To his unending shame.*

Dawn's hand halted halfway to her mouth. After two long seconds she set aside the bread and stood abruptly. "I have to go.

I should call Dirk Marcolf and read him the riot act about the attack. And I have a lecture to prepare for tomorrow."

She marched out of the kitchen.

But no more. She'd reminded him he was a demon, and of his place in her world. From now on it was back to business. The *vengeance* business.

Galen took a deep breath, paused to turn off the flame under the chowder, then strolled after her. She was standing by the entry door tapping her foot and looking furious. He came to a halt, folding his arms across his chest. "Door locked?"

She really shouldn't be so surprised. He was a goddamned demon. She'd leave when he let her leave.

"Unlock it, Galen. Let me go."

Or maybe he'd never let her leave. "No."

Her mouth dropped open. "Excuse me?"

"I said no. We're eating lunch." At the look of pure indignation on her face, his hunger suddenly shifted south. "Then I was thinking of taking you to bed."

Her jaw dropped farther. Her face flamed. "Think about it all you like."

He hiked a brow. "Is that by any chance a challenge?"

Her jaw snapped shut. "Oh, sure. One threatened rape a day isn't nearly enough. Not to mention being bartered away to a blood-sucking—"

The anger was back, clouding his vision. "I would *never*—"

"Save it, darling. Once a demon—"

Something in his face must have shown. He'd just resolved as much himself, but for some reason hearing that fatalistic sentiment on her tongue enraged him to the snapping point.

She backed away. He was faster. He grabbed her upper arms and swung her against the door. She gasped.

"You were saying, my angel?"

"Galen…"

"Since you think so highly of my personal honor, I feel it my duty to warn you—"

"You're hurting me."

"I'm a demon. Hurting is what I do."

"No. You bring pleasure. You're here to fulfill my desires, you said so yourself."

She didn't believe it. He could tell. She was just backpedaling because he was frightening her. Hurting her.

So what? He *was* here to hurt her. But not in the way she believed. She'd brought the real hurt on herself, with her dark desire for vengeance.

But she did have a point. Pleasure was so much more satisfying.

"So I did," he murmured. Sex and anger was such a volatile, exciting mix. Especially with a good dose of fear thrown in.

With steely restraint he lowered his face to hers, and brushed his mouth over her lips. They were warm and moist and trembled slightly when the tips of his tongue touched them.

He could smell her desire for him. And her fear. The scents mingled, permeating the air around them, filling his senses, quickening his body.

Much better.

He loved having this power over her. This heady, intense power that had nothing to do with being a demon and everything to do with being a man.

Couldn't she feel it? Couldn't she understand that she belonged to him?

He trailed his lips to her ear. "You want me," he whispered, and she trembled harder. "You want me all over you. You want me inside you," he whispered, drugging her with his words, with his will.

She made a tiny noise of despair. Why? Because his demon whisper compelled her to feel an urgent physical need for him? Or because she had shielded herself from his enchantment, but the need was still there, burning through her body like a brand?

Her fingers sought him, touched his torso. Her breaths were fast, shallow, uneven.

His own body was on fire. He told himself he didn't care if he didn't fit into her world. What did it matter that when she found out what he really was she'd most likely want to wipe the mortal realm of all trace of him?

He moved his grip down to her wrists and held her immobile. Apart. "You disobeyed me this morning," he said, low and rough.

She swallowed. Uncertainty hovered in her eyes, her fear growing. "You were in danger," she said. Her voice wavered. "P-Cell—"

He tightened his grip. "Sod P-Cell. There was a reason I left you behind."

"I'm not your slave, Galen. I only said that to stop Chaddiel."

"You could have been killed."

"But I wasn't."

Stubborn wench. "You could have ended up in one of those cages," he reminded her. A fate far worse than his bed, he reminded himself.

"Instead I saved your life."

Did she deliberately wish to vex him?

"Which," he gritted, "wouldn't have needed saving if you hadn't stuck your mortal nose in where it didn't belong!"

She tried to jerk away. A useless exercise. "Ungrateful bastard!"

"Why?" he demanded.

She yanked at her wrists again, avoiding his gaze. "Good bloody question."

He let one go and wrapped his fingers around her jaw, forcing her to look up at him. "Tell me, Dawn. Why? Why did you disobey me? Why did you follow me? Hell, why did you save my life?"

He really didn't want to know. It must be some terrible, self-destructive compulsion that made him ask. Any answer she gave would only inflame his fury even more.

Her eyes melted to pools of stubborn, defiant, liquid fire. "We have a bargain. I didn't want you weaseling out of it by dying on me."

Goosebumps raced up his flesh and he stared at her, long and hard. He felt suddenly as if he was on a tightrope, losing balance. Under one end was a vat of boiling tar and under the other a vast, bottomless pit.

Dare he probe what the true emotion was smoldering behind those intractable, glistening eyes?

Was her concern for his life?

Or was it only for their bargain?

"It's the Demon Stone. Isn't it?" he murmured, soft as sandpaper. "You're that worried about losing it."

For a second she didn't move. Then her chin jerked up. "Of course," she said. "What else could it possibly be?"

He swallowed down the bitter taste of some totally alien emotion. One he couldn't identify.

Relief? Self-righteousness? Disappointment?

No, surely, not. Demons didn't have such patently human emotions. Lust and anger. That was all he could feel. All he was supposed to feel.

So why, suddenly, did his heart feel so empty and hollow?

And why did he have the sinking feeling that the hollowness was just the beginning of something far, far worse?

Chapter 17

Dawn winced as Galen dropped her wrists, turned on a heel and stalked purposefully from the room. The air snapped and cracked in his wake, hot like a forest fire. The door to his bedroom opened with a thunderous crash.

She wasn't sure what to do, so she stayed right where she was, with her back pressed against the front entry.

She'd seen angry demons before. Demons she'd tracked and surprised in their lairs, demons who knew they were about to be crystallized. Demons who couldn't believe a mere mortal woman could disrupt their evil plans—and had been proved wrong. But she'd never seen any as angry as Galen was right now.

Because she'd defied him? Because of a Cadre mission statement over which she had no control? Or could he somehow sense the chaotic emotions raging within her over him, despite her best efforts to conceal them?

Emotions *she* should be angry about, not him.

God help her.

She was falling in love with Galen McManus.

Sure she'd been attracted to him—okay, had a wicked crush on him—since the first moment they'd met. But this…this was different. She'd tried to ignore it. Done her best to deny it. To herself. Certainly to him.

But this morning when he'd stalked across that huge room at Pandora's Box like an avenging angel, coming to her rescue, there'd been no mistaking the feeling that swooped down to capture her heart.

Love.

She'd felt it in every molecule of her body when she'd seen him attacked by their enemy, blood pouring from his wounds. She'd felt it deep in her soul, a primal scream of anguish when she'd thought he was about to die.

It was there now, staring her tauntingly in the face. She was teetering on an emotional brink, about to fall hopelessly, helplessly in love with the man.

Except he wasn't a man. He was a demon.

He was one of *them.* One of the fiends that had peered back at her from the void at Pandora's Box, waiting for her to be devoured, or worse. Perhaps not as evil as some. But…

He was not human.

She'd seen his awesome powers, what he could do with a mere flick of the wrist. She'd felt his bespelling magic, how he could influence her with a single thought or brush of his hand.

It scared her to death. *He* scared her to death.

She could not fall in love with a demon. She could not.

She had to keep her feelings well hidden. Not give in to them. Ever. She could fulfill her part of their bargain. Only three nights left. Sex with Galen was good. More than good, it was amazing.

But she had to stick to their original arrangement. He must come to her at night, in her dreams, as they'd agreed. She couldn't be around him any other time. She couldn't risk getting to know him any better. Couldn't risk seeing the goodness beneath his bluster, or the warmth in his eyes when he looked at her, or allow herself to feel the tenderness in his loving touch.

If she did, it would be all over for her heart.

The door to his bedroom slammed again, hurtling her back to the present. She held her breath as he stalked back into the living room and came straight for her.

Her courage teetered. It could well be all over, all right.

"Galen—"

"Give me your hand," he commanded harshly. She flinched. *"Give me your hand!"*

She did. He took it, flipped it over and smacked something hard onto her palm. It was the Demon Stone.

Shocked, she stared down at it, beautiful and sparkling black like his eyes when he made love to her.

"What— Why— What is this?"

His hot, furious breath riffled through her hair. Waves of his potent energy crawled over her skin. "What do you think?"

"But—"

Her heart quailed. She looked up into his dark, drowning eyes and almost lost herself. "I don't understand."

"I am releasing you from our bargain."

For the second time. It was unheard of. And it frightened her even more. What was he up to? Another test? She swallowed down her fear and pushed the stone back at him. "No."

A nanosecond of surprise crossed his face. He thrust the gem back into her palm. "I'm not going to argue. Take the damned stone."

She curled her hands into tight balls. "I'll take it when we agreed. After five nights."

"What is wrong with you, woman? Take it and go! It's what you said you wanted."

What she wanted was to cry. How could she tell him she'd lied? That the only thing she really wanted was…him?

No!

Why was he doing this?

It didn't matter!

She should take the Demon Stone and run like hell. Away from him. Away from the danger of his touch and these confusing feelings and the hopelessness of this wrenching dilemma. Back to St. Yve, where she'd be safe.

Safe.

Oh, my God!

She gasped as a horrible realization struck her like cold lightning. Panic swept over her. That would explain everything! His behavior. His sudden about-face on their pact.

"You think you're going to die, don't you?" she choked out in alarm. "You think Chaddiel will come for you and kill you! Or P-Cell. Or both."

He didn't think he'd be *around* for three more nights.

He stared at her as though she had just turned into a pillar of salt.

"That's absurd," he refuted flatly. "Chaddiel won't make a move without going through the Grigori first, and I can handle P-Cell."

His scowl didn't fool her for a minute. She ignored his denials. "That's why you're trying to get rid of me, isn't it? You're protecting me."

His mouth snapped closed. "Trust me, I'm not that noble."

"Why, then? Why break our deal? Why push me away now when a few hours ago you were ready to die for me?"

His eyes narrowed and his mouth thinned. "Because you are bad luck, the bane of my existence and I am finished with you. Now, take the stone and get out of here before I teach you a lesson in obedience!"

Fists bunched, he towered over her as if he'd suddenly grown two feet taller. He looked as though he wanted to tear her limb from limb. A brief dart of fear pricked her, but it dissolved just as quickly. He was trying to scare her.

She didn't scare that easily.

She put her fingers on his chest, gathered the front of his shirt. It was silky and soft, yielding. Everything his expression was not. "I know you don't mean that," she said.

"*I do,*" he roared.

"Listen to me. I have an idea."

"What are you talking about?"

"A place where they can never get to you."

"Who?"

"Chaddiel. P-Cell." She slid her arms around his neck.

He pulled them off. "Stop it. I told you, *you* are the one in danger here, not me."

She put them back. "Galen, you have to appeal to the Cadre for protection."

"The Cadre! Are you *insane?* You said if they found out I seduced you they'd lock me in a crystal for all eternity!"

"They'll never know about us. Not if we don't tell them. We'll both be safe at St. Yve."

"I'm not going near that place. Especially with you."

But the anger had seeped out of his eyes. In them was wariness instead. It was almost as if he was the one afraid—of her. Talk about absurd.

The loud chirp of her mobile phone jerked her to attention. It was in her briefcase on the floor next to the door. On the second ring, Galen stepped back, wordlessly directing her to answer it. She would have let it ring. Apparently he needed the breathing space. Saved by the bell.

"Where have you been all morning?" Aurora demanded as soon as Dawn punched the talk button. Her twin, Aurora, was second in command of the Cadre after their father, and tended to speak to everyone with a tone of authority. "I must have left half a dozen messages."

Dawn glanced at the mobile's screen. The little envelope at the bottom flashed around the number five. Oops. "Sorry. I've been, um—" Luckily Aurora didn't really care where she'd been, saving Dawn the trouble of deciding what and how much to tell her of the morning's adventures.

"The Department is in an uproar," she interrupted. "You have to—"

"Yes, I know. I was there when P-Cell started shooting."

"I can't believe that bastard Marcolf—" Aurora's litany cut off before it began. "You were?" She sounded surprised.

"Yes. Along with—" Dawn glanced up at Galen, who stood with legs braced apart and arms folded across his chest, a scowl planted firmly on his face "—a, um, friend of mine. It was him they were shooting at."

There was a telling pause, then, "What kind of friend?"

"He's…a demon."

There was an even longer pause. Her sister absolutely hated demons. As a young woman she'd been badly used by a handsome devil and she'd never forgotten or forgiven. A thousand questions were undoubtedly speeding through Aurora's mind. What would she choose to ask? Would it be business as usual? Or would she finally express a bit of personal, sisterly interest in Dawn?

"Why is P-Cell shooting at your demon friend?" Aurora asked crisply.

Dawn sighed. Ah, well. "We don't know," she said, closing her briefcase. "It's a mystery."

"You'll bring him in for interrogation, of course."

"Interro—" Dawn's feet almost came out from under her as she stood up. Galen grabbed her arm, his scowl deepening. "That won't be necessary. Galen means no harm to anyone." Except maybe Dawn. But that was a whole other story.

"If that's true, why is he on P-Cell's hit list, high enough to warrant priority execution?"

Dawn took a deep, steadying breath. "Maybe it has something to do with the Demon Stone."

"The— *What?*" Now Aurora sounded really surprised. Shocked?

Dawn smiled in satisfaction. It was so seldom one could really throw Aurora for a loop. Galen's eyes pinioned Dawn, but he made no move to stop the conversation. He let go of her arm and paced away.

"Galen has the Demon Stone. We're negotiating for possession." No pun intended. Right.

"My God," Aurora breathed. "The demon has it here, in the mortal realm? You've seen it?"

"I've held it in my hand."

"It's authentic?"

"Yes, the real thing. Inclusion and all."

"I can't believe it." Aurora's voice was almost reverent. "Father will be ecstatic! What does the demon want in exchange? When can you bring it home?"

"We're still bargaining," Dawn said, hedging.

Galen had walked to the built-in bar on the other end of the room and was casually pouring himself a drink. But his body was too rigid for casual. Oh, he was listening.

"Offer him sanctuary," Aurora said. "Here at St. Yve. We'll protect him from P-Cell until he returns to the dark realm."

Until he returns... Dawn pushed aside the painful thought and concentrated on Aurora's suggestion. "We were just discussing that very possibility. I'll let you know."

"When? Between the attack this morning and that revolting business with Marta and Dr. Cornell last night, you'll have your hands full at the Department today."

"Marta and Dr. Cornell?" Dawn's eyes rolled involuntarily.

"Don't tell me they've finally gone and killed each other?" She should get so lucky.

"Lord, you haven't heard?"

"Heard what?"

Galen glanced over, sipping his drink.

"Apparently they ran into each other at a pub last night, both well into their cups. Somehow they ended up in the back seat of Cornell's car. They were found there by a policeman this morning, passed out, naked and lovingly wrapped in each other's arms. Naturally, Marta accused Cornell of rape."

"Rape!" The woman just didn't know when to quit.

"Except Marta was on top, and Cornell's neck was covered in love bites."

"Sure they weren't vampire bites?" Dawn couldn't resist muttering.

"She didn't have much of a case. Especially after Cornell proposed to make an honest woman out of her, right there in the police station."

Dawn's jaw dropped. "Good lord, you mean *marriage?* Between the two of them?" A laugh burst from her. "Well, at least they'll be making someone else miserable for a change, besides me." For the rest of their lives. Ha. Revenge didn't come much sweeter than that. Unless you counted Roland's departure on crutches for the Greek Isles. That was pretty sweet, too.

It was a miracle, really. In the space of two days she was rid of the three most obnoxious troublemakers in the Department. At least temporarily. Someone up in heaven must like her. A lot.

Galen's steady gaze from the other side of the room brought her back to the present. She wiped the silly grin from her face and sobered.

"Aurora, please don't tell Father about the Demon Stone. I

don't want him disappointed if something unexpected happens and I can't get it."

Her sister jetted out an impatient breath. Not happy. No doubt Aurora wanted to be the one to give the earl the news, to nick what small part of Dawn's triumph she could. Tough. Not this time.

"Let me negotiate with the demon, Dawn. I'm better at these things than you."

Anger swept through Dawn, swift and sure. Anger born the same hour as she and her sister, the anger of hurt pride and pointless rivalry. Why did Aurora always do this?

Galen gazed at Dawn over the rim of his glass. She stared back.

"The demon wants sex, Aurora," she said, returning her twin's serve of hurt in kind. "Are you better at that, too? I could probably arrange for us to change places if you like."

Aurora gasped as though Dawn had struck her a physical blow. Maybe she had. She knew very well sex with a demon would be her sister's worst nightmare. Dawn felt a moment of guilty remorse. There were days she'd like to strangle her sister for her overbearing, condescending attitude. If only Aurora would bend, just a little, sometimes.

She sighed. "I'm sorry. I—"

"Don't you *dare* let that demon touch you," Aurora said stiffly. "Bring him to St. Yve."

"Aurora, I didn't mean—"

"That's an order. If you don't bring him in, I'll report you to the Cadre High Council." Which also meant their father, who was on the Council.

"Why are you doing this?" Dawn asked in heated frustration. Her sister was also on the Council, heir to the earl as leader of the Cadre. They would listen to her and not to Dawn. It had always been that way.

"For your own protection," Aurora snapped. "You don't

know demons like I do. What they'll do to you if you put your trust in them."

Actually, she knew demons far better than her sister. At least this one. "I won't bring him in unless you swear the Cadre will give him protection and not harm him in any way."

"They're evil, lying beasts, Dawn. He's just using you."

"Those are my terms, Aurora. Go to the High Council if you must." A girl had to draw the line somewhere.

The silence on the line was thick. Finally, her sister said, "Very well. The portal guardians will test the demon's mind for sincerity. If he has no harmful intent, I will grant him the Cadre's sanctuary."

It was as much of a concession as Dawn was likely to get. But she couldn't bring herself to say thank you. "I'll put the offer to Galen. It's his choice to make." She pushed the mobile's end button and swallowed heavily.

"What offer?"

Galen was standing directly in front of her. She hadn't seen him move. She stifled the instinct to jump. "Can you please warn me when you're going to do that?"

He had his hands in his pockets. "What offer?"

"The same I suggested earlier. The Cadre's protection."

He regarded her for a long moment. "You had a disagreement with your sister."

"So what's new."

"This one was about me."

"I think I mentioned before, she doesn't like demons."

A shadow had fallen over his face. He stood there looking handsome as sin and mysterious as the darkness that shrouded him. "What will happen if I refuse and she goes to your High Council?"

Dawn glanced away. The barest brush of power skimmed over her body. Controlled. Civilized. Reasonable. Yeah.

"They'll assume you've got something to hide. Are up to no good. They may put out a capture order on you."

The power prickled hotly, flowing around her like a liquid weight. "And you? What will happen to you?"

She shrugged, studying the floor. "Discipline. Restrictions. The usual. No big deal."

He took his hand from his pocket and raised it to her face, tracing his fingers along her jaw, barely touching her. She looked up into his black eyes and they glittered like midnight ice.

"Can't have that," he murmured. "You're mine to discipline. Only mine."

The glitter of his eyes was primitive and possessive. She shivered. He'd never done anything to hurt her, to subdue or physically control her. But still she shivered. Something had shifted in their relationship and she wasn't sure what. Or exactly when it had happened. But something in his eyes was different.

She wasn't sure she liked it. Or trusted it.

"Call your sister back," he said, his voice soft as velvet. "Call your sister and tell her I'll come."

Suddenly, Dawn wasn't sure this was such a good idea. What if her sister was right? What if she'd been bespelled by his potent demonic charms and her own embarrassingly unmanageable desires? What if Aurora saw right through to the truth of things?

"Galen, I don't think—"

"My mind is made up, my sweet. We'll go to St. Yve."

Chapter 18

Dawn had insisted on spending the afternoon at the Department before heading for St. Yve. Putting out fires, she'd said.

Galen snorted. More like putting off the inevitable.

He was behind her desk twirling idle circles in her office chair while she held an emergency faculty meeting down the hall. Just as well she'd left him alone. It gave him time to think. And plan.

Despite the complications, his real job was going well. Dawn's wished-for vengeance against the three antagonistic Department members had come off better than expected. Galen had no doubt he'd find equally promising opportunities among rival members of the Cadre when he and Dawn arrived at St. Yve.

And he sensed a triumphant conclusion to his work in the form of the sister. Dawn's mind was rife with jealousy and unacknowledged rage toward her twin. It was a perfect relationship to exploit for the ultimate lesson in cosmic vengeance.

He twirled another circle in the chair, parrying an unbidden stab of guilt. Guilt? He squelched it. Humans felt guilt. Not demons. Especially not for doing the job they were sent to do. Dawn's own vengeful thoughts had summoned him. *She* was the one who should feel guilty.

And she would, when he was finished with her.

The balance between good and evil, dark realm and mortal, demanded that she learn her lesson. And that he teach it to her. He must first wreak her desired vengeance upon others, but then he must wreak it back upon her tenfold. That was his Directive.

Nothing personal. It was just business. And from now on he was all about the business. He had to be. Things with Dawn were getting way too complicated. He was starting to feel things for her, because of her, that he had no business feeling. Had no desire to feel.

Demons didn't feel.

Lust and anger. Anger and lust. Nothing more.

The chair came to a stop and he stared into the empty space before him. His mouth turned down.

So why did he still feel so damned guilty?

He surged to his feet, itching to do something, anything, to relieve the hot knot of growing panic in his gut.

The door opened and Dawn walked in. Like a lamb to slaughter. Looking flushed and delectable in her coral-colored designer suit.

Well, well, well.

With a downward slash of his hand he shut the door behind her and locked it with a loud, definitive snick.

Her eyes widened. She took a step back. And hit solid wood.

He smiled.

Lust and anger.

Oh, yeah.

Chapter 19

The room trembled with silent shadows.

"So, I was wondering…" Galen's voice resonated, deep and rich, like twenty-five-year-old brandy. His dark power flowed over Dawn like a river of hot lava.

"Wondering what?" she asked.

"Is it night yet?"

She didn't need a translator to know what he was after. It was written in the hungry line of his mouth, the predatory gleam in his eyes, the tightly leashed ripple of his muscles as he advanced on her.

Her body clenched in a sudden aching desire to be taken.

Her gaze flicked to the crack between the closed window curtains. A narrow wedge of daylight spilled between the edges.

"Looks like nighttime to me," she whispered, forgetting all about her resolve to keep her distance in the thrill of his wanting. There was no sense fighting it. She'd already lost the battle.

She licked her bottom lip. He followed the movement like a tiger watching a mouse. Overmatched? Her?

The very corners of his lips twitched up.

Wrenching the files she was carrying from her hand, he tossed them over his right shoulder. Papers flew everywhere, fluttering to the floor as he put his body against hers. She gasped at the heat of the contact. He'd taken off his mac and suit coat. The molten cashmere of his cerulean-blue turtleneck slid over her silk blouse as he whisked her jacket off and tossed it over his left shoulder. The subtle scent of spicy cloves and hot desire teased her nostrils.

His mouth crushed down on hers. The front opening of her blouse ripped apart, pearl buttons joining the tempest of paper and cloth raging around them. Her skirt whipped down about her ankles. The relentless demand of his mouth, of his questing hands, the press of his hard chest crushing into her soft breasts, the taste of his sinfully forked tongue, they were an electrifying mix. She moaned, her entire body seized by a firestorm of sexual need.

Suddenly she was naked. She had no idea how or when it had happened. Things crashed all around them as Galen swept everything off her desk and lifted her onto it. Then he was on her.

The slick wood felt hard and cold against her back, the cashmere soft and hot on her front as he wrested her legs apart and mounted her. His cock, huge and wickedly thick, stabbed into her to the hilt. He captured her wild, keening cry in his mouth, devouring it as he devoured her. Utterly. Completely. Leaving nothing untouched, no part of her uncovered or unconquered.

He thrust into her and she took him in, welcomed him, surrendered to him. Gave herself over to the man…and to the demon within.

She wrapped her arms and legs around him, clutching him close. Letting him take her body with his solid flesh and his magical tongues, and her mind with his dark, seductive powers. His essence ran strong within her, making her feel his excitement, his rampant passion—for her. Her name echoed through his whole being as he claimed her.

His mouth was everywhere, his invisible tongue an unyielding presence between her legs, doing things that made her scream with pleasure. She was boneless, will-less, a slave to his sexual mastery. She wanted it never to end.

Her body convulsed in a splintering climax. He grunted a gratified acknowledgement and continued to thrust into her. Twice more she peaked, before she begged him to come and end her almost mortifying ecstasy. She could go on all night, but she'd be surprised if a crowd hadn't gathered outside her door, drawn by the pleasure cries she could not control when he was inside her.

He reared back and roared out his release. Like fiery brimstone it spurted through her, seeming to sear every molecule in her body with his hot, wet brand. She writhed in pleasure, igniting in one last, all-encompassing, body-melting orgasm.

She gasped for breath. What had he done to her? More magic? A different kind of essence?

He gazed down at her, his breathing labored, his eyes half-lidded and shuttered. His naked body glistened with sweat. When had he taken his clothes off? He shifted his knees on the desktop and she felt his cock move within her. It was still long and thick and iron-hard, even now ready for more.

What had just happened between them? Doubt thundered through her heart.

She wanted to scream, and run as far away from Galen McManus as she could get. She wanted to spread her thighs and beg him to take her again. And again and again. She wanted to turn back the clock and tell him no, no, *no!* at that first fatal meeting in the fog. She wanted to keep her arms around him and never let him go.

She didn't know what she wanted.

"What did you do to me?" she asked, barely able to speak. Her body felt wringingly depleted, not her own.

The ghost of an eyebrow raised on his harsh-angled face.

A flush ripped across her cheeks. "It's never felt like this before. So…intense."

"It's the essence. Our connection grows stronger each time our bodies become one. I can feel what you want, and I give it to you."

"You haven't…"

"Put more essence into you?" He shook his head. "I've put in too much as it is."

He pushed up on his arms and pulled out of her. She felt empty, cold. He rolled to his feet and held out his hand to help her sit up on the desk.

"What did you mean by that?" she asked, even more uneasiness creeping in at the distance he'd put between them. One minute it seemed as if he wanted to crawl inside her, the next, cool indifference.

"I mean," he said, waving their clothes to gather in a neat pile on the corner of the desk, "that we are getting too close to each other—or not close enough. This relationship between us is uncharted. I am more than your demon possessor, but you are not quite my human familiar. We lie somewhere uncomfortably in between."

"We are lovers," she said. But suddenly she was unsure of anything anymore. "Aren't we?"

He regarded her impassively. "Yes. We are lovers. Which as you know, in our circumstances never ends well."

A shudder of foreboding slid down her spine. Could it be that when he'd given her the Demon Stone and told her to go away, he hadn't been doing it to keep her safe, after all? Could he simply want to be rid of her?

Would that be such a bad thing?

"Unhappy endings are one of my specialties," she said quietly. "So, what do we do now?"

An even greater sense of foreboding sifted through her when he answered, "Now we get dressed, and you take me to St. Yve. I want to meet your sister."

Galen did his best to ignore his mounting guilt over the hurt and confusion reflected in Dawn's eyes whenever she turned them his way on the drive to St. Yve Estate. But it wasn't working.

Empathy? Him? He'd never heard of anything so outrageous. By all the devils, it was almost as if he was slowly turning human.

A frightening thought. Too frightening. Had she somehow bespelled him? A love spell maybe?

He nearly scoffed out loud. As if. Demons didn't fall in love. Ever.

Did they?

No.

Hell no.

But the fact that he could even think about the possibility reinforced one thing. He'd been right when he'd decided to get out as soon as possible. Away from her. Do his job, then scram.

Which was the *only* reason he'd agreed to come with her to Cadre headquarters at St. Yve. It had nothing to do with fulfilling the rest of their bargain. Nor was it about keeping either of them alive.

Well, maybe he was a bit concerned about keeping Dawn safe from Chaddiel….

No! That had nothing to do with it. This wasn't about her safety.

It wasn't even about the incredible prestige that breaching the impenetrable fortress of the Cadre would bring him with the Grigori and the whole dark realm, when word spread he'd been invited inside their headquarters. Invited! Unprecedented. According to the faefolk living in the surrounding enchanted forest, the only Darks who had actually been inside St. Yve Manor were the guardians and portal demons who'd resided there since the place was built five hundred years ago. And, if Dawn was being truthful, the few who had joined the Order of the Cadre as initiates. But they'd never betray Cadre secrets. He wondered if he'd run into any of them. The Grigori would be very generous to anyone who might provide their names, traitors that they were.

"Turn here," Dawn said, interrupting his scattered thoughts. "And when we get to the turnoff be sure to stay on the road. It's right up ahead."

After delving into his car collection to retrieve his treasured scuro-blue Lamborghini—a Diablo, of course, a VT roadster—to replace the shot-up Austin Healey Sprite, they'd driven southwest from London for about an hour and were now skimming along a country road through a deep wood. He didn't see a turnoff. He rolled down the window to get a closer look.

The welcome smells of the woods rushed through the low-slung car, replacing the lingering perfume of their earlier intimacy. Dank and moist, the forest smelled cloyingly green, carrying the faintest tinge of dark energy. The cry of an owl or one of the small furry creatures that haunted the woods, and the smooth purr of the engine were the only sounds that broke the thick silence.

The sun had gone down but the moon had not yet risen. Darkness cradled the Lamborghini in its arms; even the sweep of headlights on the black pavement looked more shadow than light. It was a strange, swallowing kind of darkness. Not a comforting dark as was normal for Galen. It was almost… spooky.

He laughed inwardly at his own foolishness, then pointed to two parallel dirt tracks, a barely discernible overgrown path between the trees. "Turn there? *That's* the road to St. Yve? Surely, you jest."

"It's not what it seems. Trust me, this is the way."

"If my car gets scratched—" Suddenly, he realized. "A concealment spell?"

She nodded. "We have several shields in place to prevent anyone from accidentally finding their way onto the estate. During the day, people see only a large castle perched on a hill in the distance. They never get close, and there is a spell of forgetfulness so when they lose sight of it they forget they ever saw it."

"Is that why I have to stay on the road?"

"That, and the scratch thing."

"Funny." A strange glow above the car caught his attention, and he leaned forward, peering through the windshield, up past the branches of the trees. An incredible rainbow shimmered directly above them, arching in multicolored splendor through the cobalt sky and into the distance.

He swore softly. "What the hell... Magic?"

"A beacon, to lead Cadre initiates home."

"Nice trick."

He was beginning to feel as though he might be out of his depth here. Naturally, every Dark, including himself, held a healthy respect for the Cadre, because of what its initiates were capable of. Being able to chant a spell and capture you inside a crystal, that alone was worthy of great respect. But he had never heard that their magic extended to such powerful spells as these.

What else could they do that the Grigori didn't know about?

Satan's bollocks. What was he getting himself into?

Galen wasn't even surprised when he turned onto the bumpy path and it instantly dissolved into a smooth road curving gently through the trees. The enchanted forest.

About a quarter mile in, they passed a small, white gingerbread cottage covered in vines of spicy-smelling red roses. Coach lights framed the front door invitingly. A sweet-looking old lady with a gray bun and rosy cheeks stepped onto the porch and waved. Dawn waved back and called, "Hullo, Ophelia!" through the open window. An old man peeked his head out and waved, too. "Good evening!" she called to him as well.

A tall, curlicued wrought-iron gateway with a spiked top spanned the road, but it was wide open. Galen drove through.

"Who were they?"

"St. Yve's threshold keepers."

"Demons?" he asked in surprise. They'd seemed so human.

She nodded. "The cottage is bespelled to appear wherever and whenever anyone ventures onto the estate. The uninvited are offered a cup of tea and gently encouraged to leave."

He grinned. "Tea?"

"Hawthorn tea. Ophelia claims its magical properties make a person reveal the truth about themselves." She glanced at him. "Perhaps I should ask her to give you a cup."

He frowned. "Do you want me to leave? Because if you do, I will."

She sighed. After a moment she said, "No, of course not." She took a long breath and let it out. "Normally I issue a warning about now to anyone I bring home," she said, sweeping a gaze over their surroundings.

"What kind of warning?"

"Never to go into the forest without me or a Cadre guide. But I guess you're safe, being a demon."

St. Yve was one of the rare borderlands between the dark and mortal realms. It was one of the few places in the mortal realm a demon who had not been summoned by a human could manifest without needing a familiar to bridge him over.

She lifted a shoulder. "Paras aren't affected by the old magic. But it's dangerous for a human to venture into the enchanted forest anywhere but on this road."

He figured he knew why but he asked anyway. "How so?"

"The place is full of spells and enchantments. There's an everchanging trail which unless you know the proper chants will keep you wandering on it for years, never finding your way out. The sidhe hold dances—reels—in many of the meadows that will suck you in, sap your will and never let you go." She shot him a look he couldn't interpret, then glanced away again. "Both of which are a life sentence, because if a mortal, even a Cadre member, is caught inside the treeline after the sun goes down, they belong to the forest and can never leave again."

He put his foot on the brake and stared at her, intrigued. "What happens to them?"

"They become part of the borderlands. A being neither human nor fey nor immortal. They are treated well and live a life of luxury and excess among the faefolk, but they may not leave the forest, ever. Not for the mortal realm nor the dark realm. They are stuck in limbo until they die, or…"

He started the car moving again. "Until they die, or what?"

"Some of them beg the ruling sidhe to be changed, and escape in that way."

"Changed? As in…"

"The walking dead."

"You mean…bitten by a vampire?"

She pushed out a breath. "Yeah. Or a shade. One of the species of undead. For a mortal, it's the only way out that I know of. But it happens rarely. The sidhe have a definite mean streak, and they must agree to relinquish their claim on the human. The price is always high."

Galen gave a whistle. Very interesting. "Wow. It sucks to be human."

"Tell me about it," Dawn muttered.

He let the comment pass. He wasn't about to debate the relative suckiness of being Dark versus being human with his mortal lover.

Speaking of which… "Tell me how you want to present our relationship to your father and the others." Better to get things clarified. He had no desire to end up stuck for eternity in a crystal. He couldn't even grow fangs to escape that fate.

Her mouth thinned. "There can't be a relationship. You and I must be strictly about the Demon Stone. You approached me with it, but before we could negotiate, P-Cell attacked you. I offered the Cadre's protection in exchange for the diamond."

"What about Aurora? You already told her I wanted sex in exchange."

"She'll attribute the attempt to your wicked nature, but will assume you really want something else, more in line with the stone's…true value."

He regarded her for a moment. "She always underestimates you so badly?"

He felt a flare of ancient, crackling anger swell through the small confines of the car, then recede again. "Someday she'll realize how wrong she is."

He'd been right about the sister. She was the perfect object lesson for Dawn. Too bad Aurora hadn't summoned her own demon. It sounded as though she could use a lesson or two herself.

"In the meantime she won't tell on us?" he asked.

"Not as long as she doesn't think we're actually sleeping together."

"Are we?" He told himself it was just idle curiosity. For informational purposes only. He was all about the job now. That episode in her office? One last passing fit of lust. Nothing more.

Lust and anger, remember?

"We made a bargain," she said, staring out the passenger-side window. "I live up to my word. My body is yours for another three nights if you want it."

He noticed she hadn't said, "I'm yours if you want me." For some reason that irritated him. As did the blasé tone. As if she couldn't care less.

"I'll think about it," he gritted out.

The road spilled out of the forest and into an open expanse of meadow that canted a whispering river. The dank smells of the woods were replaced by the scents of wildflowers and rushes and languid water. An elegant but ancient stone bridge arched gracefully over the slowly flowing river, looking for all the world like a bit of Roman aqueduct. Maybe it was. The Romans would have recognized a ley line when they felt it. They'd probably built one of the many ancient fertility temples under St. Yve Manor. Too bad all his jobs back then had been in Rome itself. A busy time, that.

Above the river loomed the castle. The grand facade was a pale, shimmering yellow as though made of liquid moonlight. There was no hill. Just a huge expanse of majestic lawns that sloped gently upward from the dense forest to the foot of a manicured, double-terraced rise upon which sat St. Yve Manor.

He drove over the bridge. The castle was every bit as impressive up close as it had appeared from the forest edge. Stone blocks cut so precisely you couldn't see the seams, tall windows that shone even in the starlight, rows of moldings with carved gargoyles so lifelike they had to be real. Turrets, towers, crenellated bastions. The works.

"Quite a place," he murmured. A powerful place. He could feel its magical energy tingling along his skin and scraping against his bones. *Human* magic.

"It's an ancient place of worship. It gains a lot of energy from that. There was also a fortress here, in the Dark Ages," Dawn said. "But it fell into ruin almost as soon as it was built, reportedly because it was possessed by the Devil."

"Humans were pretty superstitious back then," he recalled.

"No one would live there."

"Until your ancestor built St. Yve."

"The first Earl of St. Yve was a mystic, an alchemist, but not superstitious. He realized the strange happenings were because of the ley lines on the property. He wanted to study the phenomenon. But he got a little more than he bargained for."

"The indwellers from the fertility temples," Galen said with a wry smile.

"The place *was* possessed. By all-too human energy." She avoided his gaze. "We're here."

The bridge had led around a giant spreading oak tree to a pebbled lane which ended in a circle at the formal front door, complete with sweeping stairway and manicured topiary.

"This is the main entrance to the central part of the manor where the family lives." She pointed to the right, at a smaller car path. "That way, around in the back, is the entrance to the east wing, which is Cadre headquarters." Then she indicated a left path that branched off toward a small sheltered entrance. "We'll be staying in the family wing, but I prefer using the side door."

He pulled the Lamborghini under the tastefully pillared porte cochere and came to a stop. Immediately their doors were opened by a pair of liveried footmen.

A butler in immaculate black met them at the bottom of the low steps leading to the family entrance. "Good evening, Lady Dawn."

"Good evening, Charles. This is Mr. McManus. He'll be staying with us for a few days. Can you please put him in…hmm, the Constantinople Room, I believe."

The butler hesitated, sending a sidelong glance at Galen. He looked pained. "Yes, my lady. I'll notify Lady Aurora you've arrived, shall I?"

"There's no need, thank you, Charles," a firm feminine voice said from the doorway. "I'm already here."

A tall, elegant woman with Dawn's face—but not her softness or her smile—leveled sharp green eyes at Galen. The physical likeness between the two women was remarkable. She stood at the top of the steps, making it necessary for Galen to look up to meet her gaze. No doubt deliberate.

He offered his arm to Dawn and accompanied her up the steps. He sketched her sister a short bow. Hell, he could play milord with the best. "So kind of you to extend your hospitality, Lady Aurora."

She glanced at the ring on her forefinger, which seemed to be glowing. "I wouldn't be too sure about that, demon. First your heart must be weighed by the guardians."

Dawn jetted out an impatient breath. "Aurora, really."

Her sister ignored her. "I warn you, demon. If you fail the test, the only hospitality I'll extend will be to a crystal in our dungeon."

Galen gave Dawn's lookalike his most confident smile. The hostile gaze she returned held not one iota of sympathy or understanding.

All at once he was pricked with a dart of worry. He'd never even considered the possibility of failing the gargoyle's test. He wasn't evil. He had no malicious intent here. Not really. Maintaining balance was not malicious. Teaching a needed lesson was not evil.

Suddenly he wondered. Had he been overconfident?

What this stern woman considered evil and malicious might not jibe with his own definition. Maybe simply the fact that he was a demon who'd tried to seduce her sister was enough....

Hell's bells. Anxiety rocketed through his whole being. Could it be he'd just made the worst damned mistake of his life?

Chapter 20

Dawn's eyes rolled. "Honestly, Aurora. Is this any way to greet a guest?"

"You know the rules," Aurora said, her spine stiffening.

Galen kept his mouth shut. He didn't want any part of this argument. No sense pissing her off more than she already was.

Yeah, *either* her.

They both turned to him. He smiled, all teeth.

"Sure you want to do this?" Dawn asked.

"What the hell. It's only eternity."

Aurora twisted her ring. Dawn blanched. "Galen, is there anything you haven't told me?"

"Plenty. But nothing relevant." He hoped.

Next to the door, two giant stone half-bird, half-imp gargoyles ruffled their feathers and moved their hideous heads, as though awakening from a long slumber. Sculpted veins and bones sharpened, sinewy muscles stretched taut as they unfurled their wings. Fierce hooked beaks looked vicious enough to rip a man to ribbons. The gargoyles pinned Galen with stony gazes.

He spread his arms out from his body, meeting one then the other, eyes without hesitation. "Search my soul, guardians, and you will see it harbors no ill toward this place or those within its walls."

"Gutsy bugger, I'll give him that," Aurora murmured.

"I told you," Dawn said, "Galen is only interested in making a trade for the diamond. He has no nefarious purpose."

Her defense of him warmed his heart. He wanted to smile at her, but was too busy staring down the gargoyles.

"Then why was P-Cell shooting at him?" Aurora asked. She sounded beyond skeptical.

"He doesn't know."

"Hmph. Well, guardians?" Aurora commanded the bird-imps.

The gargoyles seemed to take flight. But it was just their ind-welling demons that lifted off, leaving the carved stone statues in place next to the door. The silvery mist-like demons swooped and circled about Galen's head. Energy flowed outward from their phantom forms like ripples of electricity. It penetrated his body, surrounding each cell with heavy, probing power, as though someone was peering at him from the inside out. A very creepy feeling.

Suddenly his arms flew up and his body locked in place, unable to move. He felt the whisper of wings against his back. At once one of the gargoyles was staring him in the face, just inches away. Primitive eyes looked deep, deep into his soul. They widened, then they were gone.

A sharp sensation stabbed through the left side of Galen's back. He gasped, breathing through the pain as an invisible claw grasped his heart and for a moment seemed to rip it from his chest. Pulsing energy swirled around the organ like a tornado. He didn't have a chance to panic, for again, as quickly as it started, it was over.

Both guardians hovered before him for a moment on silent wings. They looked at each other, then at him, then back to each other, as if undecided about something.

His restored heart started to pound like thunder. He sucked down a breath, relief pouring through him. Removing a demon's heart from his body was one of the few ways to kill him.

"What is it?" Dawn asked the gargoyles worriedly.

They bowed their heads at Galen, then swept away on wraith-like wings, melded with their stone images and came to rest, solid and unmoving.

Aurora blinked. Twice. "Well! It seems you have passed the test, demon." She looked none too happy. "When Charles has shown you to your rooms, Dawn, I'd like a word."

With that, she turned on a toe and disappeared through the door, which Charles managed to reach and open in the two seconds it took her to get there. He bowed formally as she strode through. "Shall I fetch your luggage from the car, my lady?" Charles asked, turning to Dawn.

"No luggage this time, Charles. We were— It wasn't safe to go back to the flat."

"Very good, my lady." With that, he melted into the castle and disappeared.

"Demon?" Galen asked.

Dawn gave him a quick, distracted look. "Who, Charles? Don't know. I've never asked."

Galen raised his brows in surprise. "I thought Cadre initiates could recognize demons on sight."

"Many kinds, yes. But the more evolved species, only if they give themselves away."

He nodded thoughtfully. "You spotted me right off. What gave me away?"

She was still gazing at the gargoyles as she answered. "I knew you were a para by the way you moved. Too fast for a human.

But it was your whisper that told me what you were. Only demons have that power."

"To influence a mortal's thoughts by whispering in her ear. A very handy ability it is, too. Most annoying it never seems to work on you."

She finally turned to him and smiled. "The benefit of a lifetime of Cadre training. But you do all right sometimes." She stepped closer, her thoughts obviously not on that topic. "What did the guardians see in your heart, Galen? I've never known them to react like that."

His answering smile froze on his lips. "I can't imagine."

"They seemed almost…puzzled. Are you sure you can't think of anything?"

The only thing he was sure of was that he never wanted to go through that wretched so-called test again. As for what they'd seen, or felt, within him, he was afraid to speculate. He had not been himself lately. Some of the changes were downright frightening. Maybe they'd thrown the gargoyles, too.

He forced a grin, waggling his eyebrows. "Perhaps they saw what I plan to do to you in bed tonight."

She glanced around on an intake of breath. "Shhh! You mustn't say such things."

"Can't help it. It's my wicked nature."

She made a face. "Come on, you. We should go in."

Dawn let Charles usher them upstairs to the third floor, doing her best to keep her expression neutral and play the courteous hostess rather than giving away her nervousness about bringing a demon lover straight into the lion's den.

Wicked nature. Good lord. Did he really think he could come to her bed tonight?

Of course he did. And could. He need only play incubus and no one would know. Unless they heard her screams through the walls. Or…did you scream aloud when you came for an incubus, or were the screams just in your dreams?

"My lady?"

She came to with a start, realizing Charles was addressing her. "I'm sorry, what?"

"You said the Constantinople Room for the gentleman?"

They were standing in front of the door of that disreputable room. Charles's hand was poised on the clear crystal knob. His air was bland as ever, but she could just imagine what he was thinking.

The Constantinople Room had been decorated at the height of Victorian closed-door decadence, inspired by the erotic translations of Sir Richard Burton—the real one, not that Welsh upstart. Opulent and sensual, the bedroom's furnishings, textiles and décor blended in a sumptuous feast of color and texture. There were subtle added features sure to please the most discriminating Victorian nabob: sturdy metal rings fixed here and there to the walls and the bed, a few unusual pieces of furniture with mysterious and intriguing devices attached, and sumptuous wall murals that spurred the imagination.

"It's the most…demonic room in the castle, wouldn't you agree, Charles?" she asked with mock innocence.

The room's unique ambiance was not the reason she'd chosen it for Galen. It had a secret connecting passageway to her own. She had found it by accident the summer she was six, playing hide and seek with Aurora. It turned out the manor had several secret passages. She'd never told her sister. They hadn't played hide and seek much after that. She'd always won. Aurora didn't like losing.

"The gentleman should feel right at home, my lady," Charles said, and opened the door without so much as a flicker of his placid expression.

She and Galen exchanged an amused look. Which died on Galen's face when he stepped into the room. After a quick survey, his eyes sought hers again, brows arched in mild surprise. Or was it veiled anticipation?

"You'll find a wardrobe with a variety of clothing kept for visitors," she told him in a businesslike manner. "Something's bound to fit. Cocktails at half-seven in the drawing room. Dinner at eight. I'll see you downstairs then, shall I?"

"I look forward to meeting the earl," Galen said smoothly, behaving himself under the watchful eye of Charles. Not that they were probably fooling him for one minute.

The butler pulled the door closed behind Galen, bowed to Dawn and glided tactfully away. She was almost sorry to disappoint him. She turned and headed for her own rooms so she could freshen up before her confrontation with Aurora. Wouldn't do to meet her sister with the scent of Galen's sex surrounding her like a tarnished halo.

It was too early to dress for dinner, so after a quick shower she selected a slim, long-sleeved wool jersey dress in a pretty shade of periwinkle with a black suede belt. She wore it with black heels and on one shoulder had pinned a silver and jet brooch that her late mother had left her. The outfit was very Audrey Hepburn. She always felt sophisticated and confident when she wore it. She could use all the confidence she could get for this meeting.

Aurora had left her office door open, but Dawn knocked anyway before entering. Her sister always did at the Department. No sisterly informalities between them.

"Darling, come in," Aurora said, looking up from her desk. "Close the door. We should chat."

Dawn took a seat on the comfortably shabby damask sofa that sat against the wall at right angles to the desk. Tea had been laid out for them. The pot steamed fragrantly under its cosy. Chamomile. At least it wasn't hawthorn.

"What would you like to chat about?" she asked, pouring each of them a cup.

Aurora rose and came to join her, taking the matching plush chair. "You know very well." She accepted the Royal Doulton cup and saucer Dawn extended to her. The ancient gold-and-ruby ring she always wore on her forefinger, which bore the unhappy name The Ordeal of Arwyn, flashed brilliant red in the lamplight. "Who is he and what does he want?"

"His name is Galen McManus, and I told you what he wanted."

"Yes. Sex. I trust you haven't given it to him."

Dawn looked into her cup and blew on the liquid. A drift of chamomile mist lifted to calm her nerves. "Would I have brought him to St. Yve if I were sleeping with him?" she evaded.

"Only if you are being more foolhardy than ever. If Father found out—"

"You needn't remind me. I remember what happened to James Peri."

A stricken look passed quickly over Aurora's face. James Peri was the handsome lust demon who had wiled his way to within a hairbreadth of taking her twin's innocence at age seventeen. Their father had rescued her by crystallizing the slimy bastard at the last possible second, but that second had been the defining moment of Aurora's young life. She hadn't been the same carefree girl since. Dawn doubted if she'd ever be comfortable around demons.

Aurora straightened, her cup clinking crisply in its saucer. "Exactly. And what happened to me. One of us is all the demons are getting. I'll protect you from this beast if it's the last thing I do."

She stifled the urge to protest the word beast. "Thank you, but that won't be necessary. I realize I'm not an adept like you, but this is my business and I can take care of myself."

Which brought to the surface another ongoing tension between the two of them—the continued denial of Dawn's petition to adept status by the High Council, on which Aurora sat. The Council claimed Dawn hadn't fulfilled all the requirements, but wouldn't tell her what was wanting. Aurora wouldn't, either. She should feel the lack within her, the Council maintained, if she were truly worthy of the promotion. What a load of—

"Even adepts can be fooled," Aurora said. "Their main advantage is knowing it when they are."

Another point in Dawn's favor. She knew exactly what was going on with Galen. It didn't help one bit. So what was the big deal? But that wasn't the issue they were arguing over this time.

"Don't forget the P-Cell attack on Galen," she reminded her sister. "He'll give us the Demon Stone if the Cadre protects him. It's as simple as that."

Aurora finished her tea and set the cup down. "I hope so," she said. "For your sake, I truly hope so."

The conversation then turned to the day's events at the Department. But Dawn knew her sister had not satisfied her curiosity about Galen. She should probably warn him that he was in for a grilling tonight at dinner.

On second thought, maybe not. He could hold his own as well as she. And who knew? Perhaps something interesting might slip out. Something that shed light on why he was really here.

Because after the strange reaction of the gargoyles, she was all but certain he was hiding something from her.

Something she had better find out about soon.

For everyone's sake.

Chapter 21

Charles announced Dawn's father just as she was accepting a sherry from Galen. They were standing next to the drinks cart in the drawing room. Bugger. She'd been hoping to have downed at least two of the thimble-sized glasses before facing the earl.

No demon had ever dined at their table before. This was not a casual occasion, and everyone knew it. Everyone except maybe the demon.

"Lord Lawrence," Charles intoned formally enough to set Dawn's nerves to jangling again.

Her father still cut a dashing figure despite his years, Dawn thought as he strode into the room. Retirement from active Cadre service had done him a world of good. Too bad it had done the opposite for her. Still, she couldn't blame him for her lot in life. Much.

"Lady Aurora," Charles announced, yanking Dawn back

from the edge of feeling sorry for herself. Or perhaps tumbling her over it.

St. Yve was dressed in a black dinner jacket with hematite studs and diamond cufflinks, Aurora in a flowing crimson silk gown which exactly matched the ruby of her ring. Dawn was glad she'd changed into a butter-yellow satin sheath, floor length and strapless. Her only jewelry was a pair of yellow sapphire earrings. Galen hadn't taken his eyes off her since the stairs. But then, neither had she, him. He looked killer. He was in a dinner jacket as well. She'd warned him the others would be pulling out all the stops—it was a form of intimidation in their class. But Galen hadn't been the least bit fazed. If anything, he looked far more comfortable in his shoes than she felt in hers.

"Dawn, my dear, what a lovely treat to see you," her father said, kissing her cheek. "Despite the circumstances."

So Aurora hadn't spoiled her surprise. Wonders never ceased. She smiled. "It's always good to be home, Father. May I present my friend, Galen?"

She introduced the two men, who shook hands and exchanged greetings while Charles served more sherry.

The earl looked Galen in the eye and said, "I understand you've sought sanctuary here at St. Yve, McManus. What have you done to put yourself on P-Cell's Most Wanted list?" Father seldom minced words.

"I wish I knew, my lord," Galen said. "I was as shocked by the attack as Dawn was. I'm hoping you might have a clue as to their motive."

"No sinister plots up your sleeve, what?"

"Not a one, I'm afraid."

At that Aurora snorted softly. Dawn darted her a scowl. Whatever he was up to, it wasn't sinister. The gargoyles had confirmed that. "Father, Galen came to the mortal realm to negotiate a trade."

"What kind of trade?"

Galen smiled. "An object has fallen into my possession which I understand you are looking for. I am willing to give it to you for the Cadre's protection until I can find out what's going on with P-Cell."

Her father started to speak, but before he could utter a word, Aurora interrupted. "How did you get here?" she asked Galen, her voice edged with hardness.

He blinked, taken by surprise. "Excuse me?"

"To the mortal realm. How did you bridge over? Do you have a familiar?"

His mouth opened, then closed. "Well, I…" He hesitated.

"I brought him over," Dawn jumped in. She wasn't about to let him fall on his sword for her. "I accidentally read a conjuring spell aloud during a lecture a few weeks ago." She smiled at him wryly. "One morning he showed up."

Aurora's eyes narrowed. "How convenient. What kind of a spell was it?"

Galen took over again. "Nothing terribly specific. When the spell came in and I realized who the summoner was, I petitioned the Grigori to give it to me. I managed to convince them."

"How *very* convenient. And what kind of demon are you that qualified you to satisfy my sister's spell?" She placed just the merest shade of emphasis on *satisfy*.

Dawn felt her face go hot. And her temper. Damned Aurora! She just couldn't leave it alone. Couldn't let Dawn have her one moment of glory without spoiling it for her. "That's none—"

Galen stepped forward and cut her off. "I am an incubus," he said with a charming, roguish grin for Aurora. "The spell was a general one of fulfillment. Broad enough that I could make a case for myself. I had thought—" he spread his hands in supplication to her increasingly alarmed and angry father. "Well, needless to say Lady Dawn showed me one of your Cadre crystals and told

me what I could do with *that* exchange." He made the face of a
very chastened naughty boy. "Then all hell broke loose—" He
feigned contrition and bowed. "Pardon me, ladies. When P-Cell
attacked, the whole question was moot." He sighed dramatically,
the disappointed suitor.

Aurora scowled, but didn't say anything more.

Dawn couldn't believe it. He'd told the truth—well, a distant
version of it anyway—and she'd come out smelling like a rose. She
hazarded a glance at her father. Relief etched his weathered face
as he looked at her, and in his eyes was a definite twinkle of…pride.

Her heart unfurled and basked in the rare light of paternal
approval. She pushed aside the niggling feeling that she didn't
quite deserve it.

Her father drew himself up to his full, imperious height and
turned to face Galen. "What is this object that makes you
think you can come here and seduce my daughter for its possession?" he asked.

She cringed inwardly at the word *possession*.

"Ah," Galen said as though he'd forgotten something. He
pulled a small velvet pouch from his jacket pocket and handed
it to her father with a flourish. "With my thanks, my lord, and
everlasting gratitude."

Dawn sucked in a breath. He was giving her father the Demon
Stone *now!* Which meant—what?

She tried to search Galen's face but her father's exclamation
of joy ripped her attention away. The large black diamond sat glittering on his palm.

"Good God, man! It's the Demon Stone!" He was dumb-
struck for a moment, then gasped, "Where on earth did you get
it? Do you have any idea how—" He glanced up at Galen in
wonder. "Of course you do."

Her father's gaze sought Dawn's and for the merest second
his face clouded with dismay. As though he knew exactly what

her reaction would have been to the demon's indecent proposal. Then it cleared and once again his eyes shone with excitement.

"Congratulations, Father." She hugged him and said a silent prayer of thanks to P-Cell. Who'd have thought their penchant for gratuitous, macho violence would be her saving grace?

Aurora joined in, and hugs were traded all around. Their father even hugged Galen. Aurora didn't.

St. Yve slapped Galen on the back heartily, Dawn's virtue apparently forgotten. "This calls for a real celebration, what? Charles!" When the butler appeared, he said, "Send word to the east wing. Everyone is invited to a party tonight after dinner." He consulted his gold pocket watch. "Ten o'clock should give sufficient time to organize things. Tell cook to throw something together. And we'll need champagne. Lots of it!" She'd never seen him so happy.

Even Aurora looked happy. Imagine. Because of a demon!

Dawn smiled broadly at Galen. She wanted to fling herself into his arms and cover him with kisses. She wanted to shout to her family—to the world—how wonderful he was and how much she loved him. It was the hardest thing she'd ever done, not to.

As if he knew, he lifted her hand to his lips and kissed the back of it. A gentle, lingering kiss, brushing a thumb over her knuckles. She could feel his desire. It coursed through her body, hot, intense, almost drowning. As if it were her own.

She shivered and pulled her hand from his, breaking the connection. It was too strong, too intimate. She was too needy for him. And Aurora was watching.

"Yes, and Charles!" the earl called after the retreating butler. "After you've done that, fetch the Saxon Crown!"

Dawn put her hand on her father's proffered arm and left Galen to escort Aurora in to dinner. He didn't offer his. Smart man.

The meal went quickly, accompanied by her father's animated retelling of a lifetime's worth of adventures seeking the Demon

Stone. He'd followed clue after clue, tracked demon after demon who might have knowledge of the diamond's whereabouts, making offers of ample reward to anyone who would take them to Rofocale, the demon prince of destruction who had stolen the gem from the Crown two hundred years ago.

Somewhere along the line, Charles returned bearing a velvet-lined tray, upon which sat the golden Saxon Crown.

"Ah! Here it is!" her father said eagerly as Charles set it down before him after a footman cleared his plate.

Though it had occupied a place of honor in the main salon for as long as she could remember, Dawn had never seen the Crown outside its glass case. It was absolutely gorgeous up close. Wrought of pure gold, the ornate crown was strewn with intricate filigree and delicate inlays, along with curving, mysterious figures and designs worked into the gold. Not to mention the four huge black diamonds—five now with the Demon Stone.

"Exquisite," Galen said admiringly. "Bronze Age if I'm not mistaken."

Impressed, her father smiled. "Yes, indeed. It was found in an ancient cache hidden deep in the forest by the daughter of the first earl of St. Yve. It's called the Saxon Crown, but that's a misnomer. Experts believe it to be part of a much older ritual sacrifice."

Tactfully, Galen didn't speculate on what might have been sacrificed, or to whom. "Found by the earl's daughter, you say?"

Dawn shifted in her chair and Aurora twisted The Ordeal of Arwyn on her finger. They exchanged a look.

"Arwyn," their father said, glancing briefly at the gold and ruby ring. "A young lady who endured a most unhappy fate."

"Unhappy?" Galen asked.

"She fell in love with the wrong man," Dawn told him lightly. A demon, as it happened. Not a good subject in present company. "He…disappeared. Rather than live without him, the next day at sunrise she flung herself from a parapet at the top of the castle."

Galen winced. "Ouch."

Aurora stroked a finger back and forth over the ruby. "The oak tree out front grew in the very spot where she died. It is said her grieving spirit still haunts it. Some claim to have heard her mournful cries at dawn."

"Well, I've never heard them," Dawn said quickly. She patted her father's hand lovingly and changed the subject. "Why don't you try putting the Demon Stone back in the Crown?"

Reverently, he took the gem between his fingers and held it up to the empty setting where it belonged. "A perfect fit," he breathed. His eyes were moist as he turned to her. "Thank you, my dear, for bringing it home."

Dawn's heart sang. "We should thank Galen. He's the one who brought it to us."

"By the way, you never answered Father's question," Aurora said to him casually. "How *did* you happen to acquire the Demon Stone?" Her tone was friendly, but Dawn knew the wheels were still turning, trying to find a way to implicate him in some evil plot.

"I won it in a game of chance," he answered, picking up his wineglass. "From *Ba'al* Rofocale."

"That must have been some game. For Rofocale to risk an item of such value."

Galen shrugged. "To a dark realm prince, diamonds are mere trinkets. Nothing special. The only thing he truly values is power. This was just a bit of fun."

Her father nodded. "Which is why he always ignored my offers. Wealth didn't interest him. And I wasn't willing to offer him any kind of power over me or mine. Not even for the Demon Stone."

"Then it's lucky Galen is so skilled at cards," Dawn said, beaming at him and her father.

She would remember this night for the rest of her life. The earl's happiness was an almost tangible thing, riding the air like a sweet fragrance. As was hers. All thanks to a man who by rights should be her enemy.

"Remarkably lucky," Aurora said pleasantly.

Dawn raised her glass. Not even her sister's cynicism would spoil this night for her.

"To Galen," she toasted.

The others joined in. Even Aurora. But her sister's eyes teemed with subtle misgivings. Dawn refused a tiny frisson of uneasiness. Her sister could think what she wanted, and probe all she liked. She wouldn't find anything. Dawn knew she wouldn't. There was nothing to find.

Galen was good. Not evil. Even the gargoyles had found his heart pure.

He may be hiding something, but he wasn't here in the mortal realm or at St. Yve for some foul, mysterious purpose. He wasn't like that.

On that she would bet her life.

Chapter 22

The party at St. Yve may have been impromptu, but it was no less lavish for that. Galen sipped a whiskey sour and observed the crowd as they mingled and nibbled on the delectable hors d'oeuvres being passed around by neatly uniformed footmen with silver trays. Everyone oohed and aahed over the Saxon Crown and the Demon Stone, displayed on a high table in the center of the room. Dawn, her father and sister were busy showing it off, so Galen was able to glide away to the sidelines.

The festivities were being held in the main salon of the family wing, a huge room with sumptuous antique furnishings, luxurious appointments and priceless paintings on the walls. Yet, the room was anything but cold. It gave off an aura of warmth and coziness and seemed almost alive, as though it were breathing in the cheeriness of the guests and spilling it back as convivial, hospitable vibrations. Maybe it was. The castle had a lot of strange powers.

From the corner of his eye Galen caught occasional glimpses of the indwelling house demons he'd seen on his initial visit as an incubus to the library. They flitted about the salon like gossamer ghosts, on their best behavior. No phantom fangs and claws tonight.

The magical power he'd felt upon first viewing St. Yve Manor positively pulsed through the room, surrounded as he was by the Cadre initiates who practiced it. But he'd gotten used to the hum of human magic in his body. Surprisingly, he found it rather pleasant. Kind of like a mild caffeine buzz. Drugging. Arousing. Possibly dangerous. But he was feeling reckless.

"You're new," a throaty feminine voice said close to his side. "I'm Elise. Who are you?"

Galen glanced around to find a leggy brunette in a miniskirt giving him a thorough inspection.

"And *what* are you?" she added in a purr. "For surely, such male perfection can't be human."

He raised a brow. Okay. Not *that* reckless. "I'm Galen. Lady Dawn's demon."

The brunette tilted her head, amused. "Indeed? She's keeping pets now?" Her smile turned just the slightest shade malicious. "Or is it the other way around?"

Something suddenly triggered in his memory. *Elise.* He'd heard that name before. In Dawn's mind? Hmm. Perhaps. Could this be his next vengeance victim? He sent out a subtle probe and tested the brunette's magic. Practically nil.

He turned to her with a broad smile. "A matter of opinion, I suppose." He leaned in and whispered, "I'm an incubus."

Her gaze turned calculating. "Why, you naughty boy." She gave his body another approving onceover. "And what are you doing here at St. Yve? That is, in the flesh…" She said the last word with breathy meaning.

A bit pushy, this one. No wonder Dawn didn't like her. If he was remembering correctly. "I'm the one who brought the Demon Stone."

"Ah! The guest of honor. Sorry, I didn't realize. I missed the presentation." She put her hand on his arm and raised her lips to his ear. "The earl, you know. What an old windbag." She rolled her eyes.

Actually, Galen had thought St. Yve's explanatory speech about the recovery of the Demon Stone had been quite moving—delighted and heartfelt. Not at all stuffy and sanctimonious, as might have been expected.

Moving away from the woman, Galen raised his glass in acknowledgement but didn't comment. "What about you, Elise? A Cadre initiate?"

"Three years. Still a novice, but I'm advancing to apprentice any day now," she said, preening. "My specialty is the sidhe."

"Faeries?" It was his turn to be amused. All at once the memory kicked in. *That's* where he'd heard her name before. From Raskin Rubythorn, the renegade Black Court prince he'd bought the faerie wine from. A rather risqué comment, as he recalled. Big surprise there. "I didn't think the Cadre was interested in faeries."

He felt Dawn's presence behind him.

"We're not," her voice said. "Not really, other than for research. It's almost unheard of for a sidhe to actually harm humans." She came around and slid a proprietary hand around his elbow. "Elise is mainly a recruiter. She finds individuals of the fey persuasion for us to interview. For our paranormal knowledge data base."

Elise glared at Dawn's hand. An intense aura of resentment flared around both women. "Which is a very important function," Elise said. "You as a teacher should appreciate my work."

"True enough. And trouble does occasionally brew between the faerie courts that we arbitrate," Dawn said gracefully. "Elise has proven quite resourceful in that capacity."

The women exchanged a look, all smiles laced with well-disguised antagonism. Definitely something going on there. Galen wanted to put his arms around Dawn and kiss her, to reassure her that he had no interest in the flirtatious Elise. But that would hardly be appropriate here and now. Besides, the other woman would get hers soon enough. He'd see to that, now that he knew the score.

"Come darling, there's someone I want you to meet," Dawn said to him, pulling him away. "Excuse us."

They left Elise and strolled to the other side of the room.

"You don't like her much, do you?" he asked, wondering what the cause was.

"She's talented, but a constant source of trouble in the east wing."

"What kind of trouble?"

Dawn jetted out a tight breath. "Her favorite game is to break up friendships and relationships. She's constantly trying to drive a wedge between me and Aurora. She thinks when others are brought low, her own status is raised."

"Not a very good team player." But he sensed something else between them, something more sensitive and hurtful. "There's more, isn't there?"

She was silent for a few heartbeats. Then admitted, "There was a man."

"Ah. What happened?"

"Nothing. It didn't get the chance. Elise saw to that. She seduced him and told him lies about me."

"I'm sorry."

She shook her head. "It doesn't matter now. I just wish I'd never recommended her as an initiate. Unfortunately, now she's in the Cadre there's no way to get rid of her."

He begged to differ. There were any number of ways to get rid of the woman. In fact, he was already working on an idea. Ah, vengeance, thy name is Galen.

He smiled benignly. "Once a Cadre initiate, always a Cadre initiate, eh?"

"Exactly." She tucked her arm more firmly through his. "Come meet everyone."

Like a good hostess, Dawn ushered him around and introduced him to the partygoers, including a dozen or more Cadre members. He was frankly amazed at the trust everyone showed him as they chatted. Most of them even politely shielded their magic, as he was doing with his power, so neither felt uncomfortable. True, some initiates didn't seem to like demons much. But no one tried to hide what they did for the Cadre. Dawn didn't put a stop to a single one of his questions.

Had these people never heard of spies? Demons like him lied and cheated. That's what demons did. How did they know he wouldn't run straight to the Grigori with all this juicy inside information?

He could only think that after five-hundred years of St. Yve not being breached, they must have let down their guard. Not terribly smart. If he really were a spy, it could be all over for the Order of the Cadre. He could literally open the gates of Hell over them.

Good thing he had no intention of doing so.

He sighed. How obnoxious was that? A perfect chance to give the dark realm a leg up on humanity, and he couldn't do it. What was wrong with him?

Damn, this new conscience thing was really becoming bothersome. He'd have to do something extra dastardly to Elise, just to prove—to himself at least—that he was still a real demon.

"Galen, this is Zeke Vaughan. He's an adept. And this is Felicity, his…um…"

"Fiancée," Zeke supplied with a wide smile and a thick American accent. "Nice to meet you, Galen. Hell of a thing on that Demon Stone. You've made the old man very happy."

They shook hands and Galen mumbled something appropriate. His eyes kept straying to Felicity. She was…a wood nymph. A human Cadre adept engaged to a fey? She wasn't exactly a Dark, since she lived in the mortal realm. But she was a para, as Dawn would say. He was shocked.

"You and Galen share an admiration for the hands-off philosophy regarding para deportment and crystallization."

Zeke's smile widened. "A man of infinite wisdom, I see."

"Well, I would think that way, wouldn't I?" Galen agreed good-naturedly. "Being a Dark myself."

Zeke laughed pleasantly, and put his arm around Felicity. "I firmly believe there are better ways of dealing with the unknown, without resorting to violence or torture," he said.

"I couldn't agree more," Galen said.

Violence and torture. Ouch. Thanks for the reminder, mate. He glanced around and spotted the earl talking animatedly with a clutch of his guests. But Aurora looked up and met Galen's gaze head-on. He knew if she had her way, he'd be next to experience one or the other of those delightful choices.

Better not go there. Dawn disagreed with Zeke, and Galen would just as soon there not be any discord between anyone at the moment.

So he gave her a smile and changed the subject. The four of them talked for a few minutes about where Zeke was from in the States, how he'd met Felicity and how he'd come to be at St. Yve. Galen tactfully refrained from asking how the High Council felt about their engagement. Yikes.

"How common is that?" he asked casually after the other couple excused themselves a while later.

"What?"

"A human adept pairing up with a Dark or a para."

"As in…" Her words trailed off as they watched the couple kiss affectionately on their way out.

"As in falling in love and getting married."

He didn't turn to her. Didn't so much as brush her hand. He couldn't. Because if he did, he had the horrible feeling he would sweep her into his arms and never put her down. Stand here in front of everyone and demand that the earl relinquish his daughter to him. As his mate. Forever.

Good God.

"Despite reports to the contrary," she said with a wry expression, "every once in a while, Hell does freeze over."

He made a face. "Very funny."

But his gaze lingered on the lovers. It did, eh?

Was it his imagination, or was the room suddenly getting a whole lot colder?

"The celebration was a wonderful success," Dawn's father declared after the last guest had departed for the east wing or back to their homes off the estate.

Dawn stifled a yawn. She checked the gold-and-glass clock on the mantelpiece. It was past midnight.

"Tired?" Galen asked.

She sent him a soft smile. "Very long day. Lots of excitement."

"Doubt I'll be able to sleep a wink," her father said, exhilaration still sparking off him like static. "Think I'll just take the crown and the Demon Stone back to my study and write a little in my diary." He extended his hand to Galen and shook it heartily. "Thank you again, McManus. Fulfilled a lifelong dream for me today, what? Never be able to repay you."

"My pleasure, my lord."

With that, he went off, Charles in tow carrying the glittering crown and diamond on its velvet-lined tray.

"Powerful man, your father," Galen said, thoughtfully watching the earl's triumphant exit from the room.

Dawn wondered what exactly he meant, but Aurora said pointedly, "Yes, he is. I wouldn't forget that if I were you."

Galen sent Dawn's sister a calm glance. "It must run in the family. I can feel your magic, too, Lady Aurora. Very impressive."

"What a mess," Dawn interjected, changing the subject before the two of them started testing spells on each other. She glanced around the room. "We'd better leave something extra special for the house brownie tonight. Wouldn't do to find the furniture nailed to the ceiling in the morning."

Galen chuckled. "I think Charles already took care of it. He brought those in a few minutes ago." He pointed to a stack of new CDs and DVDs sitting on the center table where the display had been earlier.

"How thoughtful," Aurora said. "Well, then. Shall I walk you two to your rooms?"

The woman was persistent, Dawn had to give her that. Her sister had kept a close eye on her and Galen all evening. No way would she leave them alone together for even a minute. She supposed it was sweet in a way, her protectiveness. But also very annoying. Dawn was a grown woman, capable of making her own decisions. If she desired to have a romantic interlude with the demon, it was her body and her heart. Her sister had no right to interfere.

Except… Of course, she did have. Every right. Aurora was responsible for the Cadre and everyone in it. If she sensed Dawn was in danger, or was putting the Cadre in danger, it was her duty to put a stop to it, whatever it was. Heaven knew, she'd done it often enough. Dawn couldn't blame her.

Shouldn't blame her. So why did she?

"An escort would be lovely, Aurora," Dawn answered. She didn't dare look at Galen. Her eyes would give her away. Both to her sister…and to him.

The plain truth was, she'd already fallen in love with the demon. Irrationally, illogically, foolishly fallen. Deeply in love. And watching him tonight as he talked to her friends and peers, interacted with her family, she'd realized how wonderful he really was. How truly worthy of her love. Charming, attentive, handsome, intelligent, honorable: Galen was everything she'd always looked for in a man.

But she couldn't let anyone see her feelings. Not even Galen. She didn't dare. Not yet. Not here, where there was a chance her father and sister might find out. If they didn't crystallize her lover out of hand, they'd surely deny him sanctuary. Until he found out why P-Cell was after him, that could prove fatal.

She fell into step beside Aurora, and Galen followed after. In the silence of the night-quiet manor, only the whisper of the women's silk gowns and the muted click of their high heels could be heard as the three climbed the stairs and traversed the long corridors to their rooms. The house seemed to follow their progress, the walls absorbing her anticipation. Her excitement.

She felt Galen's eyes on her back, felt his thoughts reach out to her, caressing her with his potent desire, his need to touch her, his fierce craving to be inside her.

"Are you quite all right?" her sister asked with a frown as they approached Dawn's door. "You look a bit flushed."

She smiled, her hand on the crystal doorknob. "Nothing a good night's sleep won't cure."

Not that she expected to get any. Galen would come to her tonight regardless of what Aurora said or did.

And Dawn couldn't wait.

She'd made up her mind. Demon or no, she wanted Galen McManus all for herself. In her bed. In her life.

And for all time.

Her father wouldn't like it. Her sister would like it even less. Dawn didn't care. Somehow she was going to make it happen. Living the rest of her days without Galen was unthinkable. She wanted him. She needed him, to be whole herself.

There had to be a way to make it work.

There just had to be.

And she was determined to find it.

Chapter 23

Wrapped in a towel, Dawn went to the wardrobe and flicked through the pretty but conservative dresses, suits and blouses she still kept in her old childhood bedroom. Finally she found what she was looking for, hanging all the way in the back. A long, sheer peignoir with matching lace teddie. White. Had she really been so naive once? The tags were still on, mute testament to a long-ago hope dashed by Elise. Dawn didn't even remember the man's name.

Okay, she did. But not what she'd ever seen in him. Not compared to Galen.

She slipped the teddie on, and the diaphanous negligee over it, eyeing the dozen tiny ribbon ties down the front. Would Galen enjoy pulling them free, one by one? She hoped he liked it. She'd never worn anything to deliberately entice him before.

Was she mad? Pinning her hopes on a demon? Risking the wrath of her father and the censure of the Cadre?

Yes. She was. But it wasn't going to stop her. Not as long as he wanted her.

She lay down on the bed and arranged herself artfully on the coverlet. Luckily, she was dead tired and sleep came almost as soon as she laid head to pillow.

Suddenly Galen was there, standing by the bed and gazing down at her with his black velvet eyes. Not the black of midnight, but the absolute absence of color, like the vast, fathomless black of the edge of the universe. A gaze as still as space itself, enigmatic, textured with a dark emotion no mortal could ever understand.

"You are a vision, my sweet. Beautiful beyond words."

Moonlight streamed in through the tall windows, picking him out of the shadows of the room. He was dressed in only a pair of black silk drawstring pajama bottoms. His broad shoulders and chest were pale and bare, pecs, biceps and six-pack abs traced in chiaroscuro relief by the kiss of moonbeams. His long black hair had been combed straight back from his forehead, gleaming wet from a shower.

Her breath caught. She'd never seen anyone so…magnificent in all her life.

"My dark angel," she whispered.

She felt more than heard low, eerie moans sift through the room, barely audible. The house demons. She knew they were watching, hopeful. As always. As was the spirit of the manor and the age-old temples below it. The walls sighed and seemed to undulate, giving off the scent of peach blossoms and musk. Silently offering her up to the act it hungered to witness.

Galen knelt on the bed and appeared above her, hands on either side of her head. Those enigmatic eyes captured hers in their spell, his potent energy spilling through her like an intoxicating wine.

She reached up, held his face between her hands. Breathed in his exotic scent. Her body unfurled, wanting him.

"I'm yours," she whispered.

His lips descended, claimed a searing kiss, then lifted. "Let's go to my room," he murmured.

She ran her fingers down his chest, feeling the warm skin, the hard muscles. So perfect. "Are you thinking of being naughty?" she asked innocently.

"Oh, yeah."

She hummed in approval. "Good."

He nuzzled her neck, licking up the column of her throat. "That room you put me in is downright decadent. It's making me crazy wanting you."

"You feel it, too? I wasn't sure you would."

"You mean the ancient spirits worshipping sex?"

She leaned up and whispered seductively in his ear, "I think they yearn for the old days. They like to watch."

His laugh was low and seductive. "Then we must not disappoint them," he murmured, brushing a hand over her breast.

She shivered. Her nipple spun to a tight point. "There's a secret passage between our rooms," she said breathlessly.

"I thought there might be." He scooped her up into his arms like a bride, her white negligee flowing around them like a cloud. "Show me."

The hidden panel opened with a touch to a corner. She whispered the way through the dank, narrow corridor that led to the Constantinople Room. He pushed on the panel at the other end and swept with her into the sumptuous seraglio.

Galen was standing in the middle of the room in his flowing black pants, looking wicked as the Devil and darkly erotic, like the reigning sultan of iniquity.

She started in shock and confusion. She glanced up at the Galen who carried her in his arms. They were identical. Exact duplicates, down to the expressions on their faces—sinful anticipation.

He gently set her on her feet. She turned as the other Galen approached. He slowly ran his fingers down the row of ribbon ties. "Surprised?"

"H-how—" She swallowed and tried again. "How is this possible?"

"I can call my incubus at will. There's no rule I can't be there, too. Close your eyes, my sweet."

He stepped closer, so his body and hers were just touching. She felt his double—his incubus—press into her back, sliding his arms around her waist from behind.

Galen lifted her chin as her eyelids squeezed closed. His mouth brushed over her lips. Another mouth trailed kisses down her cheek.

She shivered again. It felt so good. So...wicked.

"Oh-h-h," she whispered. "This is too strange."

Fingers skimmed lightly over her curves. She gasped as a hot wash of power thrilled over her skin.

"Shhh. I know you want us," he murmured. "Both of us. I can feel it in the tremble of your limbs and the heat of your flesh. I can taste it in your eager kiss."

The scent of peach blossoms grew stronger. The walls seemed to close in on them, just a little.

His face lowered to hers and hovered there. His tongue peeked out and glided over her lips, teasing with the tips, licking at the corners, flicking the bow. His incubus nibbled her ear from behind, pushed aside her hair to lick at the nape of her neck. Or was that the real Galen? Suddenly he reached around and grasped her jaw, turning her face back towards him. His mouth came over hers. She opened at his urging and his split tongue swept into her in a scorching, eating kiss.

Someone moaned. It couldn't have been her...

While he kissed her mouth, Galen sucked lightly at her throat, her shoulder, her cheek. Suddenly, her chin was tugged down and both their tongues were in her mouth. She gasped, unable to move, powerless to do anything except let them invade her totally, together. It was the most incredibly exciting thing she'd ever experienced.

She felt sinful, wanton, wicked. But how could it be wrong? One man was real, the other simply illusion. Both were one and the same man, the man she loved more than anything in the world.

She moaned again, giving herself up to the experience. She leaned back against one broad chest and the other pressed into her front. She opened to their ravaging mouths. Fingers drilled through her hair, holding her immobile to their plunder. Her own hands reached out blindly, grabbing fistfuls of thick hair to pull them closer.

She felt a tug on the top ribbon of her negligee. *At last!* It pulled apart and deft fingertips skimmed over the silk of the teddie beneath. Goose bumps shimmered over her whole body.

The next ribbon untied. Then the next. And the next. Both men's hands roamed her silk-slick body as the filmy fabric fell to the floor. They kissed and touched her, kissed and caressed her, until all she could feel, everything she smelled and tasted and heard was Galen. Only him.

She was on fire. She needed him to… She needed…

"Please," she begged. "Please."

Both men's tall, powerful bodies rubbed against her, pressing their corded muscles and hard angles into the softness of her curves. She could feel their arousals, thick and unrelenting, seeking the cradle of her thighs.

Otherworldly groans tingled up her spine like electricity, low and urgent. The walls leaned in, closer still.

"The ancient ones grow restless," Galen said, his voice rough as gravel.

"And so do I," his incubus growled.

Their arms lifted her and laid her on the bed. Before she knew what was happening, strong hands raised her arms above her head. Something soft and unyielding wrapped about her wrists and snapped tight. She couldn't lower her arms.

"Galen! What are you doing?"

He and his incubus lay down on either side of her, black eyes glittering as they reached for her. "We've shackled you to the bed."

She yanked on her bonds. "Galen, let me go."

"I don't think so."

Hot power rolled over her. She gasped at the surge of desire it brought with it. Helpless, she arched between them, as they started on the teddie.

One pushed the silken straps off her shoulders and kissed her lips while the other's tongue slicked over her bared skin. Maddeningly, deliberately slowly, they drew the slippery bit of silk down her body, lower and lower. For every inch of her they bared, Galen's clever tongues faithfully followed. She moaned in pleasure. She writhed. And begged.

It was torture. Delicious, blissful torture.

"Galen, please," she groaned when she was sure she couldn't take a single second more.

"You enjoy this," his voice whispered in her ear. "You love it when I tease your body to a frenzy."

The pleasure surged and tightened almost unbearably at the erotic suggestion of his demonic whisper. Her breath turned to deep pants. "You know I do," she managed.

He didn't need otherworldly power to influence her. Galen's powers as a man were more than enough.

The teddie lay bunched at the top of her thighs. He ripped it off her and tossed it away. She was naked.

Each man grasped a knee. They spread her legs wide.

"Galen!" she cried out. And jerked at her bonds.

He canted over her, his incubus slid between her legs.

The walls leaned in. Her heart thundered. Tongues slicked

over her breasts and between her thighs. She cried out again, in an agony of pleasure. *Too much! Too much!*

His teeth nipped, his mouth clamped. He teased sharp, deep pleasure from her body in bold strokes and subtle sucks. She gasped and moaned, calling Galen's name as he worked his wicked magic on her flesh.

He knew exactly what she wanted, and gave her everything she needed. She was helpless against him. Boneless under his incubus. Completely open to both. She had no secrets. No resistance. No caution.

They made her come. She squeezed her eyes shut and swallowed a scream.

They made her come again.

She screamed his name.

Suddenly he was on top of her, pressing down onto her, naked as she. She writhed under him, pulling at the shackles, almost terrified of what dark pleasures might come next.

His hard cock thrust into her. A brilliant kaleidoscope of power broke over her in a shower of fire, like a Guy Fawkes night sparkler.

He halted, still as a statue. "Dawn," he commanded. "Wake up." His power danced over her body. "Open your eyes, my sweet."

She dared not. She shook her head, squeezed them tighter.

The whip of energy quieted, as though holding its breath, like her. She felt only Galen's motionless body surrounding her, leashed, waiting.

"Look at me."

She swallowed heavily. And slowly opened her eyes.

The incubus was gone. Vanished.

Galen looked down at her. Suspended in time and movement, for several heartbeats they lay there, melded together in the most primitive way, staring into each other's eyes.

He leaned down to kiss her and her entire being felt it, felt his demon tongue slide into her mouth and slick slowly along her teeth, felt its tines meet her own tongue and caress it in a wet, rolling dance of seduction.

His electrifying power built and built, until it was a steady, pressing weight on her, a sensual energy pulling her tighter and tighter until surely a single thrust from him would shatter her in a million pieces. She had never been so aroused in her life.

He moved, infinitesimally, pushing himself deeper into her. She gasped. He moved again, his thick hardness stretching her. Filling her to overflowing.

"Oh, Galen."

His power suddenly burst free and whipped hotly around them, like an unleashed tempest of fire. Magic crackled through the room, potent and insistent. His skin felt hot. Burning hot. His cock became a huge, throbbing, searing brand inside her. She cried out. Not from pain, but from the incredible pleasure. It felt… She had no word for how it felt. Intense, stimulating, feverish. As though all her lover's demonic power had concentrated its heat on the surface of his body where he touched her, centering between her legs.

All for her pleasure.

The verge of climax teased her, so close, yet light years away. It jumped around like fire in her body, tantalizing, tempting, calling out to her. Growing. Threatening to undo her. But never letting her quite near enough to touch.

"Galen," she moaned. "What are you doing to me?"

"This is how demons make love."

The backwash of his power pounded in her ears. He was getting hotter and hotter. She was getting hotter and hotter. She couldn't breathe. She couldn't move.

She was going to explode.

They were both going up in flames!

His fiery tongue quivered in her mouth, sought the back of her throat, thinned and slipped deep, deep into her.

Rich, drugging pleasure surged through her body from the roots of her hair to the tips of her toes. She struggled to cry out but her throat convulsed around his slick, invading demon tongue. Or was it illusion again? His cock expanded. Thrust and hilted. Pulled out. She panted. Felt the heady rush of his breath fill her lungs. Tasted a hint of his essence, musky with clove and hot, hot spice.

His tongue went deeper still, all the way down, down, down to the burning ember between her legs. The tips of his tongue flicked and stroked the fiery center of her need. From the inside out.

His cock plunged into her again. She screamed.

Climax roared over her.

She screamed his name, the name of her dark demon. "Galen!" she screamed, and shook with the violent pleasure he wrought upon her.

"Galen!" she screamed, and knew that she had given herself over to him, heart and soul.

"Galen!" she screamed, and wondered what was to become of her now.

Chapter 24

It was only the second time Galen had awoken with a woman tucked in his arms—both times Dawn—and this was even better than the first. He smiled. Last night had been incredible. More than amazing. But this morning was even better.

Dawn was warm and soft and smelled of wildflowers and…him. The musky scent of last night's wild lovemaking drifted up from twisted satin sheets. Her fingers were tangled in his chest hair, the tingle of her touch lingered on his skin. Residual magic? Maybe.

She stirred. His arousal stirred.

He could get used to this.

His reverie was interrupted by the bleat of his mobile phone. He frowned. It was far too early for the world to intrude. Trouble? He gently eased from under Dawn and lifted the phone from the smooth marble surface of the bedside table.

"McManus."

"It's Marceau."

The vampire. Galen checked the clock. It was about an hour before sunrise. Excellent. "Have you found out anything about the P-Cell attack on me?" he asked.

"I have. You're not going to like it."

"Tell me."

"Not so fast. Aren't you forgetting our bargain?"

Galen glanced out the window. A slash of indigo quivered in the black sky just above the treetops. "There's hardly enough time for that tonight. You'll just have to trust me."

Marceau laughed. It raised the hairs on the back of Galen's neck. You had to admire the guy. He had creepy down to a fine art.

"I don't think so," the vampire said. "Meet me at the forest edge. Behind the oak tree. I'm there now. And McManus?"

"Yeah?"

"Bring the woman."

Galen quickly got dressed, then returned to the bed. He sat on the edge of the mattress and gently shook Dawn's shoulder. "Wake up, my sweet."

Her eyes fluttered open. She took in his clothes. "What's wrong? Where are you going?"

"To meet Marceau." He told her about the phone call. Except for—

"What aren't you telling me?"

Damn their connection. This was one time he did not want her reading his thoughts. "Nothing."

She sat up and took his hand. "Don't lie to me, Galen. I can tell."

He sighed in irritation. "He wants me to bring you, but—"

"Then I should go with you."

"No. I know how you feel about vampires. And you know what he's after."

She rose from the bed, grabbed her negligee from the floor

and headed straight for the secret passage. "Galen, if he's going to drink your blood I need to be there. To make sure he doesn't try anything."

He followed after as she ran quickly along the dark passageway. "But if you're there, he'll want you, too."

They emerged into her room and she went to the wardrobe. Her mouth took on a stubborn set as she grabbed clothes. "I can take care of myself!"

He snorted, calling into the en suite after her, "Like you did at Pandora's Box?"

"I saved your life, didn't I?"

He gritted his teeth. Checked the window. Stubborn little witch. "There's no time to argue, my sweet. It's almost dawn."

"I'm not arguing. I'm coming." She was already dressed. Stylish jeans and a dark-green knitted top. "I assume Marceau is in the forest. Just don't forget, I can't go in beyond the treeline," she said, leading the way down to the side entrance. "Not until after daybreak. Or I won't be able to leave."

"I remember."

"We'll wait in the meadow. Marceau can come to us. But we'll have to deal with the gate guardians."

"The old couple? Can you send them away?"

"Yes," she said. "They'll obey me."

Outside, darkness hovered over the estate, dimmed only by the glow of the nighttime rainbow overhead and a thin sliver of slate blue above the wood. Galen located the towering oak, and easily spied the lone figure standing still as death in the black void of dense trees beyond.

He took Dawn's hand and tugged her to his chest. Holding her close, he apported to a spot near the treeline behind the oak. But not too close. Marceau stepped out of the blackness onto the shadowed meadow. His gaze flicked to Galen's arms around Dawn and a fleeting smile crossed his lips.

"Who is trying to kill me?" Galen asked, cutting to the chase.

Before Marceau could answer, the voice of an elderly woman called, "Are you all right, my lady? Are you in need of aid?"

Coach lights and candles made cheerful puddles of green on the night grass.

Dawn roused and stepped out of Galen's arms. "I'm fine, Ophelia. You've met Galen, I believe."

He gave the portal guardian a smile.

The old woman nodded without returning it. "I mean the undead one." She pointed to the vampire. "He is evil, my lady. I can smell his blood lust on the air."

"That may well be," Dawn answered. "But he is here at our request. You may leave, Ophelia. But listen for my call, in case he has betrayal in mind."

In a twinkling of lights, the old woman and the cottage vanished, leaving the meadow grasses and wildflowers shrouded once again in black.

When Galen looked up, Marceau was standing in front of them, within touching distance. Galen put a protective arm around Dawn. He could smell the blood lust, too. "Haven't you fed tonight?" he asked, mildly disgusted.

"I was waiting for you, demon." The vampire paused a heartbeat. "And your lovely lady."

"I told you before, our bargain was only for me. The woman is mine. You don't touch her."

Marceau shrugged expansively. "Your choice, of course. I thought you feared for your life. But if—"

"If she's the price, I'll pass." He turned with Dawn back toward the manor and started walking.

"Wait."

Galen halted and looked over his shoulder.

"It was Rofocale," Marceau said. "He ordered the attack."

Ba'al Rofocale! The infamous demon of destruction, a

minister of Hell, one of the ruling Grigori. And the careless gambler from whom Galen had won the Demon Stone…

Galen turned back. "Impossible. I recognized the shooters. They were P-Cell. P-Cell doesn't take orders from demons."

"Are you sure about that?"

He frowned. "What are you saying…they were shape-shifters?"

Marceau just smiled and crossed his arms over his chest, looking arrogant and smug.

Confusion slammed through Galen. What the hell had he stumbled into? He glanced at Dawn, who was looking even more mystified than he.

"Tell me the rest and you can have my blood as promised. But the woman is not negotiable. *Your* choice."

Marceau's smile showed the tips of his fangs, sending an icy chill down Dawn's spine that reached through their connection, all the way to Galen's skin.

"Don't do it," she whispered.

He gave her a squeeze and waited for the vampire to answer.

"Blood first," Marceau said, glancing at the horizon. "Sunrise approaches. I must seek my rest soon."

Galen nodded. Darks lied and deceived, but when they finally sealed a pact it was seldom broken.

He had seen the blood-letting procedure a few times, so he knew what to do. He let go of Dawn, but she clung to his side as though he was in imminent danger of vanishing. He extended his left arm toward Marceau. "Go on then."

The vampire stepped up and took firm hold of Galen's arm. A backwash of old, solid-as-hardwood power crashed over him, paralyzing his own. Dawn gasped, stumbled back a step, and lost her hold on him. She flung her hand out, fingers pointed at Marceau, and chanted a few harsh words. At once the crush of power receded to a dull roar.

The vampire stared at her, his eyes still and calculating. He said nothing, just continued to stare at her as he opened his mouth and sank razor-sharp fangs into Galen's wrist.

It stung like a fucking bastard. He sucked in a sharp breath as the vampire began to suck his blood. "Satan wept," he gritted out through clenched teeth.

"You all right?" Dawn asked, hands poised in the air as though to cast another spell. She was watching his face intently, avoiding the vampire's eyes. Good girl.

"Fine," he said. "Just don't let him drain me dry."

She swallowed heavily. "Tell me when you start to get turned on."

"What?" He was so shocked, for a moment he didn't feel the vampire's lips or tongue work his flesh.

"It's a side effect. Sexual arousal."

"With humans, yeah, but not—" Suddenly it was there, a hunger in his cock he'd never felt before. It wrenched him straight up, iron-hard. "Satan's—" He groaned. "Enough!" he roared. And ripped his arm from the vampire's mouth.

The alien power ceased abruptly. He fell to his knees. Two runnels of blood drizzled from his wrist. The need for sex was voracious, knocking everything else from his mind.

He set his sights on Dawn. "Come here."

She backed up, holding her palms out. "Galen, darling. You must control it. We still have to get the information from him."

Something in her pleading eyes got through to the better part of him. He took a deep, shuddering breath, desperately fighting the urge to slam her to the ground and take her like a savage. *Damn.* He bent over and clutched handfuls of dew-laden grass with shaking, bloody fingers. He looked at her and nodded once. "You."

She seemed to understand. She faced Marceau, who was wiping his mouth with a white embroidered handkerchief. Drops and smears of bright red blood stood out in stark contrast.

She pulled a flashlight out of her back pocket and aimed it steadily at the vampire, as though it were a gun. "Talk or I burn you."

Struck by the absurd gesture, Galen let out a bark of laughter. A UV flashlight against a three-hundred-year-old vampire. That was his woman. Like David facing Goliath. God, he loved her. His ferocious arousal tightened its grip on him almost unbearably.

The vampire's brow shot up as he regarded Dawn. "I could have you so fast you'd be dead yesterday."

"I know," she said calmly. "But I wouldn't recommend it. Now, spill."

Suddenly Marceau grinned. "Feisty woman you have here, McManus. I can see why you value her. Name your price and you shall have it."

Galen clenched his jaw and straightened up, winding his shirttail over the bleeding wounds on his wrist. "You'd better be kidding."

Marceau's grin widened. "When you tire of her, then. Consider it an open offer."

Anger started to edge out the still-painful arousal. Galen managed to climb stiffly to his feet. Perhaps he should sell him Aurora instead. It would serve the bastard right. He slanted a quick glance at Dawn. Her thought or his?

She thumbed the flashlight switch as though itching to press it. "I'm flattered, Marceau. But start talking."

"Ah, well. You are right. It grows late. No more time for games, as amusing as they are." He turned to Galen. "That diamond you won gambling."

It took a second to tamp down the anger and arousal and switch gears. "Yes. The Demon Stone. What of it?"

"Rofocale lost it to you deliberately."

He blinked. "Why would he do that?"

"He set you up, hoping through the stone you would gain entrance to Cadre headquarters. He knew the earl wanted it, but would never trust him nor anyone associated with him. Very clever, using the daughter, by the way. Rofocale was quite impressed with your ingenuity."

Wait. This was about the Cadre? Okay, Galen could understand the Grigori wanting to infiltrate their stronghold. But… "What the hell does that have to do with the attack on me?"

"Rofocale engineered it." Marceau shrugged. "To make doubly sure you got inside St. Yve. He counted on the diamond paving the way."

Right. Galen should have twigged to that one. An obvious ploy. And yet— "I'm still not buying it. I repeat, P-Cell doesn't take orders from Rofocale, or any other demon."

Marceau leveled him a look. A look that said more eloquently than his cynical, "No?" that there were things going on about which Galen had no clue. The vampire spared a glance at the horizon. "I am afraid I must go." Then he whirled and vanished, more quickly than even a demon could move.

Galen stared after him, mouth agape. Dawn flicked the flashlight on and off as though unable to control the itch any longer. "Bastard," she muttered. "Bloody bastard."

He wasn't sure if she meant Rofocale, Marceau or him. "Yeah," he said anyway.

"He's lying. He has to be," she said.

"Let's hope so," he muttered. Because if he wasn't, Rofocale wouldn't be far behind.

Galen took a deep breath and unwound the shirttail from his wrist. The bleeding had stopped.

But the pulsing in his cock had not. He looked at her.

Well, they probably had a few minutes before the minister of Hell showed up….

He crooked a finger at Dawn, catching her attention. "Hey. Little girl, forget the bastard and come to daddy."

Chapter 25

Dawn did a double-take at Galen's crooked finger, half-mast bedroom eyes and the rampant bulge between his legs.

Good lord. He was serious.

She backed away. "Don't be silly. This is all just a residual effect of the vampire bite."

He advanced on her. "Doesn't make it any less real."

He had her there. Heat invaded her face. "Galen, you spent all night on top of me. I'm surprised it hasn't fallen off from overuse."

"Hardly. I'm an incubus, remember?"

"You are not." She frowned, suddenly halting. "Which brings up the point. Who exactly *are* you? And why would the Grigori choose you for their dirty work?"

He ate up the distance between them. "Who cares?"

He grabbed her and she yelped. "Galen, don't you dare!" She batted at his hands, which he'd thrust under her top.

His mouth clamped onto hers. She moaned, then twisted away. "Stop! They can see us from the manor!"

He hesitated. She cast a swift glance up at the castle. It glowed like the Parthenon in the golden light of dawn; the red rising sun reflected off the tall windows, making them look like liquid-gold ingots. Who could tell who was standing in those windows, watching?

"The trees will hide us," he said, then he was chasing her. Into the woods.

She squealed and took flight. Having grown up here, she knew the forest like the back of her hand. But he had unfair advantage with his powers. As he neared, she yelped out a spell of evasion. When he caught her, his hands slid off her as though she were made of Teflon. He caught her again with the same effect.

"Nice try," he growled.

He gathered his hands and threw a bolt of power at her. She stumbled as she felt the evasion spell splinter around her. She shrieked and took off even faster. She panted out another spell. One that would give him a little shock when he touched her.

"Ouch! Why, you little—" She laughed and he chased her around a huge tree trunk. "Ow!"

They were both laughing by now. "Stop! Galen! You'll start bleeding again!"

"What's the matter—ow!—squeamish?"

"No, but—"

"Ow! That's it." He raised a fist and smashed her shock shield to bits. He'd just pulled her into his arms when all at once they were torn apart by a dozen grasping hands, a fluttering of wings and a half score giggling faces. Sidhe.

"What-ho! Would you dance without us?" a tall man said, grabbing her. He danced her away from Galen, who was led in the opposite direction by a beautiful woman with gossamer yellow wings and shining yellow eyes. All around them, more sidhe of every size and color appeared, eager to join the festivities. The icy shimmer of glamour surrounded them all in a tingling, glittering sphere.

"A reel! A reel!" another called, and all joined hands and began to dance in a circle to bright, tinkling music that came from nowhere.

"The demon wants his mortal lover!" a tiny blue one chanted in a silvery singsong. He couldn't have been more than three inches tall.

"Then he shall have his Lady Dawn," called a dark-haired man she recognized as the self-proclaimed leader of the enchanted forest. Raskin Rubythorn was his name. Former Black Court prince and mischief-maker of the first water, his nickname with Cadre women was the Enchanter. "We shall seek the trillium meadow and there he shall take her while we dance around them!"

A musical shout went up and the laughing ring of faeries danced through the wood towing her and Galen along. She was caught up in the spell of loveliness and merriment. Her spirit filled with joy and delight. Trees seemed to dissolve before them, magically clearing a path. Galen was dancing and laughing, too. Two sidhe men ripped his bloody shirt off as they whirled about him.

"Can't have him in this thing," one called to the other.

"Must look our best for the ladies!" the second one agreed.

A quartet of sparkling, diminutive sidhe women flew up above him carrying a new, clean faerie shirt of shimmering, gauzelike fabric. Metallic threads in bright colors of purples and blues, greens and yellows, shifted in the sunlight like oil shining on water. The women dropped the shirt over his head and he slipped his arms through the sleeves. Solid, yet translucent, it molded his muscular chest like a second skin, showing off his cobblestone abs and concave belly. The blood on his arm dissolved into the air, leaving the skin smooth and clean. He looked stunning.

The women fluttered around him, touching and admiring his body, especially the thick ridge of his arousal that still pulsed like an earthquake pushing to the surface under his jeans.

"Keep your hands to yourselves," he shouted good-naturedly, swatting at ethereal fingers. "Or my woman will be angry."

Wide, jewel-colored eyes slid to her and flashed like a handful of precious gemstones being flung through the air.

"Hmph! She is but a human! What can she do to us?"

Dawn threw back her head and laughed, and as she danced she raised her hands and wove a shock shield around her lover. The sidhe seducers squealed and fell away from him like multi-colored winged dominoes. She beckoned him to her and he caught her around the waist from behind, bending to kiss her neck as he whirled her in the dance.

"The demon is mine!" she declared for all to hear, crooking her arms back to twine her fingers in his hair. His long tongue tickled the valley between her breasts.

They had made their way to the trillium meadow, a lush carpet of emerald green covered in tiny white blossoms all year round. It was a favored place for faerie reels and also for the forest satyrs and wood nymphs to gather in lascivious bacchanalia. Already couples were tangled together among the wildflowers, or reclining with picnics of gourmet treats and bottles of faerie wine. The faefolk lived a sumptuous life of luxury and instant gratification.

"Ha! So I was right!" came a familiar, haughty voice from the edge of the meadow. "The high and mighty Lady Dawn spreads her legs for a demon. Just wait till the earl hears of this!"

Elise stood in a belligerent pose that belied her lacy white ultra-feminine dress.

"Tell my father and you will regret it," Dawn shot back. She made a face at her rival. "My demon will see you regret it."

For a split second Dawn was appalled by the intensity of her vengeful feelings, and the blatant threat she'd uttered. But the guilt passed quickly. She had every right to be angry. She turned in Galen's arms and flung her own around his neck. "She will regret it, won't she, darling?"

He wrapped his tall frame around her. "If you will it, my sweet. Your wish is my command, you know that."

A delicious shiver of power ran through her limbs. Power, and something else, more malevolent. Something that turned her on…

She plastered her body against Galen and put her lips to his. The strength and hardness of his muscles as he held her, and his arousal as he pressed it to her belly, sent heat spiraling to her center. She moaned, drawing out their kiss as the sidhe danced around them in glee.

Elise didn't speak, but stood rigid with anger, watching. Dawn ignored her as she and Galen were swept up in the reel. They danced and laughed and kissed as though there was no tomorrow.

There *was* no tomorrow. They could stay here in the forest forever! Dancing and laughing and making love and drinking faerie wine. No one would ever tear them apart!

Galen grabbed her around the waist and swung her high in a twirling spin. Suddenly, she crashed into something. Someone.

Elise went spinning off balance, thrown on her backside straight into the middle of the picnic spread of a copulating satyr and nymph. Dawn gasped at the sight of Elise covered with colorful food and rich purple wine and the naked, hairy limbs of the satyr.

She clapped a hand over her mouth, clinging to Galen, trying not to giggle. "Oh, dear. I'm so sorry, I—"

"You *bitch!*" Elise screamed, scrambling to her feet. "You did that on purpose!" The woman's expression seethed with fury as she whirled and stomped out of the meadow, away from the merriment.

Good. Maybe she'd get lost and not find her way out until after sunset. *It would serve her right.*

For a moment there was complete silence. Then the sidhe

erupted in laughter. Some skipped after Elise, some rolled on the grass in mirth. Others went back to dancing, forgetting the whole incident immediately.

But suddenly Dawn jolted back to awareness. Back to herself. *What was she thinking?* She looked around. More importantly, what was she *doing?* Dancing and carrying on. It was as though she'd been...

Oh, lord! She'd allowed herself to fall into the spell of the reel! Panic crawled up her skin. My God, if it hadn't been for Elise's outburst—

She grabbed Galen's hand. "We've got to get out of here. Now." She closed her eyes and chanted the special spell to extract them from the glamour of the reel. Without opening her eyes, she pulled Galen out of the meadow.

"Dawn, what's wrong?"

When they'd ducked into the trees, she finally dared peek. "We almost got sucked in by the magic. Remember I told you about the faerie reels?"

He nodded, tilting his head. "I wasn't bespelled. I just thought you were having a good time. It was fun."

She opened her mouth, then shut it. "That's the problem. It's *too* fun. You keep thinking, just another five minutes, and pretty soon it's five days later and you're stuck there forever and never even knew it happened."

His expression grew serious. "Trust me, I would never let that happen to you. Faeries have no power over me."

She searched his face. He meant it. Her anxiety notched down a little. "They really can't control you?"

He smiled reassuringly. "Not even a little."

"Is that the same for all demons?"

"Probably not. Different kinds of demons can have very different powers. Even ones of the same persuasion don't always have the same abilities."

She sighed, shaking her head. Shaking off the creepy feeling of nearly having been caught out in such a stupid way. "No wonder we keep ending up with conflicting information in our knowledge base. I'll have to tell Interrogations."

"Interrogations?"

"That's what we call her. Our demon interviewer. I'm sure she has a name but I've never heard it."

He grimaced. "She sounds like a nasty bit of work. Remind me to avoid her."

"I'll do my best. Speaking of conflicting information… What did you make of all that stuff Marceau told you?"

He chuckled. "About P-Cell taking orders from Rofocale? Seems a bit far-fetched. I don't believe it."

"His reasoning seemed sound."

"Maybe he dropped them an anonymous tip about me. Said I was part of a plot to take over the world or something. A simple lie would make more sense than them working together."

"And the Demon Stone? What about that?" She suddenly re-membered the gargoyles' strange reaction to him. Maybe he was hiding something bad from her, after all.…

"A pretty sneaky idea, I'll admit. Too bad it won't work."

She gazed at him, praying he was telling the truth.

"Dawn, the guardians would have seen right through a lie, or if I had come to betray the Cadre," he said, reading her thoughts.

She smiled, her doubts evaporating. "You're right. I know you could never do that."

He kissed her forehead. "We'd better get back."

"Yeah. Elise will probably go straight to my father if we don't stop her."

He touched her cheek. "She'll regret it if she does, I promise."

Dawn winced. "I didn't really mean what I said back there. I don't know what came over me. I'm not usually such a vengeful person."

He just smiled and slid an arm around her shoulders as they began to walk back to the manor. "It's all right. There's nothing wrong with vengeance, my sweet. Meanwhile, it's a long hike back up the hill. Let me use my powers."

She grinned. "I don't know why you ever bother with a car. If I could do that, I sure wouldn't own one."

He winked. "It's a guy thing."

He slid his other arm around her and hugged her to his chest. She snuggled close, letting go of the rest of her anxiety. She felt so safe, so secure in his arms. She could stay there in their sheltering embrace forever. She just knew he would protect her from all dangers.

Well, except for one.

She sighed. "Don't take us too close to the manor. Whatever happens, my father can't see us."

She just hoped they'd get to Elise in time. Otherwise, it wouldn't matter if he saw them or not. He'd know about their relationship. And the danger would just be beginning.

Chapter 26

Aurora was waiting for them at the top of the steps to the side entrance, where she'd stood when Galen and Dawn had arrived at St. Yve the day before. Radiating much the same hostility.

Correction: *more* hostility.

The first glimpse of her expression and Galen knew he was screwed. Hell, *screwed* didn't begin to cover it.

"You," Aurora said, spearing her forefinger in Dawn's direction, "and *you,* demon—" she stabbed the finger toward him "—in my office."

"Aurora, I can—"

"Do not speak!" she interrupted Dawn, her voice seething. "As for you—" she waved a pyramid-shaped crystal in Galen's face "—do not even *think* about trying to escape."

He held up his palms. "Wouldn't dream of it."

He replaced his arm around Dawn and they followed Aurora into the castle. A flock of house demons dipped and swooped overhead. There must have been ten of them up there, razor-sharp claws and fangs extended. This could get ugly.

Aurora stalked into her office and slammed the door behind them, looking as pissed off as Hades on a bad night in Hell. She stormed behind her desk and stood with fists clenched. She still held the crystal. Energy rippled outward from it, pricking over Galen's skin like tiny imps with stinging pitchforks. Even the large ruby ring she always wore on her forefinger seemed to be glowing, alive with energy.

Or was it all Aurora's magic? A scary thought. Especially when he was so badly outnumbered. This could get *really* ugly.

"Please, let me explain," Dawn began.

"There's no need." Aurora's glare sliced over him, sharper than the guardians' claws. "I know exactly what is happening here. This devil has you in his thrall."

Dawn blinked. He felt a well of guilt roil up within her as vividly as if it were inside his own body. Maybe it was.

"Just how far have you fallen?" Aurora asked accusingly, her tone laced with disdain.

He felt Dawn's guilt shift swift as lightning into resentment, sharp, old and deep. "How dare—"

He squeezed her shoulder, and quickly said, "I have put no spell on your sister, Lady Aurora. I swear it. We've made but a simple bargain."

The sister's eyes narrowed. "What kind of bargain?"

"You already know what I asked for," he replied evenly.

Her face paled. "The sanctuary from P-Cell which I offered?"

Hope springs eternal.

"No. Before that. The attack happened after our bargain was struck," he informed her. "I am grateful for your protection, but it changed nothing between Dawn and me."

Her accusing eyes sought Dawn. "You lied to me!"

"Only by omission," she said defensively. "And who could blame me? I knew this would happen."

Aurora sat down hard in her office chair and dropped the crystal onto the desk. She twisted the ring on her finger in a gesture tinged with desperation. "So I'm too late to save you."

"Don't be absurd," Dawn snapped. "There's nothing to be saved from. I agreed to sleep with Galen for five nights. Just five. In exchange we got the Demon Stone. I'm sure you can sort out who got the better deal."

Dawn's self-deprecation made Galen even more furious with her sister. He could feel the ancient hurt and sense of inadequacy pressing down on Dawn like an unbearable weight. Pressing down on him. He hated Aurora for that. Or was it Dawn who hated her? Didn't matter. It was all the same. A wash of protectiveness swept over him like a burning wind.

"*I* made the better deal," he growled. "Dawn is worth a thousand Demon Stones, and a thousand of you, Lady Aurora. If you can't see that you've been blinded by your own demon."

As soon as he said it, he wanted to kick himself. Brilliant move, McManus. Insult the woman with the crystal.

Both she and Dawn stared at him in mute astonishment. They stared so long he thought about checking to see if he'd suddenly sprouted horns. Or maybe wings. And not of the faerie variety. *Satan's tears.*

He cleared his throat. "Well, if there's nothing else you want to know, we'll just be—"

Aurora came to life. She surged to her feet like a force of nature. "The hell you will. The guardians will accompany you to your room, demon, while I decide what to do with you." She rounded on Dawn. "Stay right where you are. We need to talk."

"I'd rather wait for Dawn," Galen said, "if it's all the same to you."

Aurora appeared scandalized that he dared challenge her orders. "You will do as I say or suffer the consequences."

"It's all right, darling, go," Dawn said, touching his chest. "I'll be fine. And so will you. I'll join you upstairs."

He hesitated, but she nodded encouragingly. He leaned down and gave her a soft kiss on the lips. "If you're sure. Call if you need me."

As he strode out of the office, fury flashed like St. Elmo's fire in Aurora's green eyes. *Devil take it*. The woman was after blood. *His* blood. He could practically feel his spirit going pyramid-shaped.

Another great move. Kissing Dawn probably hadn't been the best idea for a parting shot. He sighed. What the hell. The look on the sister's face alone had been worth it.

And damn. If you're going down anyway, you might as well go down in flames.

Dawn's body jumped as the door smacked closed behind Galen. She felt his absence like a physical hole in her being. Not even a glimmer of his comforting power remained in the room. The office must have built-in shields she didn't know about.

She looked at her sister. "It's not what you think," she said before Aurora could start in.

Her sister's brow shot up. "Oh, really? According to Elise, it's *exactly* what I think. Even your demon says it's exactly what I think. What makes your version different?"

"His name is Galen. I'll thank you to use it." She took a deep breath. "And I love him."

Aurora looked as though she'd been struck. "You don't know what you're saying—"

"No, Aurora. For the first time in my life, I do—"

"Dawn, he's a *demon*."

Dawn gave a humorless laugh. "Don't you think I know that? Don't you think I've been telling myself that all along? Don't you think it worries me just as much as it's worrying you?"

"Obviously not."

Dawn managed a wilted smile. "No. I suppose it wouldn't." She let out her breath in a long sough. This was the most painful subject imaginable for her sister. "Aurora, I remember what you went through. But Galen isn't like James Peri."

Peri, the lust demon who had seduced her sister as a young woman and nearly broken her spirit, had been sent to infiltrate the Cadre and had used her mercilessly. He now resided in a crystal in the dungeon, a well-deserved fate. But Galen was different.

"I know you think he's—"

"Believe me, he's not the same at all. He didn't bespell me, didn't seduce me. And he has no interest in harming the Cadre. How would he have passed the gargoyles' test otherwise?"

Aurora looked stubbornly unconvinced. "If he didn't bespell you, how did he get you to agree to…to…"

This time Dawn's smile was wry, but genuine. "I knew how much Father wanted the Demon Stone. And Galen is a very attractive man, in case you hadn't noticed. It wasn't such a sacrifice to give him what he wanted. After I got to know him, I realized what a good person he is on the inside. Aurora, I love him."

"My God, listen to yourself!" Aurora burst out. "He's *not* a good person, he's a *demon!* I can't believe—"

"I know I'm not an adept, Aurora, but I've been around demons all my life. I've tracked them, I've fought against them, I've captured them, I've even befriended some of them. I am quite capable of making my own decisions in this regard."

Her sister gripped the edge of the desk and lowered her eyes, but not before Dawn caught the sudden shine to them. If Dawn didn't know better, she'd think her sister was tearing up. Yeah, right.

"I know you're capable," Aurora said. "But you're my sister. I don't want to see you hurt." She looked up. The shine was all gone, replaced by determination. "You can't love this man! What do you really know of him? He's deceiving you. I know he is."

Dawn was sick of this. If the tables had been turned, nobody would be questioning Aurora's decisions. "Why?" Dawn gritted out. "Just because he wants me and not you?"

Aurora sucked in a sharp breath. "Leave me out of this. First of all, he's lying about being an incubus. He's a *daemon sapiens* masquerading—"

"I know that. He told me."

"Then why is he lying about it to everyone else?" Aurora demanded angrily. "What is he really, then? What kind of demon?"

Dawn folded her arms under her breasts and looked away.

"You don't know, do you?"

"No," she reluctantly admitted. "He said he couldn't tell me."

"Which can only mean he's up to no good," Aurora said. "The sole reason a demon hides his Directive is if by telling you, you might change your behavior and ruin his plans. Believe me, he's here for you, Dawn. To possess you."

Dawn snorted incredulously. "That's ridiculous. He told you already, he's here because of a Latin spell I accidentally read aloud in class."

"What kind of a spell?"

She ground her jaw. "It was about sex."

"Show me."

Aurora was so damn stubborn she was like a wolverine when she set her mind on something. The only way to prove her wrong was to show her the damn spell. Angry and irritated beyond belief at having to justify herself, Dawn walked to the glass-fronted book cases that lined three of the study walls and found the book she'd been reading from that day. It was a handwritten manuscript, beautifully illuminated and bound in thick leather with gold lettering on the front. She turned to the correct page and smacked it down in front of Aurora.

"There."

She tapped her foot impatiently as her sister read meticulously through the ancient Latin verses.

When she was finished, there was an odd look on her face. "This is about fulfilling your deepest desires."

"Exactly. Sex. That's what I've been trying to tell you."

Her sister looked her in the eye. "Dawn, don't take this the wrong way, but…sex has never been your deepest desire. Certainly not five-night casual sex. No matter how attractive the man."

"How do you know?" Dawn retorted resentfully. How could Aurora manage to turn even morality into an insult?

Her sister didn't say a word, but the look was eloquent.

"All right, fine," Dawn muttered. "I never thought so, either, but obviously I was mistaken. I must have been suppressing my libido all these years, like you do." *So there.*

Aurora's jaw clenched. "Since when did you become a bloody psychologist?"

"You know it's true. When did you last have sex?"

"Damn it, Dawn. We're not discussing me."

"What's wrong, sister dear? Jealous?"

"You'd like that, wouldn't you?" Aurora shot back. "Having your private little revenge, eh? Hurt me by flaunting your lover, your *demon* lover, in my face? What could be better?"

Dawn gasped. "I would never—"

Suddenly Aurora's eyes grew wide as saucers. "Oh, my God. That's it!" she cried.

Dawn gritted her teeth. "What's it?"

"Your greatest desire! It's *revenge.*"

"What?"

"My God. Galen McManus is a vengeance demon. He must be."

Dawn was so shocked and insulted she couldn't even think to make a comeback.

"That would explain everything," Aurora went on, a dismayed look creeping into her eyes. "Hadn't you noticed that everyone you dislike is suddenly having bad things happen to them?"

"What the hell are you talking about?"

"First Roland breaking his leg on the Department steps. Then Marta and Dr. Cornell sleeping together. And now this morning, Elise being humiliated."

That last example finally shook Dawn from her speechlessness. "Elise? Please. That was just a little spilled wine. It'll wash out."

"Maybe he's not finished with her. We should—"

"Aurora, stop!" Dawn said loudly, barely resisting covering her ears with her hands. "Galen is *not* a vengeance demon. My desire for revenge is *not* so overwhelming that it conjured him all the way from the dark realm!"

"The desire wouldn't have to be overwhelming," Aurora argued. "Because you said the spell aloud. That's all it would take. And now he's possessing you, taking over your mind and your darkest desire—for revenge—and amplifying it, making your most secret wishes come true."

"He's not!"

"You must be careful, Dawn! You know the consequences of possession by a vengeance demon. All the revenge you wreak through him will come back and fall on you tenfold."

"I'm not wreaking revenge on anyone! And I'm not listening to this, Aurora. It's just crazy!"

Dawn spun on a toe and stalked out of the study, so furious she could barely see straight. She didn't dispute that the desire spell was the catalyst for Galen's apportment from the dark realm. But good God! Her, Dawn, possessed? Wreaking revenge, her darkest desire?

Galen, a vengeance demon?

Not a chance! None of this was possible. Dawn wasn't exactly sure what her greatest desire was, but one thing was for damn bloody certain. It was *not* for vengeance.

And she'd show her meddling sister it wasn't. Somehow, some way, once and for all, she'd show her!

Chapter 27

"I'm going to kill her! I'm going to wring her bloody neck with my bare hands and choke her until—" Dawn's words cut off in a harsh oath.

Galen stopped pacing the rug and looked at her. She'd just blown into his room like a full-scale hurricane. He wondered if his fate had been decided and that's what she was upset about.

"What are you saying, my sweet? What's happened?"

"My sister, that's what's happened! Of all the arrogant, petty, outrageous, maddening—"

He went over to her, unsure if he should touch her or not. She didn't exactly look like she needed a hug. A gun, perhaps…

"Come, sit on the bed and tell me."

"I'm too furious to sit." She took his place pacing the rug, arms banded across her middle.

He could feel her fury and bitterness boiling like a toxic volcano in her body. In his body. A moment ago he'd been worried about himself. But it was her he should be worrying about. She needed to calm down. He'd take care of Aurora. That was his job.

Of course she didn't know that.

She spun to face him. "Aurora actually thinks you're a vengeance demon! I ask you. How preposterous is that!"

Galen froze. For a nanosecond he tasted his heart in his throat. Then he managed to unstick his vocal chords and say, "What on earth gave her that…ridiculous idea?"

For some reason he couldn't bring himself to flat-out deny her sister's claim. It was true. *Fires of Satan*. He'd never felt remorse in his life lying to a human. And such a simple lie, at that. But this was Dawn.…

"Because of the strange things happening to people I…I don't care for," she explained. As if it needed explaining.

"Like Roland and Marta?" he ventured. She nodded. He waved a hand dismissively. "Coincidence."

"And Elise, too."

"But—" Hell. He hadn't done Elise yet. This morning had been a pure accident. "Nothing happened to her."

"I know." Dawn put her hands to her temples. "My God, my own sister thinks my greatest desire in life is for revenge!"

Ouch. The sister was smarter than she looked.

Okay, so she looked pretty smart, too. But what to do about her uncanny powers of deduction? Never in a million years had Galen thought anyone would ferret him out until after the job was finished and his Directive fulfilled. In other words, after it was too late. Or maybe it was, already.

"Did she happen to mention what she's going to do with me?"

Dawn blinked. "Lord. I don't know. I walked out before she said anything about it." Her face slid into a scowl. "But she'll touch you over my dead body."

Not an option. "Maybe I should just go. Leave St. Yve."

"No!" She flew to the bed and threw herself down next to him. "Galen, I know she's wrong. You could never be what she believes. I won't let her win. Not this time."

He gathered her in his arms and pulled her close, carefully shielding his thoughts from her. And his overwhelming guilt.

"My sweet avenging angel," he whispered. "What did I do to deserve such loyalty? What did I do to deserve you?"

She nestled closer, sliding her arms around him, too. Her cheek pressed against his chest. "No, darling. It's what did *I* do? I'm the one who doesn't deserve you."

"You are so wrong."

He should leave. Right now. Run like hell as fast as he could, out of there, out of the danger. Away from Aurora's wrath. And away from the bewildering temptation of Dawn's love.

So, why wasn't he?

He sighed into her hair. He loved the smell of it, all feminine and flowery. He loved the feel of her body close to his, all curvy and warm. He loved the taste of her sweet, sweet lips. He loved her constancy, her tenacity, her ingenuity, he even loved her flaws. He loved everything about her.

Galen McManus, demon of the dark realm, whose only emotions were supposed to be lust and anger, was crazy in love. With a mortal woman. With Dawn Maybank, daughter to the most notorious demon hunter alive. And he couldn't make himself leave her.

If it weren't so damn depressing, he'd laugh.

God, he was so tired of the games; he hated the deception. He didn't want to lie to her anymore.

But what was he to do? If he went rogue and disobeyed the Grigori, what would become of him? Worse, what would become of *her?* They might send someone else in his place. Someone who didn't give a damn how badly she got hurt.

"Oh, Galen," Dawn murmured. "I know we have our differences. And I know at first you probably just looked at me as an amusement, our relationship just a sport or diversion. But I know how you feel about me now. I can feel the warmth of your love inside me."

He sighed. Why was he not able to shield these crazy emotions from her?

"Demons don't love, Dawn. You know that. I can never love you as you deserve to be loved." It wasn't the first time he'd said it. The words still tasted bitter, like ash on his tongue. But the last truth felt like salt being poured on his soul.

She just gazed up at him, as though she knew he was lying. But which lie did she see through?

She crawled onto the center of the bed and lay down. She reached up to him. "Lie with me for a few minutes," she whispered.

The plea wasn't sexual. It was all about comfort and longing.

He couldn't resist, though he knew he should, for both their sakes. He cuddled up to her, surrounding her body with his, holding her close to his heart as though it was the last time he'd ever get to hold her.

Because he had a sinking feeling he'd lost control of his own fate…and chances were it *would* be the last time he held her in his arms.

To their great surprise, Aurora didn't come marching up to Galen's room with an armed Cadre guard and a crystal in hand, demanding his hide. In fact, when there was a knock on the door a few hours later, Charles appeared, summoning them to lunch.

Galen couldn't help but be suspicious.

As Dawn took his hand and walked with him downstairs, she was obviously mentally preparing herself to do battle with her sister over him. But when they reached the dining room, Aurora barely looked at him. Her face was not friendly and her manners were stiff and formal, but there wasn't a crystal in sight.

What was going on?

Luckily the earl was still on a high about the Demon Stone, asking Galen question after question about its sojourn to the dark realm—not that he could answer any of them—and chatting on about the museum restoration expert he was bringing in to have the diamond professionally remounted in the Saxon Crown. The earl's joyful excitement was enough to make the meal pass quickly despite the fact that neither of his daughters said more than five words the whole time.

After St. Yve excused himself, Aurora turned and drilled her gaze into Galen. "I don't know how you managed it, but you've got yourself a reprieve, demon." She looked singularly unhappy about it, too. "I took your case to the Cadre High Council and asked for a crystallization order on you."

Dawn gasped. "Aurora!"

Her eyes didn't leave him. "It was for your own good, Dawn. He's after your soul."

"Galen is *not*—"

Aurora slashed a hand through the air. "It doesn't matter. The Council denied my request."

His heart had nearly stopped beating. It gave a stutter. "But…"

Her mouth turned down angrily. "They interviewed the gargoyles. I don't know how you managed to deceive them, but the useless buzzards supported you. They swear your heart is pure."

Dawn lit up and broke into a huge smile. "I told you so!"

Aurora stood abruptly. "For Father's sake I will keep quiet about your outrageous bargain, Dawn. It would break his heart to know—" She swallowed. Her gaze swung back to Galen, seething with loathing. "You have one more night with my sister. Then her obligation is fulfilled and you are out of here. Frankly I don't give a damn if P-Cell guns you down right outside the gate."

"Aurora, you aren't being fair!" Dawn protested in shock.

"If I ever catch you near my sister after tomorrow," she continued as though her sister hadn't spoken, "High Council or no, you *will* end up in a crystal. Do you understand me?"

Galen didn't want to tempt Aurora into calling P-Cell with the actual location of the gate, so he merely nodded. But his insides were churning.

Never see Dawn again? He couldn't imagine his life without her in it.

What could he do?

He could kidnap her and take her to the dark realm where the Cadre couldn't follow. But the other dark denizens would be merciless to her. She'd hate it there.

Take her far away, maybe to his house in Hong Kong? No, Aurora would find them there for sure. She'd find them anywhere they went. The Cadre had contacts the world over.

Neither dark realm nor mortal realm was safe. There was truly no place to hide.

"Don't worry, darling," Dawn's reassuring voice penetrated his depressing thoughts. Her hand covered his. "We'll find a way through this."

He sighed. "I fear it will take far greater powers than I possess to make that happen."

"There are greater powers," she assured him softly. She squeezed his hand. "You just have to have faith."

He gazed into her clear green eyes, and for the briefest of moments, he did. He believed.

In her. In their love.

"Dawn," he whispered. "My precious Dawn."

Neither of them had said the magical words aloud, but there was no hiding their feelings from each other. He knew she loved him as deeply as he loved her.

That knowledge was his greatest joy, their greatest strength. And yet, would surely be their downfall.

"You must promise me one thing, my love."

Her eyes widened at the endearment. Her lips parted. "Galen, what is it?"

"I need you to promise me something, my sweet."

"Anything, darling."

He took a deep breath. "Promise me that no matter what happens, you'll always love me as you do now."

Mist filled her eyes. "Of course I will," she whispered, reaching for him. She took his face between her hands and placed a tender kiss upon his lips.

"Swear to me," he murmured. "Say it, and swear."

He was scaring her. He could tell. He could feel the thump of her runaway pulse as though it was pounding in his own chest. Or maybe it *was* his.

"I love you, Galen," she quietly said. "I always will. I swear I will."

He folded her into his arms and held her tight. Desperate not to let go. Never to let her go.

Because soon she would know the truth about him. She'd see it herself, or Aurora would finally convince her. It was inevitable. And when she did know the truth, no matter how sincerely she had just sworn to love him always, she'd reject him.

And then he might as well just beg Aurora to put him in a crystal. Because without Dawn, he simply didn't wish to go on living.

Chapter 28

Galen was summoned by Interrogations.

This was bad. And Dawn couldn't figure out a way to get him out of it.

"I'll be all right," he assured her as she accompanied him to the east wing where the Cadre headquarters were located.

"You don't understand," she said. "The High Council must have ordered her to question you."

"So?"

"So, they would never insult a guest of the earl's like this unless they are taking Aurora's accusation very seriously. They denied her request to crystallize you, but there are other options, depending on Interrogations' recommendation."

He glanced at her. "Such as?"

She took him around to the lift behind the kitchens and pressed the down button. The smell of roast potatoes and onions wafted out from the dining area, plum pudding with raisins from the kitchen.

"They could deport you back to the dark realm. Immediately. No appeal."

He nodded. "I've heard of deportment. I understand you get a hell of a headache."

"This isn't funny, Galen. If you're sent back and are ever found here in the mortal realm again, you will be crystallized."

He sobered as the lift reached the basement floor. He took her hands in his. "Then I must manage a good recommendation from this Interrogations woman."

She slipped into his arms. "Oh, Galen," she whispered. "I can't lose you. I don't know what I'd do…."

He gently kissed her. "You'll never lose me, my love."

She wanted to believe him. Oh, how she wanted to. But everything seemed to be conspiring against them.

"Oi, oi, oi! Wot's going on 'ere, then?" Squire Callahan's cheerful voice followed footsteps that approached the lift.

Squire was the Cadre's demon-storage specialist, in charge of cataloging and organizing the captured demons in their crystals. Not many years past college age, he practically lived in his lab and storage facility located in the basement. The area was originally the old St. Yve dungeon and had seen some fairly gruesome times in the past. These days it was painted pristine white and was filled with high-tech equipment which Squire delighted in fiddling with all day, every day. Squire was a bit of a geek. As always, heavy metal music blared from a boom box somewhere in the depths of the dungeon.

Dawn slipped from Galen's arms and shook her finger at Squire. "This one is not one of your customers. Don't get any ideas."

"No way, Lady Dawn," the kid said with a grin and a shake of his disheveled blond hair. "And I didn't see that kiss, either, so don't bother with the spell of forgetfulness."

"As if I would. You'll have forgotten all on your own after two minutes anyway," she said with an affectionate peck to the side of his head as he walked past them into the lift. She and Squire were close. She thought of him as the baby brother she'd never had. "Is Interrogations here yet?"

He gave her and Galen each a measured look, then tipped his head toward the lab, at the far end of which was the specially built room where all questioning of paras took place. The walls were specially reinforced, but completely transparent. Interrogations was standing inside, watching them. "Ready and waiting. Good luck."

"Thanks. And wash that lab coat!" she admonished automatically as the lift doors closed on him. The kid was cute, but could use help in the hygiene department.

When they were alone again, she turned to Galen, her nerves tightening. She wasn't worried, exactly. She knew he had nothing sinister to hide. He'd passed the gargoyles' test. Aurora wasn't happy about their sexual arrangement, but it wasn't dangerous or evil. Just inappropriate.

"Don't let Interrogations fluster you," Dawn advised him. "Just tell her the truth."

His brow rose. "About everything?"

She sighed. "She'll find out anyway. No demon has ever been able to keep secrets from her. She's very good at her job."

"I see."

She tried to feel what he was thinking, but he was shielding his thoughts from her. And keeping careful control over his power. There wasn't even a tingle.

"I'll speak to her when you're finished," she said, "and ask her not to report everything to my father."

Galen pushed out a breath and looked down at the floor. "Dawn, there's—"

Suddenly, an awful feeling gripped her insides. She didn't want to know what he was about to say. "Save it for afterward." She quickly turned and practically ran into the lab.

"Dawn!"

She shook her head violently. She knew it would be something bad. Something she wouldn't want to hear. Something that would change her life, or break her heart, or maybe both. She kept running.

And ran into him. He was standing in front of her, blocking her path like a brick wall. *Damn demonic powers.*

"I have to say this, Dawn," he said, grabbing her upper arms to make her stop running.

"No."

"Tonight's our last night—"

"No!"

He gave her arms a shake. "Tonight's our last night together. But I want like hell to go on seeing you."

She stopped fighting and glanced up hopefully. Her vision swam. "I do, too."

"But I have a bad feeling about this interrogation. I'm afraid they'll send me back to the dark realm."

She shook her head in desperation. "They can't. I won't let them."

"If the worst happens, I just wanted to say…" He closed his eyes, giving a short, strangled laugh. When they opened, his face was shuttered, his expression utterly neutral. "I'm sorry," he said. "I never meant to hurt you."

A tear spilled over her lashes. "Oh, Galen. You haven't."

He gave her a smile that looked as if he'd had to chisel it onto his lips. "Hold that thought."

With that, he strode away, toward the room where both their fates would be decided.

Dawn couldn't watch. Or listen through the headphones on Squire's recording console. She didn't want to know what Galen had felt compelled to apologize to her for. So she made her way back to the family wing and ensconced herself in the library, picked out a novel and determinedly pretended to read.

Two hours later she retraced her steps down to the dungeon to check on Galen. Interrogations was still questioning him. Two hours wasn't really that long. Sometimes these things went on all night.

She repeated the procedure after another two hours. Same result. Okay, now she was getting worried. What could they possibly be talking about for this long?

She resolved firmly not to check on him again. He'd find her when he was finished. There were only a handful of people in the world who knew the intricate spells and rituals for a demon deportment; Interrogations was not one of them. Besides, the High Council would not make their ruling until morning. Galen was safe for tonight.

Even so, she was very relieved when night fell and it was time to join Aurora and her father for pre-dinner drinks. Aurora and her father were the only two people skilled at deportment currently at St. Yve. They were also on the Council. She felt better with them in her sights. Dressed for dinner, they greeted Dawn when she walked into the salon, showing no signs of anything amiss.

At least not until Jane, one of the Cadre initiates who lived in the east wing, rushed past Charles and the footman into the room and cried out, "The sun has gone down, my lord!"

Unruffled, the earl straightened and said, "Of course it has. Pull yourself together, girl," he commanded when Jane continued to weep and wring her hands. "Tell us what's happened."

"It's Elise, my lord! She went into the forest this afternoon and hasn't returned. The enchanted wood has taken her!"

For a brief second everyone froze in shock.

Aurora spun to Dawn and speared her with a look of pure outraged contempt. "This is your demon's doing," she ground out.

"It can't be," Dawn refuted. "He's been with Interrogations all afternoon."

"He's a vengeance demon, Dawn! He sets things in motion. He doesn't have to be there when it happens."

"He's not a vengeance demon!"

Their father pinned Dawn and Aurora both with a stern reproof. "Why wasn't I informed of this?"

"We have to find a way to get Elise back!" Jane wailed.

"Where is he?" the earl demanded of Dawn.

She blanched. "I told you, with Interrogations."

Standing at the door, Charles cleared his throat. She glanced at the butler and immediately her heart plummeted. Somehow she knew she wasn't going to like what he was about to say.

"Charles?" Aurora asked sharply.

"The demon, my lady. Mr. McManus…"

"What about him?"

"He was seen earlier leaving the Manor."

Dawn gasped. "What? I don't believe it! He wouldn't leave me here!"

"Where?" Aurora demanded. "Where was he going?"

"The forest, my lady. He disappeared into the enchanted forest."

Chapter 29

*S*atan's devils.

Galen watched the brunette caught in the faerie reel with a mixture of pride and fatalism. He'd done a good job on Elise. She was naked, her nude body covered in some kind of gold, glittering oil. She was well and truly caught in the reel, laughing and dancing with the faeries as if she hadn't a care in the world.

As of tonight, she didn't. This was her world now. She'd never leave it again. The faeries were delighted with her…and with him for gifting her to them.

But Galen knew this act of vengeance had sealed his fate. Aurora would have proof of her accusation. And if that weren't enough, coming to the forest himself tonight would guarantee he'd be tried and convicted by the Cadre High Council in the morning.

Dawn would despise him. She'd never want to hear his name spoken again, much less see him.

Not that he hadn't already been doomed after the grueling afternoon spent with that hideous interrogator and her unending questions. He'd told her everything—voluntarily. That had rather surprised her. But he was so tired of deception. He'd just wanted to get it over with.

The experience had been cathartic, really. He'd sat back and everything had just poured out of him. The dark realm and the Grigori, his Directive, his intimate possession of Dawn and putting his essence into her. And yes, even the disturbing emotions he'd been feeling since becoming involved with her. The woman had said nothing, just gazed at him impassively as he'd spilled his guts for hour after hour in that creepy see-through room.

"Do you want her?" a dark voice asked from behind him.

Startled, Galen turned; it took him a moment to realize the man talking meant the dancing, golden Elise. "No. Not my type," he said.

"Good," Rofocale said. "Because I've already laid claim to her. But she asked for you."

Galen regarded Rofocale. The demon of destruction had summoned him to the forest shortly after he'd left the interrogation room this evening. Even if Galen had wanted Elise—which he didn't—he wouldn't be stupid enough to challenge the powerful minister of Hell for her. He might be having some questionable desires lately, but suicide wasn't one of them.

He straightened. "Surely, you didn't come here to discuss women, my lord."

Actually, he was afraid he knew exactly what Rofocale wanted to discuss, recalling the vampire Marceau's claims this morning.

"You know what I want," Rofocale said indulgently, as though to a child.

"Perhaps you should spell it out," Galen politely suggested.

As a Grigori, Rofocacle's powers were vast. No doubt he could sense Galen's thoughts and desires. But shielding them would be a big mistake. Instead he must be very, very careful about what he allowed into his mind, and what he said.

Rofocale spread his hands, indicating a richly colorful oriental tent that had been set up in the middle of the trillium meadow. "Shall we indulge?" he asked, bidding Galen follow.

The lavishly embellished cloth sides of the tent billowed in the breeze, revealing a low, sumptuously set table surrounded by tasseled, embroidered pillows made from priceless fabrics. A man already lounged there, casually sipping from a goblet of faerie wine.

Chaddiel. The demon they had escaped from at Pandora's Box. Galen halted.

"Do not be afraid, my friend," Rofocale said. "Chaddiel acknowledges your right to the human woman. He was beaten fair and square at Pandora's Box."

He didn't know about fair, but the man's eyes didn't seem to hold a grudge. Galen allowed his anger and possessiveness of Dawn to swell within him.

Rofocale chuckled. "Down, boy. She is yours. Chaddiel can find another playmate." He glanced at the dancers as he dropped gracefully to the cushions. "Perhaps when I tire of the nubile Elise, I may give her to him."

Galen kept his mind safely blank and summoned his best obsequious voice. "I am your servant, *Ba'al* Rofocale." He bowed and took his place among the pillows.

At his host's wave, a clutch of beautiful wood nymphs sauntered into the tent bearing platters of food prepared especially for them: succulent bits of meat, vegetables that burst with exotic flavors, sweet confections that tasted of decadence and temptation. And carafes of faerie wine.

Galen knew better than to decline any of it. Or to rush the conversation he knew was coming. The princely class of the dark realm enjoyed their indulgences even more than most. And they observed a strict, if languorous, ritual of hospitality and one-upmanship before business could even be approached. During the leisurely meal and meandering conversation, he allowed his curiosity and nervousness full play within his mind. Rofocale would expect that.

The faeries and nymphs danced for them, and, in between, Galen entertained the princes with tales of previous possessions and triumphs of vengeance. It all felt far too much like an interview. Which, as it turned out, it was.

Rofocale finally came to the point of the meeting several hours later. "Galen McManus, demon of vengeance, I would ask you to join us."

Galen frowned. "I don't understand, my lord."

"You seem like a trustworthy man, loyal to your kind."

"I'd like to think I am, my lord," he said carefully.

"I am the leader of a rogue band of Dark denizens. We plan to assume power of the mortal realm, as well as our own realm. Eventually, every demon must choose which side to join. I want you on ours."

It was impossible for Galen to hide his reaction. But he managed to concentrate it to shock—and fear. Shock that he was being recruited. Fear that the other ruling Grigori would ferret out Rofocale's plan and slaughter all those involved.

The two princes merely grinned when he scrambled to his feet and protested, "I'm honored, but I would be of no use to you, my lord. An ordinary man like myself could not possibly help in such grand schemes."

"That is where you are wrong, my friend," Rofocale said, his grin fading. "You have a very important part to play."

Galen's heart threatened to beat out of his chest. He concentrated on the fear, embraced it, wallowed in it.

"What part?" he asked.

Except he already knew. The vampire had been right. All that had happened to Galen over the past several weeks had been in aid of this one moment. This one demand.

He had been set up.

"The Cadre," Rofocale said silkily. "I want you to get me into St. Yve."

Chapter 30

Dawn's heart was shattered.

Galen had betrayed her. Ruthlessly. Thoroughly.

He was a vengeance demon, just as Aurora had warned Dawn. He'd lied to her. He'd seduced her. He'd used her.

Why hadn't she listened to her training? A lifetime of experience had told her what he was. What he would do to her. But carelessly, foolishly, unforgivably naively, she had thought this demon was different. How stupid could you get?

He didn't love her. He'd never loved her. He never would love her. Just as he'd told her all along.

She should have listened to him.

Fat tears rolled down her cheeks as she lay curled on her bed. Tears so hot they scalded.

She didn't deserve to be an adept. Not ever. She didn't even deserve to be in the Cadre, much less to be the Earl of St. Yve's daughter.

A sob escaped her throat.

And yet, despite her misery, she missed Galen desperately.

But he didn't want her.

What would she do?

Oh, God, what would she do without him?

Chapter 31

Galen approached the door to the family wing of St. Yve with a determined step. At this point, his stride was about the only thing in his life he still had control over. The term *going to hell* had taken on a whole new dimension.

At the top of the entry steps, the gargoyles cracked their stony eyelids at him and fluttered their wings. Then resettled themselves and ignored him. He was almost disappointed. If they'd raised the alarm and Cadre demon hunters had come running with crystals in their hands and spells on their tongues, his problems would all have been solved. No such luck.

What a difference a night made.

He walked quietly into the house. The indwelling house demons greeted him with an almost lazy circuit around his head, no fangs, no claws, then they disappeared, too.

All was silent and dark as a tomb. But apparently not *his*

tomb. A reprieve? Unlikely. The High Council probably just hadn't expected him to have the audacity to return tonight.

He made his way to Dawn's room. He had to see her. Somehow make her understand what he had done. What he must do now.

He walked the long halls without meeting another soul, and slipped into her bedroom. She was lying on the bed, still dressed, her body curled into a fetal position. Her beautiful face carried the saddest expression he'd ever seen. Her closed eyes were rimmed in red, her lashes misty with drying tears.

His heart squeezed in a vise of regret. She looked so lost, so vulnerable. And he'd done this to her.

He sat carefully on the edge of the bed and reached a hand out to gently touch her hair.

"Don't," she said.

He stopped, letting his hand hover above her. "Dawn," he whispered. "Please. Let me explain."

"There's nothing to explain. You lied to me. You used me." Her voice was ragged from crying, filled with the pain of betrayal.

"No," he protested. "Well, yes, I lied, but—"

"Get out. You've had your fun. Now leave me alone."

"No. I won't go." He let his hand touch her hair, brushing his fingers lightly over the silken tresses. "Please, Dawn, I never meant to hurt you. You have to believe that."

Her body gave an involuntary shiver. He knew it wasn't from cold. But was it from longing...or revulsion?

"Why should I believe you?"

He swallowed. He didn't know what to do. He was drowning here. The feelings he was floundering in were all new to him. *Hopelessness, longing, need.* Those and a thousand other foreign emotions flooded through his heart. He didn't know how to control them, or how to make her see what he was going through. He wasn't even sure whether the emotions were all his, or were some of hers, leaking through the shields she had erected against him. The feelings scared the hell out of him; the intensity of them left him breathless with terror. How did humans deal with this stuff?

The only thing he knew with certainty was that he had to stay with her tonight. He desperately needed to hold her and make love with her, one last time. Before his fate caught up with him.

"I've seen Rofocale," he told her. "In the enchanted wood."

Her eyes opened, pinning him with alarm.

"There really is a plot to take over the mortal realm. Apparently the Cadre holds several of his fellow conspirators in crystals in the dungeon. He wants to get them out, and he wants me to sneak him into St. Yve to do it."

Shock swept across her face. "You? But— Why are you telling me this?"

"I'm not going to do it, Dawn. I won't betray your trust."

"Too late," she said. Her body uncurled and she reached for the phone on the bedside table. "I must tell Aurora about this so she can warn the High Council."

"Tell her in the morning. I'm not to meet Rofocale until tomorrow night."

Her hand hesitated over the phone as she weighed whether to trust him. Before she could decide against him, he slid into bed, putting his arms around her stiff, unyielding body. He pulled her wavering hand back to her side.

"What are you doing, Galen?"

"Claiming my due. I gave you the Demon Stone. You still owe me."

She let out a small cry of outrage. "I will not—"

"I won't force you, Dawn. I only want to hold you in my arms tonight." He pulled her against his chest. "I won't even kiss you if you don't want me to."

Suddenly her shields came down, and he was inundated with

a whole new set of emotions. *Hurt. Betrayal. Distress. Anguish.* He groaned under the onslaught of pain, reeling with it.

He tightened his arms around her, letting her feel his regret. His repentance. His profound need for her to understand. His profound need for *her*.

Her eyes sought his, wide and filled with cautious astonishment. She still didn't trust him. Who could blame her?

"It's all true," he said, trailing his fingers over her cheek. "I don't know how it's possible, but you were right. I do have feelings for you."

"Oh, Galen. Why did you do it, then? Why lie to me? Why hurt those people?"

"You summoned me, my sweet. It was your own wish for vengeance I fulfilled. I lied because it's the best way to do my job. To grant your greatest desire."

"But revenge *isn't* my greatest desire."

He gave her a bleak smile. "No longer, perhaps."

"No! I didn't want Elise to be caught forever in the borderlands! I didn't want Roland to break his leg or Marta to have drunken sex with Dr. Cornell. That would be awful of me!"

"That's why they are called *dark* desires, my love. It's the role of demons to illuminate the dark side of humanity."

He felt a wave of profound guilt sift through her, like a ghost walking through her body. "But Galen, you can't judge a person by their hidden thoughts, that's not fair."

"Why not? If you think about vengeance you must want it."

She shook her head. "I would never in a million years have hurt those people, even if I sometimes fantasized about it. A person's mind is like a safety valve. You can imagine all sorts of things, but your conscience prevents you from acting in a way you know isn't right."

"But then…how is one to judge a person?"

"By their words and actions. What they actually do."

Looking into her earnest eyes, he thought about what she'd said for a long, long time. It was as if a light had turned on somewhere deep in his soul. Finally he understood. "If a person really does take revenge on another, he deserves his punishment. But not for just thinking about it."

She touched his hand. "A fine distinction, but an important one. Galen, you must stop doing this. No more revenge. Promise me!"

He nodded, closing his eyes so she wouldn't see the true finality in them. "No more. I swear. I'll be gone tomorrow."

She sucked in a breath of surprise. "No, but— You have to stay," she said, her voice wavering.

"That won't be possible," he said. "I must…go." His heart felt as though it was burning to an ashy cinder in his chest. There was nothing he wanted more than to stay with this amazing woman. To live his days learning from her gentle wisdom and to spend his nights learning her soft curves.

He would give anything in the universe, give up everything he had, everything he was, to be with her. Unfortunately, the universe was not his to give. And after tomorrow, he would have nothing left to give up.

But Dawn would be safe. And he would no longer have to hurt anyone. Especially her.

One way or another, tomorrow it would be all over.

Dawn's anger with Galen slowly dissolved. How could you be angry with someone in such pain? She believed the honesty of his regret.

"This is my punishment, isn't it?" she asked dejectedly.

He opened his eyes and gazed at her uncomprehendingly. His power was barely a warm kiss on her skin, slumberous, as if he'd given up even trying to be strong or domineering.

"I know your Directive says you must punish me tenfold for my vengefulness. It's too late to change it now, isn't it?"

"Change what?"

"Losing you. That's my punishment, right?"

His lips parted. His expression softened and he sighed. "I suppose you could look at it that way. I guess it will be both our punishments."

"Why yours?"

He leaned down and kissed her tenderly. "It turns out there was very little I truly understood about humans. I've wronged so many. Cosmic justice works both ways, I suppose."

She smiled wistfully at him, and a riffle of his warmth brushed over her. She put her arms around his neck. "You've truly changed."

He reached up and drew his fingers reverently along her cheek, as though she was made of fine porcelain. "Because of you."

"What are you going to do now?"

"I…I can't go back."

"Then you really must stay. Here, with me."

He smiled, a heartrending, longing-filled curve of his sensual lips. The warmth of his energy swelled. "Yes," he said. "For tonight."

"Tomorrow we'll talk to my father," she said. "We'll make him understand. We belong together."

He kissed her again. "Your father will do the right thing, I'm sure."

Happiness bubbled up within her. It was going to be all right! She just knew it was. "Please, Galen," she whispered. "Make love to me." She kissed him, soulfully, long and deep, showing him all the love in her heart.

His power wrapped around her like a wall of liquid heat as he rolled his body over hers. A few tugs on her clothes and they were gone. Everywhere he touched, her skin came to life, heated by the fires of his power.

She loved being naked under him. Loved the sensation of being covered and coveted by his powerful body. Of feeling helpless, and helplessly in love. She loved the feeling of security belonging to him created within her, loved the feeling of belonging.

She pulled at his shirt buttons, wanting him as naked as she. As open and vulnerable as she. Except Galen would never be vulnerable. He was too strong, too commanding. His body was testament to his strength as he scattered his clothes to the floor. Muscles rippled in the solid expanse of his chest and abdomen as he levered himself between her thighs, his carved hipbones and rock-hard length contrasting erotically with her softness. His passion breathed along her skin, a hot wind charged with electricity, like the first tendrils of a mighty storm.

He thrust into her.

He held still, gazing down at her with a look she'd never seen before on his face, in his eyes. Somewhere between possessiveness and…fear?

"I know you have doubts," he murmured, "I wish I could…I wish I were something other than what I am. For you."

He pushed deeper into her. She felt his heart pound in her body as surely as she felt her own, their mingled beating fast and frantic, filled with a tangle of emotions.

"No, Galen," she whispered. "I wouldn't have you any other way than just as you are."

A ripple of his pain swept over her, from a place deep within him. "You don't understand, my sweet. I—"

"I do," she whispered. "I know all I need to know about you. I love you, Galen." *It was far too late for doubts.* Fear, perhaps. But never doubts. "I trust you to love me back."

His power swelled, gaining strength like heat lightning gathering to strike. His mouth came down on hers and it was as though a storm opened up. His dark energy boiled around her. She gasped at the suddenness and the intensity. He was the fire and her body was the vessel. Their tongues tangled and his power poured through her mouth to her whole body, wicked, molten and exciting. She trembled violently. Her center blazed with want, the place where they were joined burned with need. The flames sucked at her, tongued her from the inside, teased her to a heated frenzy.

Then suddenly she was consumed by an overwhelming pleasure. Galen threw back his head and roared. Hot, streaming fire spurted into her, exploding through her flesh as she screamed her release.

"You all right?" he asked long moments later.

She couldn't move. She couldn't speak. She could only make an inarticulate noise, low in her throat. A sated, cat-in-the-cream purr of thorough, dizzying pleasure.

"I'll take that as a yes." He kissed her again. He rolled over, bringing her on top of him. "Sleep, now," he whispered.

Her eyelids grew heavy. But as sleep began to creep over her like a slow, dark shadow, she felt something in Galen's lingering touch, in his uneasy breath, in the fleeting memory of something he had said earlier.

Something was wrong.

She struggled to think. What had he said? Something about…tomorrow. Her father? The High Council? The demon that—

"Galen?"

"Hmm?"

"What will he do to you?"

"Who, my sweet?"

"Rofocale. When you refuse to help him tomorrow night."

Galen didn't answer. His heart still beat firm and steady below hers, but she could feel a sudden tension in his body.

"Galen? What is he going to do?"

Slowly, the tension seeped from him and a peaceful look came over his face. It made her nervous. Very nervous.

He sighed and kissed her forehead. And then he said, "He's going to kill me."

Chapter 32

Dawn shot up and scrambled off Galen, staring at him in horror. "*Kill* you? You've got to be kidding."

"I'm afraid not."

He looked far too calm. Too accepting. Too— "Galen! How can you just lie there and say that as though it means nothing?"

"Believe me, I know what it means."

"Then we must do something!" She didn't wait for him to answer. She leapt off the bed and pulled his arm so hard he was compelled to roll off as well.

He balked. "What are you doing?"

"I have to take you to the High Council."

He dug his heels in. "And say what? Dawn, they aren't going to help me. More likely, they'll order me crystallized for endangering the Cadre. They'll never believe I'd defy Rofocale or the Grigori. The best we can hope for is that they simply deport me back to the dark realm. In which case I'm dead, too."

She took a minute and tried to think calmly. Hell, he was probably right. She might be able to argue and convince the Council eventually, but until she did, Galen would be in danger here at St. Yve. Especially with Rofocale lurking nearby.

Right. New plan. She ran to the wardrobe. "Get dressed. We have to go."

"Where?"

"My place in town. You'll be safe there until I can talk to my father and the Council."

He threw up his hands. "Dawn, it's no use. No one can protect me from the Grigori if they decide to side with Rofocale."

"Then we'll have to make sure they don't. Hurry!"

He regarded her scurrying around to gather her things, then relented and put on his clothes. "Fine. I'll go with you, but only if you promise you'll come straight back to St. Yve after dropping me off. I want you safe, Dawn. And that means not with me."

She didn't like it. She didn't want to leave him alone. She didn't care about her safety. Though she did pack some extra Dead Sea salt and two capture crystals in her jacket pocket in case they ran into Rofocale on the way. However, Galen had a good point. She should come back right away and talk to her father first thing in the morning. She must convince the Council to protect Galen before his meeting tomorrow night. No way would she let him be killed because of his loyalty to her.

"Okay. It's a deal."

They hurried downstairs and out to the Lamborghini. Each said a spell of protection around it and themselves before Galen sent the car rocketing through the forest toward London.

Dawn wondered briefly if it was the first time human and demonic magic had both been invoked in concert, for the same purpose. She just prayed it worked.

* * *

This wasn't going to work. He was a dead man.

Galen admired Dawn's optimism, but harbored none himself. He had less than twenty-four hours to live, and he knew it.

Strangely, he had no regrets over choosing to end his existence. Without Dawn, without her love, he had no reason to go on living. If he helped Rofocale, she would despise him. If he refused to betray her, Rofocale would kill him, and probably her, as well. He couldn't risk that.

His death was the only way out. Which was why when they made a quick stop at an all-night supermarket and Dawn ran in for breakfast things, Galen made an anonymous call to P-Cell to let them know where he would be.

Minutes later, he pulled into the gated mews behind Dawn's townhouse, which had originally been stables and carriage houses but now held cars instead of horses.

"Come on," she said as she popped the batwing door and slid out. She pressed the button to close the garage door.

"You promised to leave," he protested, jumping out to stop her.

"I will. I want to make sure you're settled in first."

"That's not necessary." He chased her through a low door into a lush garden which must be her backyard. Suddenly, a tingle of power marched along his arms, raising goose flesh. "Dawn!" he yelled, lifting his hand, surging energy in order to throw flames at whoever—whatever—was lying in wait out there.

Too late.

Chaddiel materialized in the darkness. He grabbed Dawn from behind. She cried. Her hand went for her pocket. "Oh, no you don't." He wrested her arm behind her back.

"Galen!" she screamed.

Galen rushed Chaddiel, spewing sparks from his heels and fingertips. He ran three steps before he was wrenched to a stop in his tracks. He couldn't move. His power sputtered.

Rofocale's hideous laugh came from deep in the shadows. It crept through the damp night air and coiled around Galen's body like a serpent. Cold. Vicious. Deadly.

"Let her go!" Galen shouted at the Minister of Hell. "I'll join your plot. I'll do anything you ask."

Rofocale laughed again, louder this time. Sharp, thundering laughter pounded through Galen's head like a thousand marching jackboots. The pain was excruciating. "You are a fool, McManus. You've given me the earl's daughter. I no longer need you."

Galen grabbed his head, falling to his knees. He fought the demon lord's power, crawling through it toward her. Each movement was like knives ripping through his flesh. The very air around him cut like razors. He persisted, inch by agonizing inch. By the time he reached her feet, his hands and knees were shredded and raw. His shoulders and face ran rivulets of blood.

Dawn was sobbing, crying his name over and over, thrashing in Chaddiel's grip to get free. Bent double on his knees, Galen put his arms around her legs and held her to him. He pressed his warm and blood-slippery cheek to her calf. Chaddiel ripped her jacket off her and tossed it away, then let her drop. She collapsed into Galen's arms, tears streaming.

"It's all right, my love," he whispered, gathering strength and determination from the contact. Perhaps the last… "Shhh."

Rofocale suddenly towered over them. "What have they done to you?" he boomed. "You are no demon! You stink of pathetic human emotion." For a split second Galen could have sworn fear spilled from the Grigori's mind. Then it snapped off, blocked in an instant. "No matter. You are completely inconsequential. It is your lover we need."

With that, he and Dawn were roughly dragged to their feet. Before Galen could blink, they were all inside the townhouse, standing in a dark kitchen. The only light came through the open door to the garden, which whacked open against a cupboard, vibrated, then slowly started to swing closed, bringing the dark back with it. A wide hall led from the kitchen to the grand entry foyer and front door, which might as well have been a thousand miles away. There would be no escape for him.

"A knife," Rofocale ordered Chaddiel.

The dread demon shoved Dawn into a kitchen chair. "Stay!" The barked command dared her to disobey. She didn't, cowering in the false emotion forced by her captor. Chaddiel prowled the night-dark kitchen counters and pulled out drawers, searching for an instrument for Galen's demise.

Chaddiel pulled a long, efficient-looking butcher's knife from a wooden block. He spun the lethal blade in his fingers so it flashed silver in the last beam of moonlight before the back door shut completely. Galen's breath caught in his throat.

With the strength of his power alone, Rofocale threw him against a counter and held him there. "Do it," his enemy growled.

Chaddiel raised the knife, poised over Galen's heart. *This was it.*

Dawn screamed, "No!"

Rofocale jerked her to her feet. "Swear to do as I command, mortal, or watch your lover die!"

"Don't, Dawn!" Galen told her desperately. "Let him kill me. He's going to anyway."

"Then I'll die with you!"

All at once a high-pitched whine buzzed in Galen's ears. *Where had he heard that sound before?*

Rofocale must have heard it, too, because his invisible hold on Galen abruptly ceased. Instead he grabbed Dawn and banded her in front of his chest, gaze darting to the door.

Suddenly the windows exploded. So did Chaddiel's head. *P-Cell!*

"Don't shoot the woman!" someone yelled.

Galen dove for Dawn just as the door slammed open and another volley of shots burst through it and the shattered window. Real bullets and salt pellets ripped into the counter where he had just stood. He felt the burn of salt grains as they bounced off his bloody back.

"Galen!" Dawn screamed.

Rofocale grunted as he took a shot to the shoulder. He spun around, losing his hold on Dawn. She vaulted into Galen's arms and clung to him desperately.

At their feet, suddenly Chaddiel's salt-covered body disintegrated. It just dried up and crumbled to a vaguely man-shaped puff of gray ash. *Satan wept.*

When Galen looked up, Rofocale had vanished.

"It's okay," he shouted over the din, holding Dawn tight. "You're safe now."

Dirk Marcolf and two other men stood in a semicircle pointing enough fire power at Galen to vaporize ten demons.

"I surrender," he said quickly. "Just don't hurt Dawn."

"He does *not* surrender," she said, plastering herself between him and the P-Cell goons. "If you want him you'll have to kill me first."

"Dawn, don't. They only—"

"Shut up, Galen," she hissed.

His eyes met Marcolf's over her head in shock. The other man's lip curled ever so slightly. "You heard the lady, blokes. Lower your weapons."

"But guv—"

"Let's hear what she has to say, yeah?"

She turned in Galen's arms and pressed her back into his chest, stubbornly staying there even when he tried to set her aside.

Marcolf spread his feet and cradled his M4 in his arms, looking mean and lethal and completely unsympathetic. He spared an impassive glance at Chaddiel's ash and said, "Give me one good reason I shouldn't make them a matched set."

His goons' weapons inched up. He didn't order them down.

"Mr. McManus is under the Cadre's protection. Look at his wounds! These demons were trying to kill him."

"Why?"

"It's none of your damned business why," Galen interrupted, using a thumb to swipe off the blood dripping into one eye. He didn't trust Marcolf. Plus, if one of his men *was* under Rofocale's influence, Dawn could still be in danger even if they were government agents. "I'll give myself up to you on one condition."

"What condition?"

"Galen, no!"

"Lady Dawn walks out of here and I see her drive away. Then we can negotiate."

Dawn gasped. "Negotiate? *Are you mad?* There's no way—"

"Sounds reasonable," Marcolf said. "I accept."

"I'm afraid not." Aurora's loud, commanding voice cut through the kitchen like a machete. "The demon is mine."

Everyone except Marcolf spun to see her standing framed by the garden door, tall, authoritative and unflinching in the face of the weapons that were suddenly all pointing at her. She held the room silent and immobile by sheer force of will alone. Galen was impressed.

Apparently Marcolf wasn't. He pursed his lips and turned slowly to Dawn's sister. "Lady Aurora. Nice to see you, as always."

"Agent Marcolf. Please leave my sister's house at once. I'll take care of this, if you don't mind."

A muscle jumped behind Marcolf's jaw. "And if I do mind?" he asked smoothly.

She drew herself up even taller. "That would be most unfortunate. It would be a shame if the tabloids were to find out your constant harassment of the head of a lauded university department and member of the aristocracy is because of a disturbing, not to say ridiculous, belief in otherworldly monsters." She smiled benignly. "Wouldn't it?"

Everyone in the room knew most humans didn't have a clue the mortal realm was regularly visited by demons, faeries and other creatures not human. Nor that vampires and weres existed. That was all top secret information even at the highest levels of government. Fewer still knew about the Cadre and P-Cell.

A public accusation like this could be a real career killer. Galen almost grinned. The woman had guts.

Marcolf stared at her but his expression was unreadable. "Are you threatening me, Lady Aurora?"

Her smile widened. "So we understand each other, then."

His eyes narrowed. "You are treading—"

She waved her hand as though he were an annoying insect. "How about this, Agent Marcolf?" She pulled a red, pyramid-shaped crystal from her pocket and held it up on her palm. "You and your men leave, and I'll take care of the demon."

Galen froze. Okay, not what he had in mind.

Dawn gasped, and cried out, "Aurora, no! I won't let you!"

"He's a vengeance demon, darling," her sister said evenly, her eyes still on Marcolf. "He seduced you and disrupted the Department. He's dangerous. This is the way it has to be."

"No!" Dawn lunged at Aurora.

Before Galen could get to her, Marcolf had her around the waist kicking and screaming, and the other two men were in front of Galen with their M4s jammed in his throat. It was like déjà vu but with different bad guys.

"My God, Aurora!" Galen yelled. "Don't let him touch her!"

Aurora held a hand up to Marcolf to stop. "Hurt my sister and you will pay dearly," she said, her eyes deadly serious.

"I have no intention of hurting her. Shall I let her go?"

Aurora hesitated, then shook her head. "Take her outside. And your men, too. I'll neutralize the demon."

Marcolf shook his head. "Too dangerous. We'll stay. To protect you." This time he smiled.

"If I have anything to say about this," Galen interrupted, swallowing around the two gun barrels sticking in his throat, "I'd just as soon you let Marcolf blast me. The accommodations on offer are far too small, and…I never did look good in red."

Dawn choked out a sob. "Galen, please, this isn't funny."

He looked into her tear-filled eyes and his heart ripped into tiny pieces. "I know, my love. But there's no way out for us. Rofocale will kill me anyway. At least if P-Cell does it, it'll be quick. And you'll be safe."

"But what am I to do without you?" she sobbed. "I love you!"

He swallowed heavily. "I love you, too, my sweet. Can't you see, that's why I must do this?"

The pressure of the gun barrels eased up a fraction. Their owners' faces suddenly looked uncertain. They turned to Marcolf, who regarded Galen with a calculating expression. Aurora's face was a mask of neutrality. But her eyes were shiny. Sympathy? Not likely. Not for Galen, anyway. Maybe for her sister's plight? He hoped so. Aurora would be her sister's only support when he was gone.

"Go on, do it," he told Marcolf.

"No!" Dawn struggled against Marcolf's hold, calling Galen's name over and over.

"No," Aurora said over Dawn's sobs. She shook her head at Marcolf. "As misguided as my sister is, she loves him. And I don't believe in killing. I don't care what he wants. I can't let you murder this man in cold blood."

For a moment Marcolf considered, then nodded once. "Go ahead. But I want to see it done."

She took a deep breath and raised the crystal on her palm.

Galen's heart sank. The idea of spending eternity in solitary confinement was his idea of a Hell far worse than the real thing. He thought about all the things he'd miss—books, food, warmth, driving with the wind in his face, yes, even his job. But most of all it was Dawn he'd miss. Her smile, her laugh, the touch of her hand, the way she looked at him, the way she made love to him. The way she simply loved him.

As Aurora began to chant the capture spell, he closed his eyes and fought the desperate emotions pouring through his body at the thought of losing all that was Dawn.

But his lover's soft, heartrending cries compelled his eyes to open again. He sought her desolate gaze and held it as his body began to change and grow light, sending her all the love in his heart, all the fragile new feelings of tenderness and devotion. All that he was he gave to her as he slowly lost his physical existence, and all that he could have been, if they'd only had the chance.

Aurora's voice rose to a crescendo, completing the spell.

"I love you," he whispered to Dawn, one last time.

Then his body imploded and his soul went spinning, spinning, ever inward, ever smaller. And when the spinning stopped he'd been squeezed to nothing, and he was nowhere and all around was naught but a great, red void.

Chapter 33

Dawn was gutted. Worse than gutted.

She'd watched the man she loved reduced to a thin scattering of ash on the floor, his soul captured forever in a crystal prison.

She wanted to die.

"Dawn?" Aurora was driving them back to St. Yve. Dawn had no desire to speak to her. She had no desire to speak to her sister ever again. Aurora must have sensed that because she just said, "I'm so sorry," and nothing more.

Sorry. Brilliant.

Dawn squeezed her eyes closed and rolled her head away so her sister couldn't see her tears. She didn't want to give her the satisfaction of knowing once again she'd won, she'd got—

Dawn sighed. No. She wasn't going there any more, wouldn't give in to that dark, insidious place. If Galen had taught her nothing else, he'd taught her that ugly thoughts, thoughts of hatred, and of revenge, only got you in trouble.

She owed it to his memory to honor that lesson, hard-earned as it was.

"I know," she said. "I know you were just doing what you thought was best for the Cadre. For me. I forgive you, Aurora."

It cost her a lot to say those last words. More than her sister would ever know.

Aurora turned to her in surprise. Her eyes softened and filled. "Thank you," she whispered. She turned away and continued driving. The car was still silent, but the silence was warm now, an inclusive sphere of comfort rather than a stony wall between them.

When they reached St. Yve Manor, Aurora turned toward the east wing so she could take the crystal containing Galen's soul to the dungeon for Squire Callahan to place in storage.

"Come with me," Aurora gently urged.

Dawn shook her head. "No. You do it. I can't bear to see him like that."

Funny how it had never bothered her before—crystallizing demons. How she bitterly regretted her smug attitude when Galen had questioned the Cadre's right to choose which individual was evil and which wasn't! Who was she to judge others? Thank God she wasn't an adept. Tomorrow she would tell the High Council she never wanted to be promoted. She never wanted to have to make that kind of decision. Ever. Let others be judge and jury. She didn't have the heart or the stomach.

Aurora gave her a long hug, then walked away.

"My lady?" Charles asked with concern. "Are you all right?"

"No, Charles," she whispered. "I'll never be all right again." She smiled bleakly as she said it, and hugged Galen's macintosh which she'd brought from the car and put it to her lips, then walked to the staircase leading to the top of the castle.

It was nearly sunrise. And Dawn knew what she must do.

* * *

The wind was cold as ice on the parapet. It moaned through the trees below, mournful and unearthly, like a low, keening cry.

Dawn shivered at the sound, and leaned against the freezing stone rampart. She gazed down upon the ancient spreading oak that grew from the spot where Lady Arwyn, daughter of the first Earl of St. Yve, had flung herself nearly five centuries earlier. *For love of a demon.* How little things had changed in all those years!

An orange sliver of sun trembled on the indigo horizon. In the meadow beyond the oak, faerie lights danced in a circle to the music of the dawn. But the only sounds she could hear were the moaning of the wind and the cries of her heart.

"Oh, Galen," Dawn whispered. "Forgive me."

She grasped the rough stone edge of the wall that separated her from the air beyond and tried to hoist herself up upon it. The wind howled and she stumbled, pushed back by a strong gust.

She pulled Galen's mac tighter around her and tried again. She clambered onto the stone wall and stood up. For a moment everything was deathly still, as though the whole world was holding its breath.

"Dawn! Don't!" Aurora's voice sounded from behind her. Pleading. "My God, Dawn, turn around and look at me."

She swallowed. She didn't want to look. She didn't want to look at anything else ever again. But she knew that would be the coward's way out. If Galen had to suffer an eternity of solitude, the least she could do was endure one short lifetime. *For him.* She wiped the tears from her eyes and gingerly turned.

"Don't worry, Aurora. I'm not going to—" Suddenly, Dawn saw what Aurora was holding in her hand. Her heart seized. "What are you doing with that?" *It was Galen's crystal.*

Her sister carefully set the crystal pyramid on the stone floor of the parapet. "I guessed you'd be here." She twisted the ring on her forefinger. "You love him very much, don't you."

It wasn't really a question, but Dawn answered anyway. "Yes. I love him. More than I thought it possible to love a man."

"But he's not human."

She sighed, and eased down to sit on the edge of the rampart. "Are you so sure? Demons are part of us, Aurora. A dark part, to be sure. But we wouldn't be human without that side of ourselves. We have to accept it. Once we do, we can see the humanity behind our demons. And the demons cease to rule our lives. They become human. Like us. Galen is human now, Aurora. As human as you or I."

"But how? How is that possible?"

"Simple. Through love. Galen was changed by love. My love for him and his for me."

Aurora's troubled gaze stared down at the red crystal for a long time. Finally, she said, "I heard his love for you in his voice when he pleaded for your safety. I saw his love for you in his eyes when he was facing death. I knew he'd changed. But I didn't want to believe it."

Dawn smiled despondently. "I had a hard time believing it myself sometimes."

"The gargoyles knew," Aurora said. "It's why he passed their test."

Shock went through Dawn's body. "What are you saying?"

"It's true. They told the High Council. It's why the Council refused my petition to crystallize him."

She heard the words but they refused to process. She slid off the rampart and grabbed her sister's hands. "But... But..."

"I suspected as much after tonight. When we returned, I went straight to them and related what had happened with Rofocale and P-Cell. The Council told me everything then."

Hope surged through Dawn. "I—I don't understand."

Aurora squeezed her hands. "Even Father said Galen had proven himself and his worthiness."

Even Father? She didn't dare believe… "So…what now?"

A gust of wind tore over the parapet and whipped around them, lifting their hair and clothes.

"I'm letting him out, Dawn. You can be together."

She let out an inarticulate cry and dropped to her knees next to the crystal. She reached out a trembling hand but stopped short of touching it. Tears blinded her. "Hurry, Aurora. Oh, God, please, hurry!"

The ice-cold wind rushed over her skin. She didn't hear her sister's chant, couldn't see through the watery veil clouding her vision. But she felt the power of the spell. The energy built and swelled and grew in strength until the air was crackling and swirling with the power of it. Aurora's hands lifted and she shouted the final words. A bolt of lightning cracked down from the sky, booming like a thousand cannons, lighting up the parapet like a sunburst. It hit the tip of the pyramid.

The crystal exploded, raining a thousand pieces of red.

And in its place stood Galen.

Chapter 34

Galen awoke to the deafening crash of thunder and a searing pain that burned through his body like the fires of Hell. How was that possible? He no longer had a body. Yet every cell screamed in agony. He squeezed his eyes shut and covered his ears, doubling over against the pain and the thrashing icy wind.

Then, as quickly as it started, it was over.

And he was left standing on his own unsteady feet. Warily, he opened his eyes. And saw—

"Dawn!"

She smiled and opened her arms.

He fell into them. And held her as he'd thought he'd never do again. He squeezed her tightly and kissed her and laughed with her and cried with her.

And wondered if he'd look up in a minute and she'd be gone and he'd still be captured in his scarlet prison. But she felt solid and wonderful and she didn't dissolve into thin air, but kept saying his name over and over and over, as though she couldn't believe they were together, either.

"Am I dreaming?" he asked. "Is it really you?"

"It's really me, darling." She hugged him fiercely. "Thank God you've come back to me."

The wind was icy but his trembling wasn't from cold. His body shook with the joy of being there. Back in her arms.

"You're freezing. Here." She handed him his long mac.

"No, I'm—" He suddenly realized he was standing there buck-naked. "Okay, maybe a little."

She was trembling, too. He slid his arms into the coat and wrapped it around both of them, bringing her into its warmth.

"Do I look the same?" he asked worriedly. He'd never regenerated his body before. The older *inculti* demons could shapeshift; they changed bodies regularly. But Galen's lot didn't have that power. Maybe he'd changed....

"You're even more handsome than before," she assured him with a long, loving kiss.

He kissed her back even longer, moving his body against hers. Needing the reassurance of her response. The proof of her touch that it was really her. That a miracle had happened and he really was free.

She smiled back and his whole world lit up. "Galen," she murmured, kissing him tenderly, "we should probably go down and tell the others you're all right. Aurora was very worried."

He jerked back in alarm. "Aurora?"

"The crystal shattered when she chanted the reversal spell. You should have seen the wind and the lightning. That's never happened before."

He stared at her aghast. "Wait. You're saying Aurora brought me back?" He couldn't have been more shocked. Aurora hated demons. Aurora hated *him*.

Dawn nodded. "She's a good person, Galen. Thanks to you I

understand that now. She sees our love, and respects it. It's a start. She went to the High Council and told them what happened."

"And they let her bring me back?"

"You won them over as well. They're waiting downstairs for us, too. Aurora says they'd like you to work for the Cadre, as an initiate, if you're willing."

It was almost too much to believe. "Anything," he said, wrapping his arms around her and holding her close, close, close to his heart. "I'll go anywhere to be with you, Dawn. Do anything. Just tell me what I must do and I will."

"All I want," she whispered, "is for you to stay with me always. Forever. That's all I want you to do."

"That's what I want, too. More than anything. But won't your father try to stop us?"

"No," she said, her voice filled with happiness. "Aurora said he has given us his blessing."

"But…how? Why?" Galen whispered, rocking her back and forth. He would never, ever let her go. But he just didn't understand how all this had happened. How he'd suddenly gotten so lucky. How he'd been granted his heart's greatest desire, a chance to spend his life with this amazing woman.

"Love," she said softly, holding him as fiercely as he held her. "I never understood its power before. Love is more potent than the greatest magic. Stronger than the worst evil. Love brought you back to me, Galen. Love makes anything possible."

He believed it. With all his heart he believed. It was so new to him, this incredible emotion, but he'd never felt anything more powerful. More compelling. More wondrous.

"I do love you, my beautiful Dawn," he answered gently. "More than anything. More than life itself."

"I know you do," she said, looking up at him with adoring eyes. "And I love you, too."

"Marry me," he whispered, drowning in the love he had for

her. "Take my name and be my wife. Be my love forever and ever."

She gave a little gasp, and her eyes swam with tender emotion. "Oh, Galen. I will," she whispered. "I've always been yours. And I always will be, my darling. Yours, for all eternity."

* * * * *

Secret Agent Affair
by
Marie Ferrarella

She knew better.

Of all people, Dr. Marja Pulaski knew to be alert when she was sitting behind the wheel of a moving vehicle.

It really didn't matter that the vehicle in question, a car she shared with her sister, Tania, was going at a pace that, in comparison, would have made the tortoise of "the Tortoise and the Hare" fame change his name to Lightning. A car was a dangerous weapon, an accident waiting to happen unless it was parked in a garage.

Hadn't she seen more than her share of auto accident victims in the E.R.? Marja was well versed in the kind of damage just the barest distraction could render.

Her excuse, that she'd just come off a grueling double shift at Patience Memorial Hospital, wouldn't have held water with her if someone else had offered it. And everyone knew that the cheerful, outgoing Dr. Marja Pulaski, the youngest of the five Pulaski physicians, was harder on herself than she was on anyone else.

Other than being somewhat vulnerable and all too human, there was no real reason for Marja to have glanced over at the radio just as one of her favorite songs came on. Looking at the radio hadn't made the volume louder, or crisper. And it certainly wouldn't restart the song. It was just an automatic reflex on her part.

The song had been hers and Jack's. Before Jack had decided that he was just too young to settle down, especially with a woman who'd let him know that, although she loved him, she wasn't going to make him the center of her universe.

Trouble was, for a while, Jack *had* been the center of her universe—until she'd forced herself to take stock of the situation and pull back. Pull back and refocus. Being a doctor was not something she knew she could take lightly, especially not after all the effort that had been put forth to get her to that point.

Her parents were naturalized citizens. Both had risked their lives to come to the United States from their native country of Poland. At the time, it was still bowed beneath communist domination. They'd come so that their future children could grow up free to be whatever they wanted to be.

Once those children began coming—five girls in all—the goal of having them all become doctors had somehow materialized. Her father, Josef, and her mother, Magda, worked hard to put their firstborn through medical school. Once Sasha graduated, any money she could spare went toward helping Natalya become a doctor. Natalya, in turn, helped Kady, who then helped Tania. And it all culminated in everyone working together so that she, Marja, could follow in the firm footsteps that her sisters had laid down before her.

She didn't do it because this was the way things were, she did it because, like her sisters before her, she really *wanted* to become a physician. Looking back, Marja couldn't remember a day when she *hadn't* wanted to be a doctor.

But there were moments, like tonight, that got the better of her. She'd spent her time trying to put together the broken pieces of two young souls, barely into their permanent teeth, who'd decided to wipe one another out because one had stepped onto the other one's territory.

So when the song came on, reminding her of more carefree times, she let the memories take over and momentarily distract her.

Just long enough to glance away.

Just long enough to hit whoever she hit.

The weary smile on her lips vanished instantly as the realization of what had just happened broke through. The sickening thud resounded in the August night, causing the pit of her stomach to tighten into a huge, unmanageable knot and making her soul recoil in horror. Perspiration popped out all over her brow, all but pasting her golden-brown hair against her forehead—not because the night air was so damp and clammy with humidity but because the flash of fear had made her sweat.

Her vow, to first do no harm, exploded in her head,

mocking her even before Marja brought the vehicle to a jarring stop, threw open her door and sprang out of her car.

She worked in the city that boasted never to sleep, but at two o'clock in the morning, the number of Manhattan residents milling about on any given block had considerably diminished. When she'd turned down the side street, determined to make better time getting back to the apartment she shared with Tania, her last remaining unmarried sister, there hadn't been a soul in view. Just a few trash cans pockmarking the darkened area and one lone Dumpster in the middle of the block.

You are knowing better than to go down streets like that.

Marja could all but hear her father's heavily Polish-encrusted voice gently reprimanding her. He'd been on the police force over twenty-eight years when he finally retired, much to her mother's relief. Now he was the head of a security company that had once belonged to his best friend and was no less vigilant when it came to the female members of his family.

He was especially so with her because she was the last of his daughters—through no fault of her own, she often pointed out. He always ignored the comment, saying that the fact remained that she was the youngest and as such, in need of guidance. Stubborn mules had nothing on her father.

Marja's legs felt as if they were made out of rubber and her heart pounded harder than a marching band as she rounded her vehicle. She hoped against hope that her ears were playing tricks on her. That the thud she'd both heard and—she swore—felt along every inch of her body was all just a trick being played by her over-tired imagination.

But the moment she approached the front of her car, she knew it wasn't her imagination. Her imagination didn't use the kind of words she heard emerging from just before the front of the grille.

And then the next second, she saw him.

He was lying on the ground. A blond, lean, wiry man wearing a work shirt rolled up at the sleeves and exposing forearms that could have been carved out of granite they looked so hard. The work shirt was unbuttoned. Beneath it was a black T-shirt, adhering to more muscles.

Had the man's shirt and pants been as dark as his T-shirt, she might have missed it. But they weren't. They were both light-colored. Which was how she was able to see the blood.

What had she done?

"Oh God, I'm so sorry," Marja cried, horrified as she crouched down to the man's level to take a closer look. "I didn't see you." The words sounded so lame to her ears.

The man responded with an unintelligible growl and at first she thought he was speaking to her in another language. New York City was every bit as much of a melting pot now as it had been a century ago. The only difference was that now there were different countries sending over their tired, their poor, their huddled masses yearning to be free.

But the next moment she realized that the man spoke English, just growled the words at a lowered decibel. Maybe he was trying to mask the real words out of politeness.

No, she decided in the next moment, he didn't look like the type to tiptoe around that way.

"Are you hurt?"

It was a rhetorical question, but she was flustered. Her parents thought of her as the flighty one, but that description only applied to her social life—post-Jack. Professionally, Marja was completely serious, completely dedicated. She needed one to balance out the other.

"Of course you're hurt," she chided herself for the thoughtless question. "Can you stand?" she asked. Marja held her breath as she waited hopefully for a positive answer.

Rather than reply, the bleeding stranger continued glaring at her. She could almost feel the steely, angry green gaze, as if it were physical.

It wasn't bad enough that he'd just been shot, Kane Donnelly thought. Now they were trying to finish him off with a car.

At least, that was what he'd thought when his body had felt the initial impact of the vehicle's grille against his torso, knocking him down. But now, one look at the woman's face and the sound of her breathless voice told him that she wasn't part of the little scenario that had sent him sprinting down dark alleys, holding on to his wounded side with one hand, his gun with the other.

Damn it, he was supposed to be more on top of his game than this.

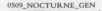
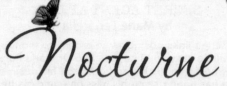

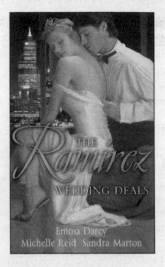

2 FREE

BOOKS AND A SURPRISE GIFT!

We would like to take this opportunity to thank you for reading this Mills & Boon® book by offering you the chance to take TWO more specially selected titles from the Intrigue series absolutely FREE! We're also making this offer to introduce you to the benefits of the Mills & Boon® Book Club™—

- ★ **FREE home delivery**
- ★ **FREE gifts and competitions**
- ★ **FREE monthly Newsletter**
- ★ **Exclusive Mills & Boon Book Club offers**
- ★ **Books available before they're in the shops**

Accepting these FREE books and gift places you under no obligation to buy, you may cancel at any time, even after receiving your free shipment. Simply complete your details below and return the entire page to the address below. You don't even need a stamp!

YES! Please send me 2 free Intrigue books and a surprise gift. I understand that unless you hear from me, I will receive 4 superb new titles every month for just £3.19 each, postage and packing free. I am under no obligation to purchase any books and may cancel my subscription at any time. The free books and gift will be mine to keep in any case.

19ZED

Ms/Mrs/Miss/Mr ....Initials ....
BLOCK CAPITALS PLEASE

Surname ....

Address ....

....

....Postcode..

Send this whole page to:
UK: FREEPOST CN81, Croydon, CR9 3WZ